THE
PENALTY
FOR
HOLDING

The Penalty for Holding
The Games Men Play Series
By Georgette Gouveia

Published by Less Than Three Press LLC

Edited by Michelle Kelley
Cover designed by Natasha Snow

Amazing
Words and Music by Henry Olusegun Adeola Samuel
Copyright (c) 2007 Perfect Songs Ltd.
All Rights Administered by BMG Rights Management (US) LLC
All Rights Reserved Used by Permission
Reprinted by Permission of Hal Leonard LLC

Extract taken from *Four Quartets* (c) Estate of T.S. Eliot and reprinted by permission of Faber & Faber

First Edition May 2017
Copyright © 2017 by Georgette Gouveia
Printed in the United States of America

Digital ISBN 9781684310166
Print ISBN 9781684310173

For my sisters

A solitary craft, writing is also always some form of collaboration.
"The Penalty for Holding" was born of my sisters' love of adventure and was nurtured through workshops at The Writing Institute at Sarah Lawrence College and the New York Pitch Conference, which I attended with my friend and fellow novelist Barbara Nachman, who offered support, advice, and inspiration.
My thanks to Westfair Communications Inc., led by publisher Dee DelBello. There Dan Viteri, associate creative director, provided promotional designs, while administrative manager Robin Costello offered technical expertise and calming wisdom.
Last but certainly not least, my thanks to the goddess who has been my right-hand woman in administering my blog and promoting my book series. I cannot thank her enough for taking this literary journey with me.

THE
PENALTY
FOR
HOLDING

THE GAMES MEN PLAY SERIES

GEORGETTE GOUVEIA

PART I

PART 1

ONE

His name was Quinton Day Novak, and as he stood in the dizzying heat that enveloped the New York Templars' summer training camp high above the Hudson—thick, glossy black curls clinging to his neck beneath his helmet—he wasn't sure where he was going or even where he had been.

He knew where he was immediately headed—or at least where the balls he was drilling were immediately headed—downfield into the sinewy arms of wide receiver Greg Moll. But whether the ability to send missiles arcing into the air would ultimately translate into the starting quarterback's job was anybody's guess. The signs from head coach Pat Smalley weren't good.

"Well, boy," he had said, "let's see what you can do."

He knew Smalley shouldn't call him, or any man for that matter, "boy." That was pure gesture politics, and the gesture said, *You're not my guy and you never will be.*

But Quinn—who had already known many Smalleys in his young life—chose instead to focus on the task at hand, sending the football spiraling twenty, forty, eighty yards into various teammates' fanning hands. When Smalley tried to pull a fast one, Quinn was ready. As defenseman Carl Knowlton came up on his right while he prepared to throw, Quinn anticipated the move and, having feigned right, broke left. He charged down the field with the ball, dodging teammates first left, then right as he ran into the end zone, reveling once more not only in a touchdown but in the sheer joy of running, nothing but the wind at his back as he broke free, heading for the goal line, heading for home. He took a knee then and quickly crossed himself, touching his fingers to his lips.

As he rose, he saw Smalley chatting and laughing with starting quarterback Lance Reinhart at midfield.

"Well, that was real impressive, Quinnie," Lance said with a smirk. "I can see why you won the Heisman as a Stanford sophomore and why Mark was so high on you."

"Was" being the operative word. As the Temps' general manager, Mark Seidelberg had signed him. Mark had believed that he could challenge for the starting QB job. And Mark was gone—another whim of owner Jimmy Jones Jefferson. So far, Quinn had encountered him just once, after an initial phone conversation that went something like, "Triple J here, Quinn. Heard great things about you and expect great things from you," blah, blah, blah. It occurred to him then that Triple J— a distant relative of the third U.S. president—was more mercurial Caesar than steadfast Founding Father.

"Thanks, sir. I intend to do everything I can to help the Temps become Super Bowl champs," was all Quinn had to say. He knew he could be cut from the roster tomorrow. Best to stick to the program—and not get your hopes up.

As he entered the locker room after practice, Quinn thought he was right to be wary. His teammates, long tethered to the starting QB, certainly were, keeping to themselves and their cliques. And that QB himself, the aforementioned Lancelot Reinhart, was in turn tied to a glamorous New York lifestyle. They weren't about to upset that carefully piled Big Apple cart for a newbie—Stanford, Heisman and Rose Bowl champion be damned.

Last year's Super Bowl was playing on a big screen. The Philadelphia Quakers were once again pitted against the San Francisco Miners and just as inevitably were their respective quarterbacks. Rumor was they hated each other as much as their teams did. It was understandable. As far as Quinn could see, the quarterbacks had nothing in common except that each was, in his own way, brilliant—and beautiful.

Quinn felt a stirring in his groin, blushed and, looking around quickly to make sure none of his preoccupied teammates noticed, forced himself to concentrate on the one thing that was certain to dampen any ardor—Smalley's banal words.

"Listen up, people. See this here video."

"We're streaming it, Coach," Greg Moll said.

"Hey, maggot, whatever," Smalley went on. "This here video is one we're going to study the rest of the year. And you know why? 'Cause at the end of the coming season, it's gonna be us in the video, us everyone's talking about and studying. Now hit the showers."

"Question is," Greg whispered to tight end Derrick Muldavey, "are we the Quakers or the Miners, the winners or the losers?"

Derrick laughed. Quinn couldn't help but laugh, too. What would they do without what passed for wit in the Temps' locker room?

"Novak, a word in my office," Smalley said. "Close the door and take a seat."

Quinn clenched and unclenched his left hand. He wondered why coaches' offices always resembled cinder-block bunkers and why people who seemed so perfectly average—round features, crimson coloring, incipient beer gut—could be so spectacularly mean.

"It says here that you had a 4.0 average at Stanford, majoring in classics. You lettered in baseball and football and speak several languages, including—"

Here Smalley stumbled.

"Bahasa," Quinn said.

"What is that?"

"It's the official language of Indonesia. I grew up there."

"Your family is with one of them big corporations, right?"

"Something like that."

"Well, well. Looks like I got myself a regular Renaissance man here."

Don't, Quinn thought, the color rising in his burnished cheeks. Don't.

"I prefer to think of myself as a man of many interests," he said. Here he paused before adding, "Coach."

He was trying, really he was. But Christ, you didn't have to be a classics major—indeed you didn't have to know Homer from Homer Simpson—to see what was going on. But if you were and you did, Smalley was Agamemnon, the boss from Hell, and he himself was Achilles, not the type to knuckle under to a bad boss. What for? It was the same old, same old—starting out as eager to please as a newborn pup, only to be dropped from a tenth-story window, your brains dashed against the pavement by someone's capricious detachment or out-and-out hostility. It was Jakarta 2.0 and he couldn't go back there—wouldn't go back there—not when he had put that Pandora's box so carefully on a shelf.

"You think you're smart, don't you?" Smalley was saying. "Well, then, understand this, boy"—-and here his broad, gap-tooth grin turned icy—"you ain't ever going to be starting quarterback of the New York Templars."

Quinn met that grin with one of his own. "Guess we'll just have to wait and see, won't we?"

He kept that smile tightly in place as he emerged from Smalley's office, but it was no use. His stomach plunged as his heart rose. His mind raced, a jumble of emotions led by those well-traveled twins, rage and fear.

I am who I say I am, he thought. But he knew that wasn't true, not entirely; knew the Smalleys of the world still had the power to hurt him, because he let them—which made whatever indignity he suffered that much worse.

Alone in the shower room, he turned on the faucet and, leaning against the cool tile, pounded it with his left fist. As he let out an animal cry, the water caressed the creamy dunes of his muscular back like a warm Jakarta rain.

TWO

Jakarta, twelve years earlier

Running: It had been his earliest memory. Running from someone. Running toward something yet unknown. Running past the smiling Nemin, with the curved, blue laundry basket always at one graceful hip and her youngest trailing close by the other; past Sumarti, polishing, always polishing the black SUV with the company plates; past Gde, who clipped the hardy, nubby grasses and had the equally unenviable task each morning of gathering the fragrant frangipani blossoms that carpeted the lawn overnight as if by magic, their pink-tinged petals seemingly touched by a fairy's kiss.

Like all budding athletes, he had his rituals to observe before bounding out the door to the city beyond and freedom. The New York Yankees cap—symbol of a team and a city he had never seen but that loomed large in his dreams—tilted slightly to the left, just so. The yellow-green shirt— a salute to one of Jakarta's greatest baseball teams—worn loose over the long, skinny navy denim shorts, matched by the yellow-green socks and navy sneakers, also just so. But most important of all, the moment of tribute to the blue, white and yellow painting of his mother and her two equally fair-haired sisters, his aunts, who lived in America and whom distance had made all the more intriguing.

His family called it *The Three Graces* though the figures were less antique than Victorian, grouped as they were after those in John Singer Sargent's *The Wyndham Sisters*. Quinnie knew nothing of Sargent and the *Sisters,* and his knowledge of the ancient Greeks did not extend beyond his mythology class. But something compelled him to touch the thickly applied, swirling paints just above the red signature of the artist, John Kalen, in the lower right-hand corner—furtively, of course, lest his mother's wrath pour down on him.

Then and only then could he singsong "Good day, Gde," making a rhyming game of his name as he scooped up a frangipani blossom and, inhaling its sweet scent, skip past the heavy metal gate, past the guards and the baying Dobermans, laughing, always laughing.

"Good day, young master," Gde would say. "You be in big trouble."

And in truth, he would be, but Quinnie didn't care. He had escaped a Yankee Doodle oasis of tennis courts, swimming pools, barking dogs, barbed-wire fences and barbecues to another world, the real one where marble mansions, sleek hotels and onion-domed mosques collided with the tin shanties that lined brackish canals. There were no sidewalks save for the raised lanes along which lumbered battered buses, fat and red, so he dodged the ubiquitous Blue Bird taxis and the mopeds and motorcycles on which modern young women in too-short skirts clung to the waists of their boyfriends. Years later, whenever reporters asked how he became a running quarterback, he would flash on his twelve-year-old self darting through traffic as if it were an obstacle course and grin at the memory.

At the Youth Monument—which to Quinnie resembled Prometheus in his mythology textbook, holding a flaming disc aloft—he would pause reverently, admiring what he imagined to be the Titan who defied the gods to bring fire to Earth and thus free mankind. He felt a ripple of pleasure as he thought of him and his powerful physique. But on the brink of young manhood, he understood that such thoughts and feelings were best kept to himself—especially as his mother, Sydney, and a reluctant Nemin, would sometimes affront his newfound manly dignity by checking him for ticks and ensuring that he was scrubbing himself in the big, claw-foot tub, while he, ashamed, would keep his knees pressed tightly up against his chest.

"Filthy, always filthy," his mother would say as she'd grab the loofah to scour his still-tender flesh, "after these excursions to God knows where. I swear you'll be the death of me."

He'd be in for quite the scrub-a-dub-dub today, he thought, as he wandered through the courtyard of the National Museum, with its elephant gods and curvaceous goddesses. He felt enormous pride in its Doric columns as well as sympathy as the museum struggled to remodel and become something greater than itself.

In a sense, he was like the museum—not yet what he would be, still becoming—and that was exciting enough.

Today, he decided to forgo communing with the warrior gods and serene goddesses for a different kind of temple—one to sport rather than art. He pressed his nose against the chain-link fence surrounding a baseball diamond as he watched teenage boys in yellow, green and white uniforms, the ball arcing in the air from the pitcher's hand to the catcher's glove or back from the hitter's bat, setting the fielders in motion. The muffled, hollow sound of the ball hitting the catcher's glove alternated with the crisp crack of bat on ball. Quinnie was slender enough to slip through a break in the fence and take a seat behind home plate. As he watched the players veer continually between stillness and motion, he remembered the book that his oldest aunt— Selena, called Lena—had sent him, describing baseball as "America's pastime." That made him chuckle. Football, he knew from scouring the Internet, was really America's game, whereas baseball, as if to compensate for being eclipsed in its own country, belonged to the world and to youths like these who gathered in the early morning mist to play for a few hours before succumbing to the heat of the day.

He longed to join them now and risked much to watch them with no other thought than someday they would let him pitch. It was one of the things he really loved to do—throw a ball straight, curving, or spiraling. It was his gift—that and running.

The players must've sensed as much, for he heard them talk about letting him play in the bottom of the inning. It was highly irregular. But Quinnie didn't care, leaping from the bench.

"What position?" asked the pitcher, who also seemed to be the team manager.

"Yours but I also play a little infield," Quinnie responded in perfect Bahasa. He could see the others were unsure of what to make of him, he who had their coloring and some of their features but whose emerald eyes and height—at twelve, he was already as tall as they were—suggested he was a foreigner. His command of their language did nothing to ease their uncertainty even as it garnered their admiration.

The pitcher motioned him to the mound. Though the batter was a few years older and heavier than he, Quinnie refused to be intimidated. "Have courage," Aunt Lena would write in closing her regular emails to him, "and life will meet you halfway." He visualized the prism of the strike zone, extending from the slightly crouching hitter's chest to his knees, kicked his right leg high in the air and, reaching back, propelled the ball forward with his left arm, sending it over the heart of the plate as his right leg drove to the ground in a lunge.

Strike one.

Clearly, this was not what the team had expected. They had expected to humor a mascot, a pet, who would follow them like one of the mangy dogs that roamed the city. The players' coolly indulgent demeanor told Quinnie that they doubted he could do it again.

So again, he squinted toward the plate, imagining the strike zone and the sweet spot he would try to hit, but this time he took a little something off his fastball and it broke sharply.

Strike two.

Now the players leaned in, putting their collective weight behind the hitter, who stepped out of the batter's box, took a few swings and stepped back in, glaring at Quinnie as he cocked his bat. Quinnie's heart was beating so fast and so loud that he heard nothing else.

This is what I long for, he thought. This is what

I belong to.

He reared back. The hitter never saw it.

Strike three.

It was the same with the next batter and the next. Nine pitches, nine strikes. Three men up and three men down.

"From now on you play for us," the pitcher said.

Quinnie was at once elated and deflated.

"But I have school," he said. "I go to one of the schools President Barack Obama attended."

"Ah," the first baseman said. "Oh bah mah."

He pronounced the name with equal emphasis on all the syllables, reflecting the uninflected aspect of the Bahasa language and the awe in which the Indonesian people held Barack Obama—a man they saw as a native son, one of their own who made good on the stage of the far, wide world. To invoke his name was to utter a password that provided entry to a magical kingdom.

"He's like a god to these people," he remembered an executive saying at one of the many tedious cocktail parties his mother gave, through which he bobbed and weaved like a player in a video game, until Nemin corralled him for dinner in the kitchen with her youngest, Adhi.

"One party is as fatuous as the next," he said to the uncomprehending Adhi, "fatuous" being one of his new vocabulary words.

The executive—who worked for the same multinational company as Quinnie's mother—had not meant what he said as a compliment but as a way of devaluing both the president and the people Quinnie had grown up among.

But Quinnie admired the president, for like

Barack Obama, he felt he belonged to two worlds. Not for him the expat life lived behind the barbed wire of the American compound. When his mother and stepfather ventured out, it was always to one of the five-star hotels like the Shangri-La or the Four Seasons for Saturday night dancing or Sunday brunch. Quinnie had studied the Indonesian culture, worked in the rice paddies as part of a school project and persuaded Sydney—he always called her "Sydney" never "Mom"—to let him visit the Indonesian friends he made at school, which wasn't too hard since more often than not she was glad to be rid of him.

Except when his absence interfered with her plans—as it clearly did now.

Quinnie's joy in being accepted by the team evaporated when he saw Sumarti waiting by the fence, arms folded across his body. The brotherly familiarity he had earned among the players vanished in an instant as they realized by Sumarti's stance and the luxury car that their rookie was a figure of some importance.

Still, the pitcher-manager said, "You can play with us anytime," tossing him the ball with which he had struck out the side. He fingered it as if it were a talisman as he sat miserably in the middle of the backseat of the SUV, Sumarti eyeing him in the rearview mirror with a mixture of sympathy and disapproval that only deepened his unhappiness. Not even the sight of Prometheus heartened him. He had braved the wrath of the gods to light the world and paid a terrible price for being true to himself. Quinnie knew he would not be half so courageous facing his Hera-mother and Zeus-stepfather.

He tried to slip into the house as Nemin

bustled about with flower arrangements, trailed by Adhi and Gaucho, the black rescue Lab whose abandonment issues were such that he was always following close behind the family or sitting on their feet, earning his mother's icy rage. Both Quinnie and Gaucho had a timeshare on the doghouse.

"It doesn't in the least surprise me that you should be out gallivanting on this, one of the most important days of my life," Sydney said the moment he entered the house. "With so much still to be done for the New Year's Eve party tonight— the first time my boss will be here—and I have to send Sumarti after you. It's just typical of your willful selfishness that you would waste my time and distract me when you know how much this means to me."

She grabbed him roughly by the arm, took him into his bedroom and closed the door.

"You listen to me now. You do anything to fuck up this party tonight and so help me God I will come down on you like a tsunami, do you hear me? You will comport yourself among my guests like a perfect little gentleman and, after a respectable length of time, you will make your excuses and come back to this room, where you will remain for the rest of the evening. Do you hear me?"

"Ooh, let go. You're hurting me," he said.

"If I tell your father, he'll do much worse."

His father: She always called his stepfather, Chandler Parquist, his father when everyone knew his real father had been someone else—someone kinder, handsomer and darker but without the money and connections of his stepfather. Or so he imagined. It was not the kind of thing, he understood, you discussed.

Instead, Quinnie sat in his room, smarting from bruises and bruising words, wiping his eyes with his forearm. After a while, having tired of sulking like Achilles in his tent, Quinnie emerged from his bedroom to hear male voices coming from his mother and stepfather's bedroom.

It was the Afghan rug merchant, Kamel, and some of his workers putting down an Indian carpet. They were not part of the party staff and in theory could've, should've come on another day. But it was typical of Sydney that everything had to be done all at once perfectly, regardless of the cost to others. How had she described him—willfully selfish? Tree, meet apple.

Such moments, though, provided what passed for comic relief in the household as Kamel, revealing considerable butt cleavage, and his cohorts strained to shove the thick, cream-colored rug under the bed.

"You do realize you're going to have to move it," Quinnie offered.

"Ah, young Master Quinn. A Happy New Year to you."

"And to you, too, Kamel. So, you realize you're going to have to move all the furniture and center the rug or Sydney's going to flip."

Kamel sighed. His men, who spoke no English, looked puzzled.

"I'll help," Quinnie said with a smile.

Afterward, they admired their teamwork.

"You have a good heart, Quinnie," Kamel said. "Just like Mrs. Syd. She a wonderful woman."

He brought out his iPhone to show Quinnie pictures of his mother, posing at her company's headquarters with Kamel, his wife and their baby. Sydney was cradling the child, smiling. Quinnie didn't know that Sydney.

But Kamel was a decent man from a war-torn country with troubles of his own. Quinnie couldn't destroy his illusions. He handed the phone back to Kamel, smiling.

"Yes, we're very proud of her," was all he said.

The success of Sydney's party did nothing to assuage her anger toward Quinnie. For days, she gave him the curtain coming down, barely speaking to him except to issue curt criticisms.

He bore all this with something approaching grace, which he had acquired after years of trying to please her followed by years of tantrums and acting out. Now he did as he wanted. The way he figured it, you could be loved the way the world loves, with strings attached, or you could suit yourself. Quinnie had chosen the latter, often meeting Sydney's criticisms with a smile that was sure to deepen her unhappiness. At least, that's what he counted on.

Still, he had to be careful. His stepfather, who was often away, was not above taking a strap to him when he was there. Quinnie might flirt with the boundary of parental tolerance, but he wouldn't cross it.

He finally achieved a fragile truce at the end of the school term, though not without some outside help from an unexpected visitor. All the Novak girls were smart, talented and good-looking. But the statuesque Selena was the most independent-minded and expressive of the three. No wonder the slim, controlling Sydney described her older sister only in the most critical of terms.

"Honestly, she's so opinionated and full of herself," "El Syd"—as Chandler called his wife behind her back at such moments—said at dinner one night shortly before her arrival.

"Oh, I don't know," Quinnie said with a smile. "From her emails, she sounds like fun."

He said this as much out of spite as out of a desire to express what he truly thought. He knew how to push his mother's buttons.

"Who asked your opinion?" she said. "You're as bad as she is. You two should get on famously."

And indeed they did. From the moment she arrived with a baseball glove and a football for him—"I know you like both," she said with a smile—Quinnie was sold on Aunt Lena. For one thing, unlike his mother—who was often too exhausted except for her company friends—Aunt Lena had a lot of energy and liked to do stuff, he observed happily. She had been the editor of the Far East edition of *Rumours* magazine—she now headed up the New York office—and seemed to know everyone and everything. But if he were brutally honest with himself, something he tried not to be too often, he would have admitted that loving Aunt Lena had the bonus effect of unsettling his mother and stepfather, both of whom were intimidated by her.

"Aunt Lena, what's New York like?"

"It's like Jakarta, kiddo—only with potable drinking water courtesy of the Croton Reservoir and an infrastructure that actually lets you get around town, even on foot."

"Of course, though the cities are about the same size, New York has ten times the murder rate," Chandler chimed in, fiddling at the dinner table with his iPhone, iPad, iSomething. Chandler had a big job with the multinational company that Quinnie's mother worked for and was now a consultant. That was all Quinnie knew or cared to.

Aunt Lena, however, was not one to be overawed. She looked hard at Quinnie's "father"—she often pronounced the word with an exaggerated emphasis that made his mother blanch—and said, "Whenever people say anything about New York, I like to remind them that on a very bad day, when we saw the worst of humanity, New York showed the very best. New Yorkers acted with courage, purpose, and without self-pity."

"Always on a soapbox, Lena," Sydney said, sighing as Chandler colored.

Quinnie merely smiled triumphantly and took a sip of Coca-Cola. He liked to make it last as he was only allowed to drink Coke—nectar of the gods, as his mythology teacher might say—on special occasions like this. Yet another reason to love Aunt Lena. So when she asked him to be her date Saturday night—"You can tell all your friends you're seeing an older woman," she offered—visions of Coca-Cola danced in his head.

"Mind your manners," his mother warned. "Be careful what you say—your aunt doesn't need to know all our business—and for God's sake, watch what you eat."

"I will, Sydney," Quinnie said, already dreaming of a night of gossip, cheeseburgers, fries and free-flowing Cokes at B.A.T.S.

With its blond wood and green leather upholstery, B.A.T.S.—or the Bar at the Shang, as in the Shangri-La Hotel—was a decidedly grown-up place. Already it was overflowing with the expat crowd bopping to a band that did serviceable Adele covers. Quinnie was in his element, taking it all in from the dining area in his new navy blazer and khakis, and nodding his head to the beat as he sipped what he hoped would be the first of at least a couple of Cokes.

Given the way Aunt Lena was savoring her Cosmo and singing along to *Set Fire to the Rain,* the prospect seemed good. Quinnie watched as three dainty young women teetered in on four-inch heels—China dolls in satiny pastels, their hair piled high—and signed a book before mingling with the crowd.

"Aunt Lena, how come we didn't sign the book when we came in?"

"Because, kiddo, we're not here to entertain gentlemen," she said.

Quinnie blushed, sensing there was something wrong with what these pretty, young women were doing. His aunt didn't elaborate, and he didn't press her for details—for which they were both grateful.

Aunt Lena waited until Quinnie was in the throes of his rare cheeseburger, sweet-potato fries and second Coke—a third would follow, along with Aunt Lena's second Cosmo—when she dropped her bombshell.

"Quinnie, how would you like to come live with me in New York?"

"Me? Really?"

He was stunned. New York—home of the Yankees, a chance to watch and play American sports in American arenas. Still, he would miss his team, his schoolmates, Nemin, Adhi, Sumarti, Gde, Gaucho, Jakarta—just about everything, he thought.

Well, not quite everything. The idea that he would be leaving his mother and stepfather bothered him not a whit, except to make him wonder why it didn't. Maybe it did, just a bit. Why didn't he love them? Why didn't they love him?

"Your mother and I were talking, and it seemed to both of us that with your athletic ability, you'll need an American high school and an American university."

What she was too kind to mention was what he had, unbeknown to her, overheard.

"I just can't do it anymore, Lee. He's growing up, becoming a man and he's getting more and more difficult to handle. Chan and I, of course, have tried. But he's just so hostile. It's a terrible thing to say you don't love your own child, but I don't love him."

"Oh, Sydie," Aunt Lena had said. "Then how could you ever hope that he would love you? How will he ever grow into a man who can love and be loved?"

"I don't know. Maybe if you were to take him..."

Tears, hot tears then. It was one thing to suspect she didn't love him. It was another to have the confirmation from her own lips.

"Think it over," Aunt Lena was saying to him.

"I don't have to," he said. "Yes."

He was packed within days, even though he wasn't leaving for two weeks. But as the date approached, Quinnie realized he had allowed what—or rather whom—he hated to blind him to what he loved.

He cried when he presented Nemin, Sumarti and Gde with the tokens of his affection—a miniature tea set for Nemin with thimble-size cups in a red, blue and yellow-colored dragon motif, a symbol of protection, and Louis Vuitton wallets for Sumarti and Gde. Actually, they were some of Jakarta's famous knockoffs, but the stitching was fine and he had insisted on paying for them with his own money. He gave Adhi a new soccer ball. And Gaucho—oh, leaving him was the greatest stab to the heart—a big box of doggie biscuits.

"Such a thoughtful boy," Nemin said to Sumarti in Bahasa. Apparently, not everyone thought he was so difficult.

He treated his baseball team to pizza from the Shang.

"Don't forget us," the manager said, shaking hands at the end of their pizza party.

Forget you? Quinnie thought. Someday, I'll return like Barack Obama, a favorite son triumphant.

But to his mother and stepfather, he had nothing to say or give.

Rather, on the day of departure, he sat calmly in the back seat of the SUV, waiting for Aunt Lena to take leave of Chandler and Sydney.

"Quinnie," Aunt Lena whispered, leaning into the back seat, "please get out and say a proper goodbye to your mother and father."

"I've already said my goodbyes," Quinnie said.

"Quinton Day Novakovic," Aunt Lena said, using his full, legal name. "You get your butt out of this car right now and kiss your mother and father goodbye." Here she paused before adding more softly, "Quinnie, we don't know what will happen in this world. Don't leave things this way."

"I'm sorry, Aunt Lena. I love you. But I won't do that, not even for you."

Aunt Lena looked sheepish as she stood by the car with Sydney and Chandler. Perhaps she now had an inkling of what Sydney meant by "difficult". Maybe she was regretting her offer to take him. She seemed weary, and it was only 7 a.m.

"Take care of yourselves," he heard Sydney say with surprising emotion.

But it was not enough to melt him.

"Goodbye, Sydney," he called out, waving from the car. "Goodbye, Chandler."

They rode to the airport in silence as the intermittent rain that punctuated the rhythm of Jakarta's days and nights fell. Soon the dry season would be in full swing, ushering in a wave of tourists. Quinnie was glad for the quiet as it gave him a chance to take in every mosque, canal and shanty. Even the fatuous billboards with the politicians standing stiffly—their chests puffed out like pigeons on a perch—filled him with longing. This was his home, his native land, and Quinnie had no illusions about what was to come. Someday another place would lay claim to his affections, and Jakarta—indeed, all of Indonesia—would recede, even as it receded now in the rearview mirror.

Perhaps sensing his regret, Aunt Lena brightened at the airport.

"We'll have a few days to relax in Singapore and Hong Kong before we have to start thinking about a new school for you. And you'll need new clothes, too. It can get pretty cold in New York."

He had never seen snow, he thought as he strapped on his seatbelt. A video droned on about new improvements to Eagles Airlines. The plane leaked. Ironic, he thought, using the last new word he had learned in his English vocabulary lesson.

"It is ironic that the plane is leaking as the airline's video boasts of improvements."

His English teacher would be proud. His English teacher: She, too, was part of the past, while his future lay 10,000 miles ahead. Aunt

Lena took note of the leak and smiled at him.

"It'll stop when we're above the clouds," she said.

They began to taxi.

"Well, here we go," she said, squeezing his hand.

She crossed herself. Quinnie followed suit. They hurtled down the runway, the green fields and red-tile roofs passing in a blur that would fade to blue.

Goodbye, Jakarta, Quinnie thought. Goodbye, Indonesia. Goodbye, my home.

He started to cry. Aunt Lena leaned over and whispered, "Have courage, and life will meet you halfway."

As the wheels lifted, so did his spirits, and he felt lighter than wings.

THREE

"The trick, kiddo," Aunt Lena used to say, "is to be happy in the moment."

But Quinn knew that for some—himself included—it was easier to appreciate "the moment" once it had already passed. He missed Aunt Lena, missed everything about Jakarta— well, almost everything—but never more so than on those raw November days when the prospect of winter stretched out before him like a vast, frozen wasteland and he paced the sidelines of Templars Stadium with a clipboard and a ski cap.

They were the kind of days that offered no comfort. The wind would blow off the marshes— land that some clever reporter discovered had, ironically enough, once belonged to Quinn's French ancestors—bringing with it a dampness that seeped into the bones and made it impossible to sit, stand, pace or play too long before every joint and muscle throbbed. Still, Quinn was convinced that it would matter not a whit if he were doing what he was born to do—play. Instead, it was all Lance all the time, even though the Temps rarely won. And on those plays when Lance came out of the game, Smalley called on third- string quarterback Dave Donaldson.

So Quinn compensated for the humiliation by over-preparing—memorizing the playbook (he had an eidetic memory); watching game film until he was bleary-eyed; absorbing everything the coaches said; throwing until his arm felt like it would fall off; and working out until his feet were calloused and his hands, raw and bleeding.

It was one thing to prepare for a game, another to play it. The annals of QB history were filled with the urban legends of men who were all parade, no battle. And Quinn feared not only that his lack of field time would stunt his development as a QB but that it was also what he secretly desired—to stay safe on the sidelines. But that was not what quarterbacks were born for. So he kept himself primed to such an extent that he didn't need the cuff other QBs wore with a cheat sheet of the various plays. He knew them by heart.

That comforted him a bit, as did the fans' encouragement.

"No-vak, No-vak, No-vak," they chanted, while girls in fetching outfits that revealed plenty of cleavage and thighs reddened by the autumn chill held up signs saying, "Quinn for the win."

The man with the aptly rhyming moniker, however, had no illusions about the fans. They were the mob, the modern equivalent of the ancient Roman rabble. They liked him, because they didn't know him and could write whatever narrative they wanted on what they thought was a tabula rasa. The minute they discovered who he was, they might turn on him, especially if he didn't deliver.

But he knew he would never disappoint—if given the chance. He also knew that nothing short of a miracle would give him that chance, certainly not a mere dismal trouncing by newbie franchise the Orlando Copperheads.

"Smalley, Smalley, burn in Hell," the fans shouted along the railing as the team skulked toward the locker room at halftime, trailing 35-7.

"Muldavey, Moll, you're worthless. You're all maggot bastards. Not you, Novak. We want you in there for the second half."

When the press criticized his teammates and gleefully reported their transgressions—an easy pursuit, for they were many—Quinn tried to remember the vomit of vulgarity that fans spewed in their faces week after week. Not since his days at Stanford, when rival fans would text him death threats before a game, had he encountered such viciousness.

The Templar fans' rage was equaled only by Smalley's halftime rants, which rhymed four-letter words in surprisingly inventive ways: Pornography, meet poetry, Quinn thought. Or at least anatomically impossible rap. (He himself tried to refrain from cursing until Thursdays, figuring if the week hadn't improved by then it was unlikely to do so, and even then he reserved it for moments of high emotion.)

During these tirades, he had learned to stay transfixed on the litany of verbal abuse else Smalley might think you weren't paying sufficient attention.

"Having a low-blood sugar moment, are we?" Smalley said the day Greg Moll had the temerity to unwrap a Mini Snickers during one of these "Poetry Slams." Smalley took the candy then and shoved it down Greg's throat so forcefully that he began to gag and Quinn and the others had to intervene.

Such volatility was the tip of the globally warmed iceberg. That most of the team wasn't serving time in Sing Sing was its real accomplishment, Quinn thought. There was safety Cesare Dalton, who had beaten an involuntary manslaughter rap after he choked his girlfriend to death during rough sex; punter Indigo West, who had been arrested trying to buy weed and coke from an undercover cop in the shadow of the George Washington Bridge; and ever-prolific tackle Jeremiah Dupré, who had 15 kids by 12 women in 11 states. Such was the achievement that Greg and Derrick Muldavey, who would've fancied themselves team ironists had they understood the concept of postmodern irony, once presented Jeremiah with a framed map of the United States containing diamond push pins where he had "multiplied, filled the earth and subdued it," in the words of the Good Book. Jeremiah was so touched he broke down and cried, hugging his generous teammates.

Sometimes, some of the Jeremiah juniors visited the locker room, where they clung to various players like barnacles to a boat, for Jeremiah was an affectionate if understandably distracted daddy. Quinn felt sorry for the Jere juniors and tried to be patient with them and their endless questions, their touching of things that didn't belong to them and general interference. Perhaps they reminded him of himself. They certainly reminded him of his long-cherished dream and the reason he tolerated everything the NFL had thrown at him—to build a new, state-of-the-art orphanage and school in Jakarta.

"Get these bastards out of here," Smalley would yell at the risk of offending Jeremiah, who was one of his best players.

No worries: The actual Jeremiah Junior, the oldest of the litter at age 10, gave as good as he got.

"You're kind of fat," he said to Smalley, who turned beet-red.

"Kind of?" Greg whispered to Derrick, who caught Quinn's eye, and the three dissolved into giggles, which was why they were running an extra ten miles in the rain the next day.

"That's right," Smalley screamed. "When I'm finished with you guys, you'll be too tired to laugh, let alone suck dick."

Such punishments were worth it, though, Quinn thought, for the opportunity to savor the way Jere Junior had stood up to Smalley—Quinn never called him "Coach" except to his face, preferring to refer to him instead as "Small E"— and for the look on his face.

At least no one questioned Jeremiah's sexual prowess. Whereas, if you weren't doing it with a woman or talking about doing it with a woman every five minutes you were suspect. Quinn hadn't been with the team long before the, "So, dating anyone special? If not, I know this chick," conversation began.

It's not that he didn't find women objectively attractive. It's just that he was sexually excited by men, two in particular—Tamarind Tarquin, the quarterback of the San Francisco Miners, and Mallory Ryan, the Philadelphia Quakers' QB.

Often late at night, when he couldn't sleep, Quinn would imagine the three of them in bed, engaged in a water-dance with himself in the middle, melting into their arms as he surrendered to and received their strength. While he stroked his erect cock in a soft cloth slathered with lube, he thought of Tam pinning his arms behind his back as he entered him and Mal sucked him off, then came, smearing the come on his belly.

The fantasy would leave the shivering Quinn sticky and sated but also ashamed as he was one of those men for whom sex was not enough. He wanted to love and be loved.

Of course, it was a dream too far, Quinn knew. That's what made it so delicious. In reality, Mal was rumored to have a girlfriend or two, while Tam was said to be a player, with a different date for every red-carpet event. Even if they were free and gay, they hated each other, perhaps owing to their having been rivals since their high school days in Philly—an antagonism that reached its pinnacle when the Quakers drafted Mal instead of Tam, which sportscasters couldn't stop mentioning.

But it would be exquisite, wouldn't it, Quinn thought, to test his mettle against them on the field and then off it in an arena of another kind, one buffeted by cool, silky 600 thread-count sheets, soft pillows and whispers of things you did only in the dark.

"So, got a girl?" Jeremiah asked Quinn after the Temps' 48-7 loss to the Copperheads.

With that, Brenna James of The New York Record came rushing into the locker room and proceeded to spill the contents of her huge, green suede hobo bag.

"Oh, God, I'm sorry," she said as Quinn helped her collect her compact and cell and their eyes locked. "I'm so clumsy."

"Not at all," Quinn said, smiling at her.

He watched as she tramped to Smalley's office.

"Sometimes," he said to Jeremiah, "you want what you can't have."

Jeremiah nodded as if he knew what he didn't.

FOUR

In life, there is only narrative, Quinn realized.

Control the narrative, and you control public opinion. That was real power.

Brenna had that kind of power. As a columnist for *The Wreck,* she had alluded to Smalley's prejudice against Quinn in the past. Now she actively lobbied for him to replace Lance. In a column titled *Free Quinn Novak,* she delivered the coup de grace:

Pharaoh was forced to free the Israelites from bondage in Egypt.

Lincoln liberated the slaves.

It's time for the New York Templars to get off their assets. Play Quinn Novak or trade him to a place where his many admirers can thrill to this transcendent talent.

Soon, *Free Quinn Novak* T-shirts, mugs, banners, and parties began cropping up around New York. Others tweeted, Instagram-ed, Facebook-ed, blogged, and—oh, yes—wrote about him, or Brenna writing about him. He became a cause célèbre even among those who knew nothing of football.

It wasn't the kind of fame he wanted—to be known for who he was rather than what he did. But he could hardly complain when the perks and endorsements that came his way helped others, including the orphans back in Indonesia. Then came the backlash.

"I want that bitch muzzled," he overheard

Smalley say to two men in one of the "catacombs"—the yellow-green and blue cinder-block tunnels that snaked through the bowels of the stadium. "I don't care how you do it, just do it."

Alarmed, Quinn texted her.

"Don't worry (lol)," she texted back. "I can take care of myself."

Still, she was subjected to death threats, received packages containing used condoms, and was even hit in the back with a football "unintentionally" by tight end Taylor Higgs, one of Lance's henchmen—which led Quinn to call him out.

"Stay away from her," Quinn told him, "or you—and anyone else who tries to harm her—will answer to me."

"Ooh, I'm scared," Taylor said, laughing.

Quinn smiled. Then he decked him. Hey, he figured, some people never learn.

"I don't want you to stick your neck out for me anymore," he wrote Brenna in a note that accompanied a dozen red roses interspersed with stargazer lilies. "Still, I appreciate it more than I can say. If you ever need anything, you come to me."

"She's nothing but Novak's whore," a teammate,Taylor? Lance?, was quoted anonymously as saying, which raised a momentary firestorm in the press once again about the NFL's continuing female trouble—this despite new regulations implemented after its domestic abuse crisis—and the way men fought one another on the battlefield of female sexuality.

Though everyone denounced the remark, it suggested that the columnist and the quarterback were secret lovers, which both were quick to deny, thereby only stoking the rumors.

Those rumors had their advantage. The "So, got a girl?" questions ceased. It was, Quinn knew, a sad world when a lie and a possible breach of journalistic ethics were preferable to him than revealing the truth that he was a gay virgin. He continued to say nothing, though. And that was sad, too. But then, he was no Michael Sam. At least not yet. Why declare his preference for a certain "team" when he had yet to play for it, right?

The *Free Quinn Novak* campaign came to a head in a stunning way when Lance broke his left leg in the wee hours of a Sunday morning before the big game against the loathed Philadelphia Quakers and quarterback Mal Ryan.

"There is indeed a God," one fan tweeted, "because Lance-o-little couldn't stink up the joint more."

That was before the Twitteratti got wind of how Lance broke his leg. It seemed that he and "muy caliente Argentine soul-mate"—as she was invariably described in the press to such an extent that it became an epithet, like "rosy-fingered dawn" in *The Iliad*—had been engaging in some lubricious foreplay involving the new Black Orchid body lotion when Lance slid off her and the bed, suffering a freak stress fracture.

"'What a fall was there,'" one surprisingly literary poster wrote on the Temps' blog, echoing that great coach known as the Bard.

"In a fall worthy of Adam and Eve," *The New York Gazette* intoned, "Lancelot Reinhart slid off *muy caliente* Argentine soul-mate Ileana Cardenas and into a maelstrom of controversy and uncertainty, throwing the Temps' season into doubt."

"Season? What season?" Derrick said after reading the story. "Do we have a season? And what doubt? The way I look at it there's no doubt where we're headed—the bottom of our division."

Smalley was so inconsolable that he started hyperventilating.

"We have to win this one for Lance," he gasped between sobs.

"Not quite *Brian's Song*, is it?" Greg whispered to Derrick.

"Hey, hey," Smalley yelled at them, his face growing so red that his players feared blood would start gushing from his nostrils. "The leader of this team is hurting. Have some respect. Donaldson, it's on your shoulders tonight. Make Lance proud."

Stunned, embarrassed silence. Quinn knew Smalley hated him. Now he knew just how much. To pass him over for Dave, it was more than humiliating. Even Dave himself didn't think he should start.

When the Freers or Quinnies—as Quinn's fans were known—found out, they exploded.

"Since when is the second-string quarterback passed over for the third?" Brenna texted. "Oh, right, when they play for Smalley."

"Just want to wish you the best, man," Quinn told Dave, giving him a bro shoulder bump.

"I can't do it," Dave said.

"Of course, you can," Quinn said. "As my aunt always said, 'Have courage and life will meet you halfway.'"

"No, you don't understand," and with that Dave let loose a stream of projectile vomit worthy of Linda Blair in *The Exorcist*. Whereupon the trainer and team physician were summoned—to say nothing of the clubhouse man with a mop and bucket—and Dave was pronounced ill enough from the flu to be sent off to the hospital.

Smalley didn't say anything to Quinn before the game. He didn't have to. Quinn was feeling enough pressure. This was the nationally televised Sunday night game, and the stakes were made clear by the mediocre-former-players-turned-commentators who bloviated on the pregame show.

"Boy oh boy, Coach, with Lance Reinhart out for the season and Dave Donaldson a scratch, facing perhaps the greatest team the NFL has ever produced, the entire Temps' season rests on the lean shoulders of one rookie quarterback Quinton Day Novak," Rufus Washington salivated with his usual ungrammatical earnestness to former coach and broadcast partner Joe Nowicki. "And you know, Coach, the Temps' fans have to be wondering about now if he's up to the challenge."

"Well, Ruf, we'll know in a few hours, won't we?"

Yes, Ruf, we sure will, Quinn thought as he passed the TV. Jesus Christ, no wonder people thought football players were no-neck neo-Neanderthals.

"Look," Quinn told his teammates before play began, "I'm not going to make a big speech, because we've had enough drama for a whole season, let alone one day. All I want to say is, we can make the drama worthwhile by winning this."

Early on, it looked as if that would be impossible as the Quakers' defense boxed Quinn in. But then he remembered himself. Finding he couldn't get rid of the ball, he simply ran with it. And suddenly he was no longer at Templars

Stadium but back there—back in Jakarta with Nemin, Adhi, Sumarti, Gde, his baseball teammates and Aunt Lena—all the people he loved and who loved him. He would not break faith with them.

In the end zone, he raised his arms triumphantly. He could've kept on running, so great was the rush. Instead, he dropped to one knee quickly and, just as quickly, crossed himself. "Thank you, God," he prayed. "And thanks, Aunt Lee."

He jogged back to his position, acknowledging neither the cheers, which were now all-enveloping, nor the steam pouring from the nostrils of the opposition.

The Quakers sacked him, and his brain pushed against his aching skull and helmet. His mind longed to slip the confines of bone and plastic as his body—ravaged by the opposition's pile-on—was buried alive.

"Get the fuck off him." His teammates were yelling now, the sounds indistinct at first as if he were underwater—or beyond the grave. Only slowly did the words come into focus as his teammates clawed their way to free him, bringing with them a lightness of feeling. He knew then that they had his back, knew he would rise again. For this was what he did; this was who he was; this was all he had to give.

He was under center again—clear-headed once more, cool, collected, commanding.

"22, 55, hut," he directed, his trained baritone channeled and strong. On the field of battle that day, Quinn found his voice and knew it would pierce the cold, the crowd, anything.

The Quakers struck back—the empire always

does—but they would never recover from the shock of Quinn drawing first blood as they lost 21-14.

After the game and all the following week, the story was about Quinn—"Rookie QB Stuns Super Bowl Champs."

This is what the Quinnies wanted, Brenna wrote in her postgame column, which was equal parts glee and schadenfreude, *to see their man have his moment in the sun. And he didn't disappoint. All his promise and all the tragedy and heartache he's endured—the long road from Jakarta, the waiting on the sidelines as other men got the call—all of it was fulfilled today.*

He was, as *Rumours* magazine noted, "the toast of the town." Even talk-show hosts who had made fun of him were deluging the Temps' easily exasperated PR guy, Harvey Soffel, to book him.

"Thank you for this," Quinn said when he caught up with Brenna after a practice session.

"You're welcome for this, but I did nothing. It was you. You're on your way."

"That remains to be seen," Quinn said. "People recover from the flu. Broken legs heal."

Brenna shook her head. "They'll have a hard time putting this genie back in the bottle."

What he remembered most from that strange, wonderful day, though, was not what she said or the fans or the crush of media but Mal coming up to congratulate him in the postgame ritual in which winners and losers exchanged words of bland grace that rode on plumes of breath in the night air.

"I guess we'll be seeing more of each other," Mal whispered in his ear.

His splayed fingers—with their massive ten-inch span from thumb to pinky—spread like tentacles around Quinn's coiled waist, and he in turn experienced an electric thrill he still felt forbidden to know.

FIVE

As the November possibility of snow turned to December certainty, the Temps' record improved in inverse proportion to Smalley's mood. Dave Donaldson, it turned out, didn't have the flu but colon cancer. With him and Lance out for the season at least, it was all on Quinn. Another man would've considered it a stroke of luck—no, a blessing from the gridiron gods—to have lost two quarterbacks and not only survived but thrived. Coach Smalley, however, was not another man.

"You're supposed to stand in the goddamn pocket and throw the ball," Smalley would scream at Quinn. "Stand and deliver. That's what a pure pocket passer does. But you'll never be a pure pocket passer, a real quarterback, because you're too fucking stupid, stubborn and gutless to do anything but run."

"That's a load of crap, Coach, and you know it," Quinn would say. "I can deliver from the pocket. I do deliver from the pocket. But if no one's open, I like our chances with my speed."

"And risk getting injured when we have no one else right now? And then what am I going to do, smart ass, huh? You'll end up like all those other running quarterbacks. You'll run yourself right out of the league."

Quinn knew Smalley had a point. (Was there anything more annoying than someone you hated being right?) But he also got the not-so-subtle

45

subtext of these supportive chats. "Running quarterback" was code for the QBs of color who made up the vast portion of that category. The 411 was that they were athletic enough, all right, but not smart enough for the job. Quinn knew that wasn't true, knew that while some people had brains or talent—wasn't that the theme of one of his favorite films, *Bull Durham*?—he, like his running QB brothers, had both.

"You are brilliant, beautiful, talented and kind, my Quinnie," Aunt Lena would say. "Someday you'll be rich and famous, too. So you must give to others, even if it hurts. And I fear it will."

"I'm trying, Aunt Lee," Quinn would mutter under his breath after these go-rounds with Smalley. "But it ain't easy."

The more the team won—often with just Quinn's combination of charismatic, strategic leadership and late-game heroics—the more Smalley made him and his teammates suffer in ways that left the guys, including those who, for whatever reason, had not previously been in Quinn's corner, shaking their heads. These included grueling workouts that might have you retching, yet Quinn never minded. He liked pushing his body—and mind—to their limits. He figured it was all he really deserved. Besides, wasn't that what the NFL called character-building? he wondered with a bitter smile.

The failure of anyone to complete any portion of such workouts resulted in more weightlifting, running, cycling and sit-ups for the entire team. Quinn thought of filing a grievance with the players' union on behalf of his teammates, but what was the point? Half the team was already in violation of league dress and conduct codes to the tune of tens of thousands of dollars—fines that you still had to pay in part even if you won your challenge--so what good would a formal complaint do?

Quinn tried to shut out the pain that ran from both sides of his neck up through his ears. He didn't know which was worse—the workouts or Smalley's voice blaring from a bullhorn or loudspeaker.

"Come on, you nellies," he'd yell. "What're ya gonna do someday when you have real problems, like Dave? Pick up the pace or I will make you start from scratch."

"You know what this reminds me of?" Greg told Derrick and the others as they collapsed in the locker room, panting like porno stars. "That movie with Mel Gibson."

"That really narrows it down," Derrick said, barely able to get the words out as he lolled on a bench at last, his head rolling from side to side in ecstasy. "You mean, *The Passion of the Christ*?"

"No that's by Mel Gibson. I mean the one with Mel Gibson and the guy who played Hannibal Lecter—*Mutiny on the Bounty*."

"I think that version was just called *The Bounty*," Quinn offered quietly.

"That's it," Greg said to Quinn. "*The Bounty* and you're the guy the Hannibal Lecter guy keeps yelling at and we're like the ship's crew."

"Please," Derrick said, heading to the whirlpool bent like a creaky old man. "You know how I get seasick."

With Templars Stadium a dry-docked HMS Bounty, Quinn tried to serve as a buffer and distraction between Smalley's Capt. Bligh and the crew, er, players.

He visited Dave at Memorial Sloan Kettering, where he was undergoing tests.

"I'm scared, real scared," Dave said, tenting his eyes with one arm to hide his tears.

Quinn was scared, too. Should he pat that arm, or would that be too intimate? Oh, hell. He squeezed Dave's forearm.

"Pray," Quinn said, "and I'll pray for you. The whole team will."

Quinn organized his teammates around Dave's illness. They wore his number, 35, on their sleeves and flashed it—three fingers then five—whenever they got on the tube. They donated $10,000 to the American Cancer Society for every touchdown they scored. They sent him cards, flowers and teddy bears and rotated visits among themselves and their families—reminders that even on the road, they had him on their radar. The effect was twofold: It buoyed Dave and it made the team at once looser and more cohesive, putting its *Bounty*-full situation in perspective.

The Temps' other patient, though not nearly in as tough a spot, was more of a challenge for Quinn. He and Lance were rivals first, teammates second. But Quinn felt the need to set an example. So he circulated a get-well card among the team and organized a rotation of visits among Lance's pals, himself excluded.

The team was better than it had ever been. Everyone was happier with its play. Well, almost everyone.

"How could you?" Smalley shrieked. "How could you have allowed that interception?"

"We won, didn't we?" Quinn said.

"That's not the point," Smalley screamed. "We may not always be that lucky. It's gonna take more than luck to beat the Miners this Sunday."

That was true. If the Quakers were the best the NFL had produced—so far—the Miners were the only team capable of beating the best on any given Sunday. And in their QBs they had a pair of fascinating mismatched bookends—Mal Ryan and Tam Tarquin, two guys out of rival Philly high schools (Quaker Latin and St. Michael's respectively) and rival colleges (Penn State and the University of Pennsylvania), two stars once vying for the starting QB spot on the Quakers' roster. The Quakers went with Mal and Tam, incensed, signed with the Miners. The rest may not have been history, but it made for one hell of an ongoing sports conversation.

"And you know, Coach," Rufus Washington was saying to broadcast partner Joe Nowicki before the Sunday-night game. "Except for that legendary high-school championship game in which Tam Tarquin's team stunned Mal Ryan's, Mal has always had a beat on Tam."

Ah yes, the legendary all-city conference game in which the St. Michael's Tigers beat the Quaker Latin Panthers—a game so famous and so stunning for its outcome, with the underdog Tigers squeaking by the undefeated Panthers in the last moment of play on a Hail Mary-pass from Tam, that even people like Quinn, who was still growing up half a world away at the time, felt as if he'd been there.

It was true what Doofus, er, Rufus said about Tam and Mal, Quinn thought. Even their looks echoed their places relative to each other: At six feet four inches, Tam was an inch shorter, his thick hair a darker gold. The gray of his eyes was a warmer, kinder, more relaxed complement to

Mal's otherworldly aquamarine. Quinn found both men intoxicating, with their cut bone structure and builds. Indeed, when teammates dared wonder aloud how he could take the constant beatdown from Smalley, he dared not speak the two reasons. He parsed Mal's "I guess we'll be seeing more of each other" like a schoolgirl mooning over her first kiss. Had Mal meant on the field? Yes, of course, that was it. What else could it be?

But it was possible he meant personally, wasn't it? He had looked into Quinn's eyes and then whispered the words into his ear as he held him in a gesture of intimacy. The whole thing had lasted no more than a few seconds at best. But to a lonely virgin who had never been touched by a man, Mal's gesture was like a few drops of rain on a crimson succulent. Quinn's parched spirit soaked it up and stored whatever it could, replaying the moment constantly.

He was still blossoming under the memory of Mal's touch when he remembered that Tam and his Miners were coming to town. Quinn imagined the two rival QBs together and with him, Tam holding him gently from behind—his arms scooping under Quinn's, drawing his shoulders back—as Mal approached him.

"Mmm," Mal would murmur, "I love me some white chocolate." Then he would go down on him, sucking him as hard as he could, his teeth raking Quinn's cock as Quinn cried out and Tam—entering him from behind and cupping Quinn's buttocks as he thrust him forward into Mal's voracious mouth—would rasp, "It's OK. I've got you."

Tam was nicer than Mal—in imagination and

reality. When the Temps lost to the Miners 38-35—a gutsy effort in which Quinn played with a sinus infection—there was none of the exercising of control in victory that Mal had in defeat. Instead, Tam wrapped Quinn in a bear hug.

"I know you're gonna be one of the greats," he said as he pulled away, laughing and patting Quinn's stuffy, ski-capped head.

And then he was gone. It wasn't the fantasy-inducing prelude to a boner that Mal's seductive gesture had been—it was too big-brotherly for that—but it was warmer, more direct, more honest.

The thought that he had the love, respect, admiration, affection—whatever—of the two finest quarterbacks in the league, not to mention the two objects of his desire, was enough to sustain Quinn through the latest round of Smalley abuse.

"You know, the only thing worse than a niggah, is a half-niggah," Smalley said afterward. "You cost the team this game. I just hope your lousy play doesn't cost us a playoffs spot as well, you hear me?"

Loud and clear, Quinn thought as he ran his punitive extra laps around the field amid flurries, his head pounding. He imagined Tam cupping his chiseled jaw in the shadow of the stands and himself holding Tam's gray-eyed gaze with his own big green eyes peering out from under curling lashes.

"You are so beautiful," Tam would say. "How could anyone be so cruel to someone so lovely?"

Then Tam would tug at Quinn's waistband. "You know what the sexiest part of a man is? Right here," Tam would whisper thickly, exposing and tracing the café-au-lait-colored flesh and throbbing vein to the right of Quinn's mossy man-fur. "As smooth and perfect as marble. Only you're not cold and white like marble but dark and so warm."

Quinn jerked his head around, as if the empty stadium could read his thoughts. How pathetic was that—to be afraid to be who he was, even in his own mind? In his headphones, Seal sang:

Pretend you don't see it, that we can live a lie, so you run, so you run.

SIX

Smalley needn't have worried. The Temps made the playoffs easily. It had been a foregone conclusion, Quinn reasoned, not because he was arrogant or the team was even that good but because in the NFL, it was possible to have a losing record and still make the playoffs. The Temps, at 9 and 7, were certainly better than that. Maybe not much better but still good enough for a system that was like The Grammy Awards, with its zillion categories and nominees.

Indeed, Quinn was surprised that his dead grandparents weren't in the playoffs or Sami, who owned the newsstand he frequented. It was a system that rewarded mediocrity or the merely good, particularly in the early rounds. To make it beyond the division championships, however, the Temps were going to have to be better than good. They were going to have to be lucky. And, as Quinn well knew, no one was lucky forever.

Smalley stalked the stadium as if his luck had already run out, telling any reporter who was willing to listen that the Temps were no match for whomever.

It is, Brenna noted in one column, *as if he were willing the team to lose, now that Novak is the signal-caller and not Reinhart.*

That certainly seemed to be true, Quinn thought. And it was equally true that Smalley was careful to credit the team's success to its steady defense, its surging offense, anything but Quinn's play.

He didn't care. Quinn knew that success had many fathers. Whereas failure, in Smalley's view, had only Quinn as parent.

If Smalley walked around as if his best friend had died, New York was elated—lit up in the Temps' colors, with a vibrant attitude to match. For his part, Quinn was determined not to let Smalley rob him of his joy. All adulthood, he knew, was but a reaction to childhood. You were trying either to replicate memories you cherished or make up for those you lacked—though more often than not you wound up repeating a troubled past. In a way, Smalley was nothing more than Sydney and Chandler revisited. It made Quinn doubly happy to know that his happiness pissed Smalley off. No doubt Quinn had his enemies in mind when he agreed to pose for a layout in New York *Rumours* magazine, although he quickly wondered what he had gotten himself into.

"Watch your back," Brenna had warned when she heard about it, "to say nothing of your clothes."

"Meaning?" Quinn asked, blushing.

"Let's just say my former editor, Vienne Le Wood, is well-known for dressing famous male athletes—and undressing them just as easily."

He hadn't been on the set of the photo shoot five minutes when she arrived, a tall, angular woman with a surprisingly mincing gait, given her height—as if those size eleven tootsies had failed to escape foot-binding—a dyed black bob parted on the side and lacquered behind her ears, florid coloring and an understatedly luxurious black pantsuit that whispered, even to fashion novice Quinn, "Armani."

Vienne—who preferred animals to people unless they were young, beautiful, male and distinguished—had one distinctive accessory, a rescue Papillon named Steve McQueen who was the bane of everyone else's existence since he bit anyone he came into contact with, forcing Vienne's poor, put-upon assistants to wear oven mitts when trying to corral him whenever he ran away, which was often. The minute Vienne opened her mouth, Quinn understood why.

"Of course, I have to be here," she said grandly, framing the space like a demented Erich von Stroheim with her fingers forming a rectangle. "Few people have my eye."

"That's for sure," Quinn heard one assistant say, sniggering to another.

All her presence did was unnerve Quinn, who felt quite like Steve McQueen—the dog, not the movie star or British film director---and enflame Elliott Gardener, whose onetime ad campaign for Dusk cologne with former tennis superstar Tariq Alí Iskandar Quinn had so admired. He had heard that Vienne had tried to seduce Iskandar, but he demurred, in part because she was so enamored of one of his rivals, Etienne Alençon. Good for him, Quinn thought as he stood before her in a black-and-gold brocade Alexander McQueen robe that was one of the props.

"All right," she said, eyeing him up and down, then whipping the robe from him as if she were offering him up in a sex club, "let's not be shy. Let's see you."

She patted his crotch, which sent a lightning bolt of pleasure through his nervous system.

"I want to make sure these compression undies fit properly."

The gesture had Gardener apoplectic while two young female interns tittered.

Quinn wasn't sure why it was necessary to make sure the underwear fit as he was supposedly going to be swathed in yards of purple velvet and animal print bedding "made" by beauty empress and Vienne favorite Estrelita Gonzalez, with only his head, chest and arms exposed.

"Now in this scene," Vienne said as if she were directing a big-budget Hollywood movie, "you've just awakened and are greeting your lover as she returns to the bed. Make love to the camera," Vienne said, leaning in—eyes wide, lips parted—as if she were Norma Desmond, ready for her close-up.

The look on Quinn's face must've said less "eager lover" than "deer caught in the headlights," for he saw Elliott motion quietly to his assistant Annabelle to move behind Vienne and then gestured for Quinn to look at Annabelle instead.

When Quinn looked at her, he saw not just the delighted, blushing young woman before him but the girl Brenna might've been as well as the commanding Mal and the devil-may-care Tam. Quinn's eyes—the color of absinthe in bar light—blazed as did his smile and he shifted comfortably, supporting his classically sculpted head, framed by a halo of curling black hair, with his right arm while his left met it, revealing a molded shoulder and a peekaboo nipple in a high, rounded pec. The photo was an immediate sensation, making Quinn a household name. Not since Farrah Fawcett had a mane and an insistent nipple done so much for pop culture—at least outside Templars Stadium.

Inside, a trembling Harvey Soffel quickly deposited a copy of the magazine in Smalley's empty office—and just as hastily left, making sure his cell phone and pager were off, knowing that the outrage would be heard across the Hudson all the way to the offices of *New York Rumours* at One World Trade Center.

"This, this," Smalley screamed in the locker room, "is the reason we'll lose. Because instead of preparing himself, our so-called leader is making porno pictures for some fag fashion magazine."

Given Smalley's wrath, the team thought it wise not to remind him of the sex tape that Lance had made with a barely eighteen-year-old Long Island girl, although to his credit, everyone guessed, he thought she was twenty-one.

Did Quinn think of any of this as he hurled an 80-yard pass into Greg's waiting arms in the last 30 seconds against the Copperheads to advance the team to the divisional playoff? Indeed, he had thought only of connecting.

"Go, go," he shouted as he ran down the field after Greg, watching him throw off one Copperhead after another.

Trailing him—in freedom, joy and certain triumph—Quinn leapt into his arms. He knew in that moment that he had passed from celebrity into stardom, and maybe even from stardom into legend.

SEVEN

In a Twitter era, Brenna James still had newsprint in her blood when it wasn't smudging her nose and fingers. That was partly because she was the daughter of Mort James, who had risen from sportswriter to editor-in-chief of *The New York Record,* the city's most influential newspaper. But mostly it was because Brenna was obsessed with print—books, magazines, newspapers, maps, scores, anything that allowed her to turn pages. The computer, despite her facility with languages in any medium, left her cold.

Terrified that she would wind up the slave to news and locker-rooms that her husband had been, Brenna's mother, the former Catherine van Duzen, had steered her daughter through convent school, Sarah Lawrence College, a PhD in art history at Harvard and an early career as arts editor of New York *Rumours* magazine, where Selina Day Novak—perhaps not-so-coincidentally another graduate of Sadie Lou—had been a legend. To no avail. When a sports job opened on *The Wreck,* as *The Record* was known, Brenna used PDFs of her writing, along with her retired father's still considerable influence, to wrangle an interview and then the job.

"Nepotism is never a bad thing where talent is concerned," Brenna told *Vanity Fair* in its exposé on *The Wreck* as one of the print media's last hurrahs.

She was equally frank about her love of art and sport. She had written her thesis on homoerotic influences in both.

"I love them, because I love looking at beautiful men," she told Vanity Fair. "On the whole, I think they're the prettier sex though not the smarter."

Such remarks, Mort James swore, led to his quadruple bypass and early retirement. Secretly, however, he admired the way his daughter gave everyone hell. As she was giving Smalley now.

"Coach Smalley, Coach Smalley," she yelled, rapping on his office door. "I have a few more questions. I know you're in there. I can hear your labored breathing. You never answered my question about how you can ignore Quinn Novak when Lance Reinhart is playing so badly. Coach Smalley, Mark Seidelburg signed Novak with great fanfare. So the question remains—not to mix a sports metaphor here—but when will it be Quinn Novak's inning?"

It was no secret that the press in general—and Brenna James in particular—was the bane of Smalley's existence. Her endless probing had led Smalley to contact *The Wreck's* current editor-in-chief, Cecil Walton, who had been brought over from *The London Record, The Wreck's* flagship, and knew little of American football but loved a good story—particularly if it carried a whiff of scandal.

Unfortunately for Smalley, Walton was of an equally volcanic temperament, one that did not take kindly to anyone questioning his writers or his authority. Their shouting match—or at least Smalley's profane side of the phone conversation—echoed through the Templars' locker room, causing Greg and Derrick to roll their eyes at Quinn, who shrugged.

Brenna was an enigma to them, a self-possessed woman in a man's world.

"So, how'd you do her, Quinn?"

"Huh?"

"How'd you, you know, do her?" Jeremiah wondered. "Me, I'd take her from behind. That big booty was made for some man love. You know what they always say: 'The bigger the cushion, the better the pushin'.'"

Quinn was appalled not only by their sexism but by their vulgarity. But he laughed when he realized that in any romantic matchup between Brenna and Jeremiah there was no doubt who would come out on top.

"I'd be careful if I were you. I think you might be the one crying 'Uncle,'" Quinn said.

"No matter," Greg said. "A fugly guy like Jere has as much chance with her as I'd have with Rihanna. Now Quinnie here's another matter. Look, he's turning all red. I seen her look at you, Quinnie, and I seen you look at her."

It was true there was something about her. Maybe it was the Venus de Milo figure—encased in navy stretch jeans, matching heeled boots and a form-fitting olive green pleather moto jacket—or the long fishtail braid of thick, auburn hair; or the wide cheekbones and pert nose.

Brenna confused Quinn. He liked looking at her, liked imagining those high, well-shaped breasts in a tight corset set off by a thin, jeweled collar. (Greg and Derrick really had to stop trying to interest him in porn, he thought.) But he liked looking at Tam and Mal more. And she was, after all, a member of the press.

"Forbidden fruit," Derrick said. "Just

remember, Quinn, it would be like sleeping with the enemy, you know, like being a Nazi collaborator."

"Yeah," Greg said sarcastically. "'Cause an American newspaper is really the equivalent of Hitler. Of all the dumb-ass things to say."

"Hey, who are you calling dumb?" Derrick said. "I went to Ole Miss."

"Where you majored in what? Shop? Home Ec? No, wait, basket-weaving. This chick went to Harvard. Harvard. Face it. Even if she weren't working for the enemy, and wasn't, like, you know, forty, she'd still be out of reach. Quinn at least went to Stanford and got a perfect score on the Wonderlic test. He's from another world, man, one closer to hers."

"Hey, thanks for going to bat for me, so to speak," Quinn said when he caught up with her after another tough loss and testy Smalley press conference.

"Now whose mixing metaphors?" she said with a laugh. "Anyway, I know how I'd feel if I weren't given a chance to write at *The Wreck*. You deserve a shot, especially with the way Lance has been playing—or not."

"He's had some bad breaks," Quinn said, "no pun intended."

"I know you have to say that kind of stuff. But we're not on the record now."

She paused. "My mother and I went to the same school as your aunt. And I worked for the magazine she loved so. There wasn't a day that someone didn't mention one of her favorite sayings. Mine is 'Have courage, and life will meet you halfway.'"

Quinn smiled at the memory. It kept him from

weeping.

"She used to tell me the same thing."

"You must miss her," Brenna said. "Of all the stupid things to say. Forgive me."

Sometimes when you lose something—or someone—it comes back in a different way, he thought. How could he tell her she was so like his aunt?

"No, it's all right," he said. "I do."

EIGHT

Though Smalley often accused Quinn of courting the press—the *New York Rumours'* spread being Exhibit A—he didn't, not really. Reporters found him. And Quinn saw no reason to be unfriendly, particularly when it helped his causes, like the proposed orphanage and school.

But, as with most stars, he had learned soon enough that cultivating the press was like trying to ride a tiger. There was no way to control it.

"Novak, will your parents be coming for the big game?" a reporter asked after practice.

"Oh, no," Quinn said. "They live in Indonesia, where they work for a big multinational company. It wouldn't be fair to tear them away. They sent their best wishes, though."

It was all plausible. What it wasn't was particularly true. They could certainly tear themselves away, though it was a long schlep—twenty-two hours by air. But Quinn hadn't asked them, in part because he assumed they wouldn't want to. The one time Sydney and Chandler had seen him play, at the Rose Bowl, all she could say was, "I assumed it would be bigger."

And sure enough, they soon sent their "Congratulations, sorry we can't be there but best of luck" wishes via email.

In a way, he was relieved. He had enough stress at the moment without the strain of having to tease out a relationship with them under a New York microscope. He was glad he could rely on them not to show up.

If only that were true of Aunt Sarah. Whenever there was good fortune to be shared, she could be counted on to exploit it.

"There's someone at the gate here to see you," security informed him after the press conference. "Says you invited her, a Sarah Novak?"

He never invited her. But then you never had to invite Aunt Sarah. Like the Devil or a vampire, she invited herself.

"Yeah, tell her I'll meet her in the family lounge."

"Hi, honey," she said, hugging him warmly. "Congrats. This is awesome."

"Thanks, Aunt Sarah," Quinn said, looking around to ensure no one had seen them. He tried not to be embarrassed by her, but he was.

From a distance, she was a babe—blonde hair and form-fitting white leggings, turtleneck, boots and fur vest. All three of the Novak sisters had what passed for conventional beauty, but Sarah, the youngest, had a thicker nose, which gave her a little toughness, as did the smudged blue eye shadow, the unkempt hair, the chipped nail polish, the constant sniffling, the forays into her purse for Hello Kitty breath mints, which weren't mints, of course. Not that she was well-acquainted with mints, soap, shampoo, or deodorant. She often smelled.

It didn't stop men from lusting after her.

"Who's the hottie, Novak?" male members of the press would invariably ask after his high school games.

"The lady is my Aunt Sarah, and I'll thank you to mind your manners."

Politesse was lost on the paparazzi.

"Hey, Sarah, are those M & Ms, or are you just glad to see me?" one yelled as she posed with Quinn in one of her skintight outfits after a Stanford win.

"You men are disgusting," Quinn said. "Have some respect."

But all Sarah did was giggle and thrust her erect nipples, visible through her thin cotton sweater, out farther. It made him sad.

Once Quinn overheard her tell a reporter that the secret to his success was that he had been a love child. After that, Quinn tried to shield her—and his private life—from interviewers. But she was unstoppable, an artist—at least that was what Quinn told anyone who asked. Not that she ever sold anything or even did anything, except a lot of sketches. She was very good at sketching and planning, as were all her friends. They were artists, too—aspiring novelists; actors on the verge of that big break—or professional mistresses who were arts patrons, hospital volunteers, animal rescuers; people always on the move, with no fixed incomes to accompany their lack of fixed addresses.

"Whatever you do later in life, never lend your Aunt Sarah any money," his Aunt Lena had warned him. "A loan implies a return, and you'll never see a dime back from her. If she needs food or clothes, you buy them for her. But don't give her money."

Aunt Sarah must've gotten wise to that for she started asking for more expensive things. It wasn't just a coat she needed; it was a Dolce & Gabbana coat, red and green floral on a black background. Kept on a tight budget by his agent and financial planner, Quinn found himself going without to give to Aunt Sarah. How fucked up was that? But then, we're a badly fucked-up family, Quinn thought.

Aunt Sarah wasn't here for Dolce & Gabbana, not this time. She was looking for playoff tickets for herself and her friends.

"You know they only allot you so many, Aunt Sarah."

"Oh, come on, we're gonna have a nice, big cheering section for you," she said. "I just know you're gonna do great."

Great, no, but very good indeed. And yet, it wasn't enough to defeat the Quakers. The Temps went down 21-20 as Quinn's Hail Mary pass just went wide. Still, no one blamed him except for Smalley and himself.

"Had we more seasoning, fewer injuries," Smalley said at the postgame press conference, barely trying to contain his glee, "we might've pulled it out."

Everyone understood that what he was really saying was that had Lance been in for Quinn, the Temps would've won, which wasn't necessarily so.

"What about when the defense failed to contain the Quakers in the first half, Coach?" Brenna piped up. "What about the failure of the offense to capitalize on opportunities in the third quarter?"

"The quarterback leads the team on the field and off, Ms. James," Smalley snapped.

Quinn agreed. "Hey, I make that last play, we're AFC Championship-bound. I don't make it, we go home. I didn't make it happen."

"But do you think you got the support this season you deserved, I mean, particularly from Coach Smalley?" a reporter from *The New York*

Gazette asked.

Quinn paused. He and everyone else knew the answer to that.

"I think it was my fault we lost."

Sarah was oblivious to all of it—the game's politics, Smalley's loathing of Quinn, Quinn's guilt, which was only partly about his sense of responsibility for and to the team.

She had left somewhere in the third quarter. Quinn tried to reach her by phone afterward.

"Oh, honey-bunny, I'm so sorry, but we wanted to beat the crowd. You were just wonderful. But, darlin', that team leaves a lot to be desired."

"Yeah, well, you know, we're a work in progress. Still, to make it to the divisional playoffs when we started out so badly..."

"Honey, I can hardly hear you."

No surprise. There was a lot of music and laughter wherever she was.

"I said why don't we meet for a late dinner," Quinn shouted. "I feel like I let the guys down, you know? I—"

"Honey, honey, if you're gonna be in the spotlight, you're gonna have to learn to cut it short. Think tweet-size, you know?"

"Oh, yeah, of course, I guess, I—"

She had hung up.

I'm a fool for caring, for letting my family hurt me. But I do and they have, he thought dully as he slipped into bed at the Mark Hotel in Philadelphia. He had asked GM Jeff Sylvan if he could stay overnight, using his family as an excuse. The truth was that he could hardly breathe for the pounding he and particularly his ribs had taken in the brutal third quarter. But he hadn't said anything, because, well, who else was there to call plays?

Besides, he was afraid that if he ever stopped playing, he would not only lose his job but cease to exist. Now he could barely turn in bed.

He dreamt his heart was pounding against his ribs, like the wings of a bird beating against a cruel cage until he realized someone was knocking on the door.

Sarah, it's got to be Sarah, he thought. Or the police. She was a breaking news story waiting to happen.

But it wasn't Sarah. It was Mal Ryan, his molded features ripe with drink and lust.

"Called some PR guy named Sofa or Softy or Selfie or something under the pretense of congratulating you on your efforts only to find out you were still here in Philly," he said, bursting into the room and shutting the door with the finality of one sealing a crypt. "God, how I want you."

He embraced Quinn roughly, tugging at his clothes, inhaling his scent and covering him in kisses until the two fell awkwardly back onto the bed, and Quinn was naked.

"God, look at you. You're gorgeous," Mal said.

Quinn scooted back near the headboard and drew his knees up instinctively, hugging them.

"Aw, come on. Don't be bashful," Mal said. "I'll show you mine," he added, stripping off his clothes in a few seamless movements to free his erect cock.

There was something faintly ridiculous about men's bodies, especially their penises, Quinn thought, even when those bodies were as Michelangelo-perfect as Mal's. Women's sex organs conjured images of seashells and flowers with all the promise of secret beauties to be revealed. Whereas men looked like they were sticking their tongues out—way out.

And yet, there was nothing ridiculous about Mal's confident stance or Quinn's own pounding need.

Kneeling on the bed, Mal slinked forward on all fours with the power and grace of a panther, then doubled back, moving forward again. Quinn laughed and Mal followed suit, despite himself. But humor didn't suit him, and the lighter mood didn't last for long. Mal took Quinn in his arms, gulping his mouth as if he were dying of thirst—or drowning.

"Shouldn't we talk, get to know each other first?" Quinn asked when he could come up for air.

"What are you, a girl? I'm not interested in foreplay or a relationship or anything but the fierce hunger of now. I'm not that way, you know—gay. It's just something I need from time to time, something that I do privately, quietly, no questions asked."

"It just seems so sudden."

Mal pulled back and made as if he were gathering his clothes to leave.

"Your call," he said, as he narrowed his focus on Quinn. "In or out."

Quinn understood instantly that this was one of those moments that would somehow determine the course of his life. "In," he said, as Mal covered him like the night.

Contrasts, Quinn thought, concentrate on the contrasts—the hardness of Mal's desire, the softness of his own yielding; the cool of the sheets, the heat of their bodies; the excruciating initial pain of Mal thrusting deeply into his voluptuous buttocks; the exquisite pleasure as he fondled Quinn's swollen cock—stroking the spongy spot where it met his balls in rhythm to the thrusts and the ebb and flow of his ragged breath and grunts against Quinn's damp neck.

Quinn only hoped that he himself wouldn't come too quickly. Indeed, he wished he would never come at all but live in this state of heightened, almost unbearable anticipation.

As he strained to hold back, Quinn focused on Mal as the Eros to his Psyche, a secret lover in the dark whom he could neither ignore nor acknowledge. What kind of crazy love was that?

Afterward, Quinn thought how different everything would be now. Before he was a virgin; now, no longer and ultimately changed. He was giving Mal something that could never be regained. And yet there was a part of Quinn that couldn't be breached, that remained one-in-himself, that would always be secret, sealed off, inviolate, ever new. Then why did feel so sad, so lonely?

Perhaps because they slept apart, or at least Mal slept—muttering, even crying. Quinn longed to hold and comfort him but sensed it wouldn't be appreciated. You didn't cuddle a cougar. In truth, Quinn wasn't sure what he should do or how he should feel. He had never had a lover before. Maybe this was the way they all were. So he tried to rest his aching ribs, which he had forgotten about amid their orgasmic exertions and waited until Mal nudged those painful ribs unwittingly, saying, "I have to have it again, baby," in a low voice that nonetheless pierced the darkness and later the dawn.

Then Quinn watched him dispose of the used condoms carefully and, freshly showered, dress just as deliberately, as if he could wash away the scent of him and the memory of the night.

"I'll be in touch," Mal said, kissing him and peeling three crisp bills from a fat silver Tiffany money clip with the letter M. "Buy yourself something real nice."

"I'm not a whore," Quinn said, trying to rise, his chest throbbing as the door closed, and he wondered if Mal and the night had happened at all.

Sore and breathing hard, Quinn struggled to shower and shave, pausing every once and a while to rest. Toweling off, he felt a little wetness in the crack of his butt—his virgin blood.

Quinn took his time with his appearance, like the driver who doesn't want anyone to know he's drunk so he drives too slowly. It was no use.

Leaning against the wall in the elevator—he was glad to ride down alone—he willed himself across the lobby, went outside and had the valet hail a cab.

"Take me to the nearest hospital," Quinn told the driver.

Inside, all he had to say was, "I'm having trouble breathing." There were no forms, no questions about insurance. Just a gurney and people stripping away his clothes with an urgency that Mal and Vienne might've envied.

His six-pack laid bare, electrodes, monitors: He thought one said "Eighty over forty." A doctor leaned over him—blond, handsome, smiling.

"I'm Dr. Matthew Harrington. It's OK. You're not having a heart attack." Hand on his shoulder— compassionate, brotherly. "You're going to be all right."

"You're going to be all right"—another hospital, another doctor, comforting his younger self screaming in Bahasa for Aunt Lena.

He shut out the image—remembering the words of T.S. Eliot, memorized in a Stanford English class, as he drifted off:

We die with the dying:
See, they depart, and we go with them.
We are born with the dead:
See, they return, and bring us with them.

NINE

When Quinn woke, he thought for a moment he was in Jakarta again. The TV quietly carried the nature sounds and images that hospitals used to try to soothe—check that, control—patients. As his eyes adjusted to the darkened, antiseptic room—drawn curtains and blinds, monitors, metal beds—the old dread rose and leveled off. Then he flipped the channel, and all hell broke loose.

"Sources close to the New York Templars tell me that they'll discipline quarterback Quinn Novak for failing to return to New York after Sunday's loss to the Philadelphia Quakers," Ric Wynters was intoning. "Novak was believed to have been partying with a blonde and friends after the defeat. I spoke just moments ago with Coach Smalley, who was livid, just livid about his MIA star. Here's what the coach had to say."

"Well, it shows you the gutlessness of the guy and the contempt he has for the fans, the media, the whole organization that he couldn't bother to face the music with us in New York."

Quinn reached for his cell. But his clothes and phone weren't there. He rang for the nurse.

"Do you know where my cell is?" he asked.

"I wouldn't worry about that," she said, as if addressing a child. "You need to stay quiet and rest."

When she left, he reached for the phone by the bed, despite a stabbing pain in his side.

"Hello."

"Brenna, it's Quinn," he said, breathless.

"Quinn, thank God. The whole town's looking for you. I thought the Small One would blow a gasket at the press conference. Where the hell are you?"

"I'm still in Philly. Brenna, listen: Smalley, Ric Wynters, they're bullshit. The blonde is my aunt and I wasn't out with her. I don't even know where she is."

He almost said, "I thought she was the one knocking on my door early Monday morning," but caught himself.

"I'm in the hospital. I think I busted some ribs. But that's not the point. I had the team's permission. Check with Jeff."

"I will. What do you need?"

"Nothing except to set the record straight. I'll be fine. I was just uncomfortable after the game, stayed the night in Philly, and when I woke up, I couldn't breathe very well. Can you get the word out?"

"I'm on it. Feel better, and don't worry about a thing."

When Quinn was finally able to secure his phone from Nurse Ratched, he checked his Twitter account.

"Quinn's in hosp. Busted ribs," Brenna tweeted. "GM OK'ed Philly stay. More at nyrecord.com/red zone."

The next thing Quinn knew, his room was flooded with teddy bears, flowers, balloons, and cards from well-wishers, and he couldn't breathe for a whole different reason. He paged the nurse and asked that the lot be distributed to the pediatric, geriatric, and maternity wards.

As usual, the media seemed to know more

about his condition than he did.

"OK," Dr. Matthew Harrington was saying on the International News Network (INN). "I'm not going to be holding these chitchats daily, only when there's real info. Mr. Novak is alert, stable, and in good spirits. He thanks everyone for his concern and good wishes. But as his doctor, I have ordered complete rest for the patient and no visitors. He was admitted with a couple of broken ribs, one of which punctured his left lung. And it's this that we're most concerned with."

Yikes. Had Dr. Matthew told him all this? Probably, and just as likely he didn't remember.

"So we're going to have to keep a lid on things while he heals. That's all for now, ladies and gentlemen. I'll be back if and when there's news."

Quinn surfed the tube, stopping at INN's sister station, Sports News Network.

"We won't be disciplining anyone," Jeff Sylvan was saying. "Quinn had my permission, and, looking back on it, it was the right decision. Who knows what might've happened had he not rested the night in Philly and sought medical treatment the next day."

"But Jeff," Ric Wynters spoke up, "did he have Coach Smalley's permission?"

"Coach Smalley's permission, my permission, Mr. Jefferson's permission, he had permission from someone in charge," Sylvan snapped. "He didn't have to get it in triplicate. This isn't the IRS."

"The point is I should've been informed, and I wasn't," Smalley countered at a later news conference. "Yes, we're all part of the same team. And last time I checked, there was no 'I' in team."

No, but there is in egomaniac, Quinn thought.

So escalated the war of words between Sylvan and Smalley that Quinn had not so innocently started. It was true that he had gone over Smalley's head to Sylvan, in part to annoy him. But he was also certain that Smalley would've said "No" to his request to stay overnight in Philly and given him the usual long song-and-dance about what a prima donna he was, how inflexible he was, blah, blah, blah, blah, blah.

Smalley always finished these diatribes behind closed doors with this flourish:

"You mustn't take this personally."

No, of course not. Because it wasn't meant personally, right? Quinn thought, disgusted.

As opposed to the time when some reporter for *Sportin' Life* magazine had done a less than flattering profile on Smalley and the missus.

"You're dead to me, you hear?" he shouted into the phone, presumably at the reporter. "Dead to me."

"We should all be so lucky," Derrick said to Quinn as Smalley's voice exploded from his office. "Never to hear his fat-ass mouth again, God, that would be like you stopped hitting your head against a wall."

Instead, Derrick and the rest of the Temps had been condemned to that special circle of Hell known as Smalleyville. Still, Quinn was ashamed of himself. His cross wasn't particularly heavy. He thought of the men and women in Jakarta who worked the tin shacks clustered on the corners of the streets bearing the McMansions that resembled the 10,000 block on Hollywood's Sunset Boulevard, huddling under palm fronds in the rainy season as they displayed their shiny goods.

"I'd like a New Year's horn, Sydney," Quinn's child self asked as they drove by.

"Would you also like tuberculosis?" Sydney replied by way of "No."

He remembered the women in the coolie hats on the beaches with their pearls for sale and their patter, the merchants who stroked your arms and your ego on the streets of Kuta in Bali.

"Get your hands off me," Chandler would say.

"Try to relax, Chan," Sydney would offer. "They have to make their rupiah now, because for them now is all there is."

In Kuta, watches and wallets weren't the only things for sale. At night, Quinn had heard, the Kuta Cowboys plied their trade on the public beaches, searching for rich, lonely European women.

"You're excused from the table," Sydney would say whenever that conversation arose. And Quinn would blush in shame.

Better to be a whore honestly, Quinn thought now, than merely to be treated like one.

It could be worse. He remembered a beggar woman beating her stumps against the window of his family's car near the statue of Prometheus as he and Sumarti waited for the rare traffic light.

Quinn went to open the window to give her some of his allowance.

"No, no, young master," Sumarti said, checking that the windows were shut and the doors locked as they sped off.

I see you. I will always see you, Quinn thought then as he turned back in his seat and gazed at a flitting butterfly. But not before he watched her hobble away undaunted, patiently waiting for the next red traffic light, the next possible benefactor in what Mal would call "the fierce hunger of now."

TEN

Quinn received an offer from Sports News Network to serve as guest commentator for the Super Bowl pre and postgame shows, and so, against Dr. Matthew's orders, gingerly prepared to leave the hospital for his new gig after a two-and-a-half-week stay.

"As your physician, I advise against it," Dr. Matthew said ruefully, arms crossed as Quinn packed the stuff he had accumulated. "But as a fan, I guess I understand it."

"It's not that, doc," Quinn said. "The money will come in handy for the orphanage I'm building in Jakarta. I think that's what I was really born for. Football is just a means to that end. Anyway, I want to do it. My Aunt Lena always said you should say 'yes' to life's opportunities."

"Well, just remember there are no life opportunities without life. Your health has to come first."

"I know it does. It will," Quinn said unconvincingly. He stopped packing to consider Dr. Matthew in an attempt to hide how winded he was.

"Now I know where I remember you from," Quinn said. "I thought I recognized you the morning I came into the emergency room, even in the state I was in. You're the doctor who treated the tennis player Alí Iskandar after he was knifed by that deranged fan."

"That's right," he said. "And if you know that, then you know I can't talk about my patients, beyond what they and the hospital may permit me to say. That goes for you, too."

Here Dr. Matthew turned all sotto voce.

"I would advise you always to use condoms."

Quinn started to protest, blushing.

"It's OK. I'm not here to judge. I'm gay myself. So you're using protection, right?"

Quinn nodded.

"And just as important, if I thought for a moment some of the bruises I saw on you were from domestic abuse rather than the football field, I would have to report them to the police immediately."

Quinn flashed on Mal unthreading the belt from his pants and snapping it between hands.

"No, no, it was from the game where I cracked my ribs."

"Uh-huh," Dr. Matthew said, unconvinced. "I have no proof, and that's the hell of it." He offered Quinn a card for a domestic abuse hotline. "I don't want you to be afraid to use this. And I'll expect to see you in a week."

Dr. Matthew was a toughie. But Quinn knew he was right. He'd have to be careful, not that there was much chance of seeing his "boyfriend" with him playing in the Super Bowl. Plus, just preparing for his commentating stint was a huge deal. The digital playbook on each of the two teams alone would engage him, never mind the camera angles he had to note.

"Don't be nervous," executive producer Neal Morocco said.

Didn't people realize, Quinn wondered, that saying "don't be nervous" only tended to make people nervous?

"I won't, sir," he said.

"Please, it's Neal. OK, places everyone."

As if memorizing the Super Bowl media guide and learning the camera angles weren't enough, dealing with hyperactive analyst Rufus Washington was almost more than Quinn could bear. Rufus had been a linebacker with the Chicago Brass, and he and former Brass Coach Joe Nowicki were now together again on the SNN team.

"And you know, Coach," Rufus would always begin, "I think, Coach, for a team to win today, Coach, it's gonna take offense and defense."

OK, Coach, Quinn thought, not exactly Hamlet, is he? Worse yet, whenever Quinn tried to throw in an observation, ooh-ooh-ooh-teacher-pick-me Rufus cut him off at the pass.

"I'm so sorry about that, Quinnie," he said during a commercial break. "After all these years, I still get so nervous."

"No problem," Quinn said, smiling. He couldn't figure out if Rufus were that much of an idiot or just a passive-aggressive Macchiavel.

Finally, it came time for each analyst to give his Super Bowl prediction.

Everyone—including Rufus, after saying "Coach" forty-five more times—predicted the Quakers would win. Everyone, except Quinn.

"I'm going to have to go with the Miners," he said. "I think it's going to come down to quarterbacking. In last year's Super Bowl, Tam Tarquin kept the Miners close. I think this time he and they are going to do it."

After the Miners won 17-14 on two last-minute bullet passes from Tam—who somehow managed to remain poised and upright despite the onslaught of Quaker defensemen—Quinn looked like a genius. So much so that Morocco selected him for the postgame on-field interview. Quinn tried to appear objective when what he wanted to do was hurl himself into Tam's arms and say, "Take me."

Instead, he said, "Tam, a great win, a magical win. What was the difference between this year and last?"

Tam laughed as the crowd at Arizona Canyons Stadium erupted.

"Well, um, divine intervention. No, I think faith in myself and my team. And I guess I just got tired of being number two all the time. I knew our guys were better than that, and they proved it."

"Again, a memorable win. Congratulations, Tam."

"And congratulations to you on a great rookie season with the Temps."

"Thanks and back to you guys upstairs."

Upstairs, Morocco was as giddy as a lottery winner.

"You were terrific," he told Quinn, "and the chemistry between Tarquin and you—the present and the future of the NFL—also terrific. Listen, you don't have to worry about your post-gridiron career. It's here."

It was nice to know his future was secure. But it looked to come at a steep cost to his present.

"How could you, how could you pick him over me?" Mal asked, barging into his room at the Sonora Desert Inn at 3 a.m. "What are you, fucking him?"

It was one of those instances in which a lie voiced a wish, Quinn thought. No doubt it was why he felt so guilty when he said, "Of course not. But they asked me for my professional opinion. Now if they had asked who'd win the bedroom Super Bowl, I'd have gone with you, but then, I have nothing else to compare it to."

It was a flippant answer, for which Mal slapped him hard across the face.

"OK," Quinn said, stunned. "Get out. Get. Out."

"I say when I leave, and I'm not leaving till I get what I came for."

He grabbed Quinn, who fought back with a fury that surprised them both.

"Oh, you want to play rough?" Mal said. "Baby, nothing gets me hotter."

Finally, he pinned Quinn and his aching ribs to the carpet but instead of mounting him collapsed on top of him, sobbing, the salt of his tears mixing with that of their sweat.

"I wanted to win so bad, so bad," Mal kept saying.

"I know. I know," Quinn said softly. "It's OK. Why don't you let me turn over, and I can hold you."

Mal slid off him and curved against Quinn, fondling his chest and then sucking one of his nipples as Quinn held him in his arms.

"Why are you so good to me," Mal whimpered.

"I don't know, maybe because others have been kind to me."

"You won't tell about our little game, will you? It's just a game men play."

Quinn turned his throbbing head toward his pinging phone, among the items that lay scattered beside him. There was a text from tmt@miners.com—Tam. "Breakfast this morning?"

Quinn's heart leapt as his stomach sank—a dangerous game indeed.

"No," he told Mal. "I won't tell a soul."

ELEVEN

Crazy, just frigging crazy, Quinn thought as he sat in the Tombstone Diner outside Phoenix, jiggling one leg under the table and flipping through the song titles in one of the old individual jukeboxes that stood at attention at each table. He had to be crazy in love, or just plain crazy, to be out on what he assumed was a date with the chief rival of his volatile lover.

Or maybe not. Maybe the invite was just that—breakfast at a diner. Anyway, he loved diners, loved the way the early morning light slanted through the windows, as in a Hopper painting, slicing through the space with the promise of a new day.

Mostly, he loved the huge menus. You could get anything you wanted, from banana pancakes to fried clams, maybe both at one sitting. (He really did love to eat.)

Normally, a diner menu would set his mouth watering. Now the mere thought of sipping water left him ready to retch.

"Can I get you something while you wait, darlin'?" the waitress—part mother, part vixen—drawled.

Why did diner waitresses always look like something out of the movies—big, dyed black hair, big makeup, big crimson lips, big boobs, bigger-than-life personalities?

"No, ma'am, I'll just wait."

"Not even a cup of coffee?"

"Uh, no, ma'am."

"Well, then at least make yourself comfortable, honey. Take off that baseball cap so we can see that gorgeous face and all that lovely, curly dark hair. Mmm, mmm, if I were twenty years younger... Well, never mind. Though you would do nicely for my niece, Ruby Junior."

"Yes'm."

As if on cue to rescue him, Tam sauntered in, wearing fitted, khaki-colored jeans and a short-sleeved, three-button, camel-colored shirt that teased the skin and fine bones at his throat, offering the possibility of so much more. His sandy hair, which was swept back from a high forehead, and his tawny, sculpted features were a thousand shades of blond and brown—like the luxuriant fields in a Thomas Hardy novel or a Van Gogh landscape or an American song. Amber waves indeed. The wheat palette offset Tam's limpid, lushly fringed gray eyes—oh, how Quinn long to plunge into those pools—which wore the amused expression of one of those rare people who finds life perpetually delicious, perhaps as a safeguard against its actual disappointments. But then, why shouldn't he? Quinn thought. He was "F***ing Tam Tarquin," as *Sportin' Life* magazine called him, no longer a mere golden boy but a desert god, a gridiron Apollo, born of the sun.

"Well, well, two such beauties," the waitress said. "This must be my lucky day."

She poured the coffee now and leaned in to whisper, "Yes, gentlemen, I know who you are, and I'll be expecting a big tip."

"Count on it, Ruby Senior," Tam said, glancing at the name on the pin that held her frilly uniform handkerchief in place but saying it as if he'd known her all his life. He had that gift, Quinn thought — the uncommon common touch.

"Sorry I'm late," he said sheepishly to Quinn. "They have me doing these early-morning-after-the-Super Bowl calls. I don't think I slept an hour."

He certainly didn't look the worse for wear, Quinn thought, a ripple of pleasure washing over his groin.

"No worries. You should enjoy it. You deserve it. Everyone will want a piece of you now." Including me, Quinn added to himself, but would they love you as I could? Before Tam walked in, he was ready to flee. Now he couldn't imagine leaving. Isn't that when you knew it was right?

"I guess," Tam said. It took Quinn a minute to realize Tam wasn't responding to the question in his head but to the idea that he deserved all the adulation. "Frankly, I'd rather forget all the hoopla and concentrate on the reason I asked you to meet me."

Heart pounding, mind racing, stomach dropping, body ready to bolt through his hot skin. Chris Isaak's *Wicked Games* playing ironically on the jukebox. What god of mischief—perhaps Eris, the goddess of discord—put it in the mind of a patron to select that?

Saved by Ruby Senior. "What'll it be, boys?"

It was a double order of eggs over easy, bacon, whole wheat toast, blueberry pancakes and sausage; a pitcher of pineapple-orange juice; and more coffee with cream.

"Lord, if I ate like you fellas, I'd be two of me six feet under. Life is so unfair."

"Why, Ruby Senior if you ate like us, that spectacular figure would be in jeopardy," Tam said.

Ruby waved him off in a way that suggested she was pleased.

"That's right, boys, you keep slinging those compliments, and I'll keep refilling these cups."

"So the reason I invited you to breakfast," Tam said, suddenly shy.

"Yes," Quinn said, drawing the word out humorously as he hoped against hope.

"I was hoping you'd agree to take part in the pro-am tournament for my foundation later this month. We do so much for children through the arts. It's really the perfect San Fran charity, and it would mean so much to me to bring one of the NFL's young guns into the mix."

Quinn was alternately flattered and crushed. Tam didn't have to take him out to breakfast to invite him to a golf outing. He could've emailed or texted him or had his people call Quinn's people, not that he really had people except for the mother hens of an agent and a financial planner. There had to be more to breakfast than, well, pancakes. Or was desire trumping Quinn's better judgment?

"Good, I'm glad that's settled," Tam said, looking genuinely relieved as Quinn nodded. "I figured you've become such a big celebrity that the demands on your time must be extraordinary."

"Me?" Quinn paused to consider whether Tam might be mocking him. But though a playful sort, ridicule wasn't in his repertoire. "I'm just the backup quarterback."

"Is that how you see yourself? Because I gotta tell you, you're the real deal. And don't you let anyone tell you otherwise. Pat Smalley—what a jackass. Props to you, though, for putting up with him and turning the Temps around. I couldn't have done it."

"Well, I'm sure you could do anything. But thanks, that means a lot coming from you."

They fell into a comfortable silence, savoring their blueberry pancakes. That was how you knew it was love, Quinn thought. It didn't require chatter or action. It could just be pancakes. When Tam finally broke the spell, it was with the kind of mundane question that a long-married couple might share: "What for today?"

"Mm?"

"I was wondering how you're going to spend the day?"

Quinn was startled, not because he had no plans but because people rarely asked him anything personal—how he was, what he was doing for lunch. He was so used to being on his own, entertaining himself, or caring about others that he was both pleased by Tam's interest and ashamed at how emotionally one-sided his life was.

"I thought I'd do a little sightseeing, take a little time to relax. We rush from city to city so much during the season that I thought it'd be nice to stop before catching a flight back to New York tomorrow."

Tam grinned. "I'm the same way. I like to get to know a place, even during the season, else what is this life for?"

And so it was that Quinn found himself driving with Tam improbably to the Grand Canyon. Quinn didn't have an overwhelming desire to see it. Even when he found himself before this cathedral of God—humbled by its vast, terra-cotta, prehistoric mystery—he could conclude only that it was very Grand Canyon-y. But he loved being on the road—especially with Tam. It was Tam who made it different, Tam who made it seem exciting and new. Later when he was gone, Quinn would remember something that being with Aunt Lena had taught him: It wasn't where you went or what you did but whom you were with.

"Think of all these rocks have seen," Tam marveled. "We come and go. They remain."

Tam notwithstanding, Quinn didn't quite see it that way. He saw the remnants of a river—soft in its overwhelming power, powerful in its soft currents—that had carved fissures in the earth over time. People were like those now-phantom waters, wearing away the bedrock of your soul.

Not Tam, though. He didn't have it in him. There was no malice about him. How Quinn longed to present him to Mal, Smalley, Sydney and Chandler—indeed to the whole world—and say, here's my lover. He's kind and funny and sweet and gentle and he chooses me above all others. Me.

It was just a fantasy, of course, wasn't it? When Tam said that he had put his family on a plane for Philly in the wee hours of that morning—how blissfully normal they sounded, with their medical practices and teaching positions to go home to, Quinn thought with a sigh—he wondered if there were a girlfriend on that plane, though Tam didn't mention one. He would've mentioned one if there had been, wouldn't he?

Of course, if there were a boyfriend, he would hardly have mentioned that. Besides, Mal—who flew away, perhaps even on the same plane, as easily as he flew into Quinn's life—would never let him go, particularly to a hated rival. Mal would not quit the field that Quinn would become. And even if he did, where was the place for Tam and Quinn amid the brutal beauty of the NFL?

"You're the first person I've seen shiver in the desert," Tam said later back at the Sonora Inn.

"Oh, that," Quinn said, covering for his desire and fear. "That's because I'm in awe of your prowess at miniature golf."

"And well you should be," Tam said, "because I'm the Jordan Spieth of the mini course. Let me show you something."

He lined himself up with a shot at a tiny windmill. Then he took a beige print bandana from his pocket and tied it around his eyes. He paused, oscillating the club, and putted: Tam came within an inch of the hole, a wondrous example to Quinn of how a superb athlete retains a sense of his body even in sightless space.

"You try," Tam said.

He tied the bandana around Quinn's eyes loosely, then guided him to the hole.

"Relax," he said. "You're too tight. Trust me."

Moving behind him, Tam directed Quinn using only the voice that commanded the best O-line in the NFL. How to describe a voice, Quinn wondered? It was as ineffable as music and just as indispensable, something that was often overlooked in a visual culture, yet nonetheless worked its magic nonetheless subliminally. Tam's dusky baritone was like everything else about him, easy and fluid.

Sightless, Quinn was aware at first of that voice alone, and that naked distillation sent an erotic shock coursing through his body. But then everything about Tam became heightened for him– his tone, his heat, his powdery sandalwood cologne. He longed to lean into him, savoring his warmth and heady scent, and meld with his honeyed muscles if only for a moment. A moment would be enough, Quinn lied to himself.

When he whipped off the blindfold, he saw that with Tam's vocal prompts, he had sunk the put.

"High five," Tam said, clasping Quinn's hand and quickly weaving his fingers through Quinn's.

"I had help," Quinn said.

"Everyone needs a little help now and then," Tam said, smiling.

Back in his suite, he guided their lovemaking, too.

"I can't, I don't, I," Quinn said as their lips reached for each other, their arms still holding back, bent and taut, as they tasted that first kiss.

"Yes, I know, I understand," Tam said, finally embracing him gently. "We don't have to rush. We don't have to do anything you don't like."

Tam took him for the virgin he wasn't, Quinn thought. But perhaps it was possible to be a virgin reborn, like Aphrodite rising from the sea, a male Venus on the half-shell. Quinn knew how to fuck—Mal had made sure of that—but he didn't know how to make love. He had never been kissed, not properly anyway. Tam knew how to suck Quinn's bow-shaped mouth, slowly teasing apart his parched lips with his tongue. Quinn thought kissing the most erotic thing in the world, next to the way Tam slowly circled his nipples with a moist fingertip or drew back the hood of his stiffening cock or the way he did everything—gently laying him back on the bed as he settled on top of him, stroking his cheek, talking to him as he entered him, his dancing eyes never leaving Quinn's face.

He wasn't used to being the center of someone's delighted attention, and the effect was narcotic. Quinn couldn't get enough of Tam. He rose to meet him—stroking his back, cupping and parting his buttocks as he drew him deeper inside himself, the pain in his ribs creating a sharp intake of breath as their bodies strove together.

"I have an idea," Tam said, breathless, turning them on their sides to face one another. "There, that's more comfortable, isn't it?"

They were complements, Quinn thought as he considered Tam's lightness of being—his beauty, poise and goodness. And what did Tam see? Quinn wondered, a figure as brackish and opaque as the canals of Jakarta, a mystery, a fraud.

After, Tam lay on his back, relishing the moment, while Quinn curled up beside him but apart, eyeing him like a dog unsure of his master's affection. He needn't have been.

"Come on," Tam said, smiling at him, holding out an arm. "Come on, scooch over."

Quinn brightened, snuggling in his arms.

"I wasn't sure you liked to cuddle," he said.

"Are you kidding?" Tam said, laughing. "Listen: After what we've shared, I think we're past formality."

Quinn carried the memory of Tam's touch back to New York, to the other side of the Hudson where such tenderness was in short supply.

As he finished cleaning out his locker for the season with a few other players, a bouquet of white roses and hydrangeas arrived for him, laced with savory sprigs of rosemary.

"That's for remembrance": Quinn thought of Ophelia—mad for love, lost to it. This was madness—a lover who would never let him go and a great love that might not be but would not be denied.

He read the card. "I love you. T."

"Ooh, somebody's got a girlfriend, somebody's got a girlfriend," Derrick sang as he grabbed the card from Quinn's hand.

Somebody's acting juvenile, somebody's acting juvenile, Quinn thought.

"T. Let's see—Toni, Terri, Tonya, ooh, Tiffany. Could it be supermodel Tiffany Turkova?"

"Ooh, could it be that someone should mind their own business," Jeremiah said.

Turning to Quinn, he added, "I'm happy for you, man. And you don't have to share the lady with no one."

At his spare Manhattan digs—where canoe paddles, a gamelan and other Indonesian artifacts stood out against the ascetic backdrop—Quinn thought of his "lady" as Mal, blown in like a late-season nor'easter, buffeted him.

"Who's T?" Mal said, contemptuously flicking aside the card from Tam's bouquet, which graced a night table.

"Tante Josie back in Misalliance, Missouri," Quinn lied readily. "Tante is French for aunt. Our family is part French."

"Mm," Mal muttered, neither interested nor entirely convinced but unable to penetrate the lie and Quinn both at once. "No one's ever sent me flowers."

He drew Quinn back against himself and, wrapping him in a chokehold, bit him on the neck and hissed, "You be my rose."

TWELVE

May brought mini-camp and maxi uncertainty. After a moment of desert bliss, Quinn wondered if that was all he and Tam were meant to share. He played in Tam's pro-am, which was fine professionally but frustrating romantically.

Golf was golf. He really didn't like it, even though he had learned to play as a high school caddy in Misalliance. Made good money, too. But he didn't understand why it was a sport, all those paunchy guys in polo shirts riding around in golf carts only to strike a ball for a second and then retreat to the clubhouse, where they downed more than a few drafts and popped more than a few beer nuts. Golf was a game rather than a sport, pool played in wide, open spaces. Tam liked it, though. The tournament got a lot of publicity. And Quinn was paired with Tony Herrera, one of the greats of the game, er, sport.

But there was no time for Quinn and Tam to be together, let alone intimate. Quinn didn't know what he expected—for Tam to take him on the seventeenth hole? He had a tournament to run, for God's sake. Still, having experienced love, Quinn wanted it all the time. And the old insecurities that dogged him like a golem kept insisting he might never have it again. Even when he received a thank you from Tam, a Swarovski crystal golf ball paperweight, he told himself Tam's foundation probably sent them to all the participants, until he saw what it was wrapped in—Tam's tawny print handkerchief.

Bet the other guys didn't get one of these, Quinn thought, grinning.

He carried the hankie with him everywhere as a talisman against the bad days. And there were many bad days, with Lance back in camp—his leg "99.9 percent," as he kept telling the press—and Smalley saying, "Now things can get back to normal," plus a challenge from newbie QB Nero Jones out of the University of Tennessee. Not only was Quinn probably not going to be the starting quarterback, he was probably not going to be the backup quarterback either. Whenever Quinn started feeling sorry for himself, he went to the one place where he knew it would be impossible to experience self-pity—Dave Donaldson's home.

The former third-stringer had several feet of his intestines removed and a colostomy. Quinn recoiled at the thought of what that meant—shitting through a hole in your gut into a bag you had to empty. He had read all about it, knew it had improved since the early days of the procedure. But still, jeez.

And he looked like shit, to stick with a metaphor—thin, ashen, hollow, sunken-cheeked, a husk of the football player he had been. One look at Dave's wife, Kelly—a blonde whose prettiness was worn with care—and their kids tiptoeing around, far too somber for preschoolers, and you knew that the family's otherwise typical split-level Jersey home was nothing but a death house. Dave must've known it, too, for he kept crying and apologizing.

"Dave, look, man, you don't have to apologize," Quinn said. "How you feel about your illness is how you feel. You want to cry, cry. You want to talk, we'll talk. You want me to leave, fine. Or you want just to sit and be, that's fine, too."

Sometimes they'd talk—about the team, the weather, anything to get his mind off his cancer—and Dave would nod off, then come to with a start, embarrassed.

"It's OK," Quinn would say. "Take a snooze, and I'll watch you."

Once when Quinn rose to leave, Dave grasped his hand and kissed it.

"Don't forget me," Dave said.

Quinn kissed the top of his head. "I never will. Pray, and I'll pray, too."

He kept up the pressure on the Temps to remember Dave—with cards, visits, texts, tweets, and posts. He even enlisted Brenna to write a column about Dave's battle with a foe greater than any he had encountered on the gridiron. The support, Kelly texted Quinn, was one of the few things keeping her husband alive.

Not long after the column ran, Brenna got the idea for a cancer fundraiser in honor of Dave.

"We'll get my parents to sponsor it at their Park Avenue place. They're very cause-y."

Dave was too weak to attend, and Kelly had her hands full with him and the kids. But Quinn was there, as were Greg, Derrick, and Jeremiah. Quinn wondered if they were thinking what he was: I so don't belong here. The duplex was filled with 20th century masters, photographs of Brenna's parents with various presidents, and guests who, knowing one another, treated Quinn and company like an exotic species.

"I think he's part Polynesian," he heard one guest whisper to another behind his back. "There was some family tragedy. I'm sure I read about it."

The way Quinn figured it, life was a series of concentric circles, and you were lucky if you were born into the one your heart desired, because the chances of making the leap to another were slim and none.

Oh, some did, like Brenna's father, a newspaperman who married into the Van Duzens. But they were the exceptions that proved the rule.

For his part, Quinn knew how to leapfrog, never alighting in one place too long. Years of behaving himself during his brief appearances at Sydney and Chandler's parties had taught him how to talk to anyone about nothing while making it sound like something. Now he stood smiling, holding a china plate with a piece of chocolate mousse cake in one hand and a cup of latte in the other, surrounded by admiring ladies, who, he soon realized, were content just to gaze at him.

"Excuse me, ladies," Brenna said, extricating him. "I need to borrow this gentleman for a moment."

"Poor you," she added as she led him to her father's study. "How would you ever eat dessert? My mother, what a hostess. My father wants to talk to you. At least in here you can have your dessert in peace. I hope you don't mind the smoke. It's the only place in the apartment Dad can."

"Dad" was Mort James, a wiry man—smaller than his imposing wife, the former Catherine Van Duzen—with white hair, a bald spot and the quick manner of the ace newsman he had once been.

"Cuban?" Mort asked, offering him a redolent cigar.

"No thanks, sir, I don't smoke."

"Sir? Mort, please." He considered the cigar in his hand.

"To think these lovelies were once illegal here. But you'll find in life that plenty of things that were once illegal aren't now and vice versa. And that what's legal isn't always moral and vice versa. But where are my manners? Sit down, have your cake and eat it, too," he said with a laugh, adding, "let me Irish that for you," as he poured more than a wee drop in Quinn's latte and Quinn eased into a soft-as-butter red leather chair.

Mort's study was a classier version of a man cave, complete with first editions of works Quinn knew he would never read. One, however, popped off the shelf like an old friend.

"This is a particularly good translation of *The Iliad*," Quinn said. "We used it at Stanford."

"Brenna tells me you studied classics there."

"That's right."

"You're something of an oddity for a football player, aren't you, Quinn?"

"I'm something of an oddity for a human being, sir, er, Mort."

"That's right. You'll get the hang of it. I like oddities, being one myself. How else can you explain a mutt like me winding up in a place like this?"

"I think, Mort, some people are just meant to make the leap and others aren't."

"The leap, huh? I sometimes wonder if it was worth it. The Van Doozies, as I like to call them, were fated for vessels. The first Van Doozies came to America on a seventeenth-century Dutch ship, where some, having landed and looked around, puked their guts out and promptly expired. But a few survived and thrived to amass vast quantities of property and wealth in Manhattan and the Hudson Valley.

"The most famous Van Doozie, Cyrus Senior, sailed on the Titanic, where he did the gentlemanly thing and required his manservant to go down with him and the ship. They say the ghost of his wife, Amelia, who did not accompany him, still haunts the docks of Manhattan's West Side, waiting for the husband who will never return.

"It may have been a fitting metaphor for their marriage. As Cyrus Junior escorted his mother from her vigil-in-vain, another son, Hugo, awaited the rescuing Carpathia and Cyrus Senior's surviving mistress, whom he whisked to the countryside, where she and her illegitimate Van Doozie baby were never heard of again— illegitimacy being such a thing in those days.

"You're shivering. Are you cold? It's this damn air conditioning. Spring has barely sprung but already Her Highness—my wife, Catherine— insists on keeping the temperature set on Arctic."

Mort got up from his favorite bottle-green leather chair and adjusted the thermostat, pretending to shoot it when it refused to budge, which made Quinn laugh.

"Catherine: When I met her she was Kate, sometimes Katie—a rebel with a cause and without a pause. But everything ends, including the sixties, and yesterday's radical is today's conservative. Catherine, as she is once more known, is more Van Doozie than thou, if you get my drift."

"I think I do," Quinn said, imagining an icy smackdown between Catherine "Van Doozie" James in one corner and his own mother, "El Syd," in another.

"All of this is by way of telling you what you're up against, but don't let that stop you. You and

Brenna have my full support. I know you're a bit young for her. And, as a former editor, I don't believe in shitting where you eat—perhaps not the best expression in these circumstances. But if you're what makes my daughter happy, who am I to stand in your way?"

"Mort, I—"

"No, please, let me finish. I try to be a supportive parent, but the truth is I hate Brenna covering you guys for *The Record*. Being beside men but not with one: Call me old-fashioned but to me, it's no good for a woman. Someday if you're lucky enough to have a daughter, you'll understand. Did you ever hear my son?"

"Cy James? Yeah. Great acoustic singer-songwriter."

Mort nodded. "Plunged off his apartment balcony—or fell, some said. That's what drugs will do to you. After that, I wanted Bren, our only surviving child, just to be safe. I wish she stayed at *New York Rumours*. But she couldn't stand working for Vienne Le Wood. Now if it had been back in the day when your aunt ran it—there was a newswoman. Terrible business that. Loss is something we never outgrow."

Quinn didn't respond. He couldn't go there—not without getting emotional. And that, he had learned, was not something a man did, particularly in the presence of another man. Instead, he watched Mort puff on his cigar as if he were playing a wind instrument, contentedly creating rings of smoke. There was something satisfying in savoring the enjoyment of others, Quinn thought, even if smoking were a filthy habit. For his part, he continued eating his cake and sipping his latte in silence—grateful for the dessert, the company and Mort carrying the conversational ball.

"Anyhow, speaking of Vienne, no doubt you received an invitation to her American Arts Club Ball in a couple of weeks? Don't look so surprised. I know, because she and Her Highness are part of the coven that runs what passes for polite society in New York. You've accepted?" Quinn nodded mid-sip. "Good. It would've done you no good to refuse. Work with Vienne, and doors in this town will open for you. Cross her, and you'll live to regret it.

"Besides, you won't be the only representative from the sports world. Vienne always stacks the deck with idle football studs—baseball players being immersed in the start of their season and hockey and basketball players at the end of theirs. So there will be plenty of gridiron guys like Mal Ryan—he always gets an invite—and Tam Tarquin. You'll have lots of support."

Yep, lots of support, Quinn thought as he made his way out of Mort's study in a stupor. He'll be the belle of the ball, the Cinderella from Hell with both Prince Charming and Prince Not-So-Charming in the same place. Quinn was still mulling the prospect—which thrilled him as much as it terrified him—as he bid the other guests good night and thanked his hostess, who seemed to be as relieved to take her leave of him as he was to depart. He didn't have to look far for Brenna. She was right at his elbow.

"Let me walk you out," she said, taking him by the arm.

"Listen, I know what my father wanted to talk to you about, and I'm sorry. He was a newsman for so long, but he forgot the cardinal rule of journalism: Don't believe everything you read—or write.

"I'll let him know that while you and I are friends, we're both too busy with our careers. You won't mind ending a relationship that never existed?"

He paused and smiled. "We'll always have Park Avenue."

As she shut the car door, she had a look on her face that Quinn had seen once before, late at night when, too tired to read but not tired enough to sleep, he was surfing the tube and came across some old movie in which Gregory Peck was a reporter and Audrey Hepburn, the princess he loved and lost. Brenna looked at him just the way Peck looked at Hepburn—with all the wistful longing for a love that could never be.

Guess that makes me Audrey, Quinn thought, as Brenna wrapped a pink paisley shawl tightly around her sleeveless gray silk sheath and walked back into the apartment building, sheltered once again from the night.

THIRTEEN

Every year, The American Arts Club Gala was billed as "the party of the century." And every year it seemed to live up to that billing, leading Quinn to wonder, even in the age of digital hyperbole, how many "parties of the century" could there be? And how could anyone judge, given that the century was still quite young? Nevertheless, this year's had to be one of the parties of the century, Quinn thought. He was used to being photographed, but never had he seen as many flashes as went off when he stepped onto the red carpet. He staggered back, surprised and a little frightened, as if he had suddenly been punched in the gut.

"Quinn, Quinn, over here," the paparazzi shouted. "This way. One more. That's right. Beautiful."

The directions were punctuated by questions like, "What'd'ya think of the Temps' chances this coming season?"

It seemed to Quinn that the paparazzi worked overtime to keep up a steady stream of chatter—as if the quality of the photograph were determined by the amount of conversation.

"I think our chances are great."

"Do you think you'll be the team's number one quarterback?"

"I think you have to earn it every year. Thank you, ladies and gentlemen. I hope you have everything you need," he said, adding his traditional news conference sign-off.

He was glad to escape inside until he realized the red carpet continued up the grand staircase, atop which Vienne Le Wood stood rooted like a Roman empress. The Temps' entire O-line could not have gotten past her Imperial Majesty, clad in her usual severely elegant black.

"Good evening, Ms. Le Wood. Thank you so much for inviting me."

"Delighted to have you, my dear," she said, drinking him in from head to toe. "And don't you look splendid in that fitted Armani Collezioni tux," she added, squeezing his right bicep in a way that suggested she'd prefer he be wearing nothing at all.

"Yes, well, I best press on to the show," Quinn said, blushing.

The arts club was not a club, or at least it hadn't been for a century, but a museum and library that held regular exhibits on American art, mainly in a vaulted Romanesque space. Lately, the museum had been featuring edgier fare like Terence Benchley's jagged antiwar installations, one of which, *After Baghdad,* consisted of a room of broken glass. It became the subject of controversy when a woman fell into the display in another city, cutting a femoral artery on a piece of glass. At the arts club, it was roped off in the museum's new, white, modern wing, as was a sculpture of a couple, bloodied and naked, making love. The configuration of the space—to say nothing of the crowd gathered around the nudes—had guests and pool reporters jockeying for position, locked in an awkward, "excuse me" two-step. It wasn't long before Quinn ran into Brenna—literally.

She cleaned up real good, Quinn thought, the

vintage strapless silk floral gown—with its fitted bodice, baroque bow at the waist and cascading pink-purple palette—flattering her swan neck, superb shoulders, and toned arms.

"I didn't think *The Wreck's* sports department went in for this sort of thing," Quinn said, bussing her cheek. "You look beautiful."

"Thanks, but I'm not here in my usual guise. I'm subbing for the society columnist, who picked tonight of all nights to have her baby."

"Well, I imagine she didn't do it on purpose," Quinn said.

"Oh, I wouldn't be so sure about that," Brenna said, uncharacteristically cross. "And, of course, I work for a guy who has told me in no uncertain terms that my job is whatever he says my job is. Who knows? Maybe next week I'll be emptying wastepaper baskets with the one janitor who wasn't laid off. Honestly, it just galls me. But then, I think, I could be out on my considerable ass. And I am an actual newspaper columnist, the last of a dying breed. More like a dinosaur, if you ask me. Anyhoo, despite my Van Doozie pedigree, I'm hardly a trust-fund baby. So I borrowed one of my mother's gowns, corralled my curls in my best imitation of a chignon and here I am."

Her mood softened. "I'm sorry, Quinnie. It's just the low blood sugar talking. I'd kill for one of those fried salmon dumplings I saw floating around."

"Waiter," Quinn said, calling over one of the pieces of man candy who worked any Vienne party. "The lady here would like a dumpling—or two."

Quinn winked at Brenna.

"Mmm, ambrosia of the gods," Brenna said,

almost orgasmically.

"Ah, Brenna, I see you're on the scene for *The Wreck* tonight," Vienne said, coming up behind them.

"Oh, hello, Vienne," Brenna said, shooting Quinn a "just-my-luck" look as she tried to polish off the dumpling.

"We all miss your writing at *Rumours*," Vienne said, adding, "I wouldn't be eating too many of those if I were you."

Brenna smiled sweetly. "Thanks for the diet tip, Vienne. But at least my IQ is higher than my weight."

"Meow," Brenna purred to Quinn as Vienne moved on. "And therein lies the reason I'm no longer at *Rumours*, that and well, I couldn't stand the pressure. There was no end to the work and no hope for a raise or a day off. But then, you know what it's like to work for someone who doesn't appreciate you."

Quinn nodded, shrugging. "What choice do we have but to go on?"

"Precisely," Tam said, smiling and embracing them both at once as he snuck up on them. "Brenna, you look absolutely stunning," he added, kissing her cheek.

"Thanks but I think not as stunning as you guys," she volleyed, taking in the effect of Tam's blue-black tux. Leave it to him, Quinn thought, to wear something unusual but totally appropriate. He never misstepped, did he? He was that sure of himself.

"Hello, you," he said to Quinn, giving him a bro shoulder bump as he clasped his hand. The effect on Quinn was like a cloudburst on the parched land.

"Quinn?"

The voice belonged to Mal, who had Tiffany Turkova in a slinky red strapless ball gown on his arm. She flashed Brenna a big cat grin before air-kissing her.

"Nice dress," Mal said to Brenna in a perfunctory manner as he looked around. He and Tam didn't greet each other. OK, awk-ward, Quinn sing-sang to himself.

"Tiffany, gorgeous as always," Brenna said, cutting through the tension. "Why don't I get some pix of you with the NFL's three quarterbacks of the moment?"

As Tiffany obliged, flashing a shoulder and a grin, Mal glowered, Tam looked slightly less than his usual amused self and Quinn posed stiffly, wishing the night were already over.

"Now for a few quotes," Brenna said. "How did everyone like the exhibit?"

"Oh, I was so, so moved by it," Tiffany said, putting her short, fire-engine red nails to a neckline in which every bone was articulated.

"Well, of course, I don't know much about this stuff," Mal said, flashing his trademark frat-boy grin as he squeezed Tiffany into silence, "and I'm happy to support Vienne in whatever she does."

And well he should be, Quinn thought, since she'd been giving him advice, dressing—and, if the rumors were true, undressing—him for years.

"But—"

Here it comes, Quinn thought miserably.

"I just want to say I hope none of our tax dollars are going to support this."

"Naturally," Tam said, smiling, "because nothing says 'democracy' quite like the suppression of artists."

"I'm not saying suppress them," Mal said, his rising voice threatening to pierce the icy veneer that separated his cheesy, toothsome image from his true narcissistic self. "I'm just saying I don't want to pay for this crap."

"But if I may," Quinn jumped in nervously. "I think it said in the introduction that the artist had been a soldier in Iraq and turned to art in a VA hospital as a form of therapy."

"If I wanted a tour, I would've used the audio guide," Mal snapped.

"He's entitled to his opinion," Tam said.

"Hey, hey," Brenna said, flashing them the time-out sign. "Flag on the play, guys. Otherwise, I'm going to have to penalize you, Mal, for unnecessary roughness."

And so it went all night, with Tam, who seemed to be entertaining some private joke, casting furtive glances at Quinn, who caught Mal looking at him Mal-evolently as if to say, "Why's he looking at you?", which in turn caused Tam to shoot Quinn a "Why's he being so possessive of you?" reaction—and no Brenna, stuck with the pool reporters, to run interference.

Nor were they helped at their table by Tiffany, who decided to flirt with Tam, leaning into him and gazing adoringly after consuming the one lettuce leaf that was the supermodel allotment. It made Quinn long for Brenna and a platter of those gluten-loaded fried salmon dumplings.

"Is it TURK o va or Tur KOV a?" Tam asked, egging her on.

"It's TURK o va," she chirped, flashing a set of pearly whites set off by her rich red lipstick.

Quinn's dinner companion was Jennifer Seabert, a young woman oblivious to how lucky

she was. Her husband, venture capitalist
Jonathan Seabert, was on business in Shanghai.
Would that he had taken her with him.

"I don't know about all of you," she said, "but I
find this time of year so stressful, preparing the
house for the Hamptons' season. Do you frequent
the Hamptons?" she asked Quinn.

"Ah, no, ma'am, we're football players so we
spend the summer in training camps and
preseason games around the country."

"Oh, right," she said. Quinn could see she was
mentally crossing them off her list.

"But surely if you could, you'd be in the
Hamptons."

"Oh, I don't know, I'm more of a Jersey Shore
guy myself," Tam said. "I've spent some of the best
moments of my life there."

He looked away, sadly Quinn thought, as if to
add, "and some of the worst."

"Well, then, you must be a Jersey boy,"
Jennifer said. It didn't sound like a compliment.

"Close. I'm from Philly."

"And where do your people live on the Main
Line?"

"My people," Tam said, smiling, "have done
very well for themselves in this world, but they are
hardly Main Liners."

"But you're right. The Hamptons is the place to
be," Mal said, as if Tam's remarks, and thus the
speaker himself, didn't exist. He put an arm
around Tiffany before adding, "We love it."

Dinner arrived, and the group fell into a silence
but not because everyone was enjoying his meal.
When had food become so complicated? Quinn
thought. A piece of meat, vegetables, maybe a
potato, some bread or a little pasta: It wasn't

rocket science. But everything had to be artistic. This chef d'oeuvre was buried under some sauce.

"Isn't the veal exquisite?" Jennifer said. "But the sauce is too rich." She took a few bites then pushed the dish away, scrunching up her face.

Veal: Quinn ate no baby animals.

"What are you, a Buddhist?" Sydney had asked, after he refused to eat the lamb chops she had procured for an Easter feast in Jakarta one year. But Quinn had stood his ground.

"All right, then, you'll get no dinner."

He thought of that as he pushed the veal to the side subtly and ate the vegetables. He noticed that Tam ate little and drank less, while Mal ate whatever was set down in front of him, presumably without coming up for air. He was like a shark—an efficient eating, sleeping, fucking machine.

Dessert offered no respite. It was silver-frosted yellow cake shaped like an amulet that was one of the arts clubs' signature treasures. Quinn didn't mind looking at silver amulets. He just didn't want to eat something that looked like one.

Thoroughly at sea, he excused himself to say hello to Mort, who looked no happier wedged between his wife and Vienne. He was if not two sheets to the wind then at least two napkins.

"I've been watching you tonight, my boy, and I like the way you handle yourself. You've got to stand up to these people in a nice way. It's all about attitude—well, that and a case of single malt Scotch. Yes, you'll do very well in the Van Doozie world."

Quinn wondered why Brenna hadn't told him they weren't a couple as he wandered off for a men's room break only to encounter Tam outside the door.

"Loitering outside the men's room?" Quinn asked. "That could get you arrested."

"It might be worth it if I could eat you with a spoon. You're just about the only delicious thing here. What say we blow this place, go to my hotel, order some real food and have our own little gala?"

In Tam's suite later that night, they shared a sausage pizza and a bottle of wine.

"Now for the real eating," Tam said, "the taking and being taken."

It was funny, Quinn thought. In the museum, he himself had been shy about the erotic works. He barely looked at the bloodied couple, their expressions caught somewhere between orgasmic ecstasy and howling pain. He didn't want to invade their privacy, as it were.

"They're not real, you know," Tam had said to him. "They're just art."

But here in the real, private world, Quinn had no trouble watching himself in a mirror as Tam took him from behind, stroking his throbbing cock as he panted in lust, his come arcing like a fountain spray.

"Be your own work of art," Tam whispered thickly as he nibbled his neck.

FOURTEEN

Quinn longed to go on holiday—not the brief, bittersweet *Roman Holiday* of the Gregory Peck-Audrey Hepburn movie—but a month-long vacation to Indonesia where he could show off the country to Tam and Tam off to the country. He knew it was impossible with summer training camp looming. But then Tam called with the next best thing:

"Listen, a friend of my family has a house in Lyndwood on the Jersey shore—very secluded, with a private beach. What say we escape for a couple of days?"

"I'm already packed," Quinn said, heart singing.

He toyed with the idea of leaving his cell at home, the better not to receive Mal's constant 'Where are you and why aren't you at my beck and call?' texts. But what if something happened to Great-aunt Josie and Great-uncle Artur or—God forbid and more likely—Aunt Sarah? He had to have that constant, instant lifeline to Patience, their appropriately named aide, who looked out for Aunt Sarah as well. Otherwise, he might've ditched the cell. There were few he needed to respond to urgently—certainly not his parents, who rarely contacted him, and certainly not Smalley.

It irked him, though, not to have parents for whom he was the sun that rose and set. Maybe that's why he gave Tam's hand an extra squeeze as they drove down I-95 and headed for the Garden State Parkway—counting the water towers as their official car game and singing along to The Mamas & the Papas.

They were careful to wear sunglasses as well as baseball caps that had nothing to do with San Francisco and New York when they stopped along the way. And they made sure to pay cash. How nutty was that—to be on your guard, no, to feel like a criminal—for loving? That was no way to live, Quinn thought. He longed to break free and to live a life that required no self-consciousness. He could see that Tam was ready for it now. But Quinn wasn't. Not really. Not yet.

The house in which they could be free would probably have never measured up to the Hamptons standards of the Jennifer Seaberts of the world. But to Quinn, it was heaven on earth.

Built by a sea captain, it was a ramshackle, eggplant-colored clapboard and cinder-block affair with three porches the length of bowling lanes, including a screened-in porch that fronted onto the street and a screened-in back porch that opened onto a deck and the ocean.

It was on the gray and white deck that they sat mornings, enjoying the paper, their coffee and fresh, powdery rolls from the Lyndwood Bakery. They'd spend the day walking the beach, or chasing each other there as they played touch football, wearing each other's jerseys—a tribute not only to their mutual love and admiration but to the privacy in which they could express them. When they were brave enough, they took a dip in the Atlantic, which was still cool at that time of year.

Afternoons, they read and dozed on the deck until Tam invariably woke and said, "Why don't we go in for a bit?"

In the light-dappled bedroom that opened onto the gingham back porch, Tam would kiss Quinn deeply, slipping his shirt from his shoulders or pulling his T-shirt overhead to fasten his arms momentarily. He relished the leisurely pace of Tam's lovemaking, the way his large hands with their long, exquisite fingers ranged over every inch of him; the way he looked directly into his eyes, smiling, talking to him, ensuring his comfort; the way he stroked him, bringing him to the edge but not over it until he could enter him and they could come together. Tam's lovemaking was like his quarterbacking—measured and commanding. What must it be like to have such a rock-solid, unruffled sense of yourself? Quinn sometimes hurried in the pocket, anticipating the sack.

"That's 'cause you're still a rookie," Tam purred. "You need a little seasoning under a vet."

He'd trace Quinn's nipples with his thumbs as he lightly held the rib cage that buoyed his high breasts then worked his hands down to the inside of Quinn's briefs, cupping his tight, well-rounded butt.

"You have the most beautiful skin," Tam murmured as he stroked the small of his back and kissed his quivering eyelids slowly.

Where were you, Quinn thought, all those years to shield that skin from hate-filled eyes?

He remembered standing in line with Aunt Sarah at the old Bijou in Misalliance, glancing around and tapping his hand against his thigh, waiting for the movie and one of her loser boyfriends.

"Hey, boy, what are you doing sniffing around

here," or words to that effect, Kevin, Darrin, Steven—pick an "en-in" name—would say.

"Devon (Marvin, Arlen), " Aunt Sarah would respond, giggling, "you know this is my nephew."

"Ain't he a little dark to be your nephew?"

"Don't be like that. You know he's from Indonesia."

But they didn't know, the Aunt Sarah beaus, Quinn thought. Nor were his bosses any less ignorant.

"Just turn around and lift your hair off your neck," the team physician had directed him, almost embarrassed.

He stood with Quinn in the trainer's room, while Smalley, team owner Jimmy Jones Jefferson and former GM Mark Seidelberg watched with varying degrees of interest nearby. Quinn felt the color rise in his cheeks and his heart beat faster as it did when he knew something was terribly wrong. Yet he felt powerless to do anything but comply. He had signed a contract— not great star-quarterback money but more than he had ever seen. He wanted this job. He needed this job. And, more important, he aspired to Lance's starting QB job. So if he had to prove that their backup quarterback was as perfect a specimen as every other Temps' quarterback had been, well...

He turned around in one graceful gesture, gathered his chin-length hair in one hand and lifted it, like a woman waiting to be nuzzled by a lover, to reveal a pristine neck.

"Take off your shirt," Smalley said.

"It's OK, son," the doctor said.

Quinn didn't turn around but slipped it off his shoulders. How I loathe you, he thought.

"What's this?" Smalley barked at the doc. "Is this skin cancer?"

"It's just a mole," the doctor said, sighing, "a beauty mark."

"A beauty mark?" Smalley said. "Well, what have we got ourselves here, a beauty queen? Are you a girl, boy?"

"No sir."

"Turn around."

Quinn turned around for Smalley to consider him skeptically.

"A little lightweight for a quarterback. I'm surprised you don't have tats. I thought all your people did."

Your people? Quinn fumed. Would that be the Indonesian people? It was all he could do to keep himself from grabbing Smalley by the throat and shoving him into a wall.

"Well, I've seen enough," Jefferson said, "a healthy young man in excellent condition. Doctor, you can continue your evaluation in private."

Afterward, he sat in front of his locker, rubbing the knuckles of one hand with the other, hot tears stinging his eyes. Jeremiah Dupré came by, shook his head and simply put a hand on Quinn's right shoulder in a gesture he had never experienced before. It was fatherly.

Tam touched that shoulder now in a gesture that was anything but—massaging it as they lay facing each other—tracing a line down Quinn's right hip and buttock as he lifted his leg to enter him. Theirs was the most egalitarian of relationships, Quinn thought, two equals mirroring the struggle to fulfill the other's desire and their own need to come. After, Quinn nestled happily in Tam's arms as his lover dozed, caressing the lighter, caramel-colored skin of his biceps and comparing it to his own tawnier canvas.

"Tam," he whispered.

"Mmm," Tam murmured dreamily. "What do you want, my heart, my love, my own? Ask me anything."

"I was just wondering, when you joined the Miners, did they, you know, inspect you?"

"Inspect me?"

"You know, look you over."

"Well, I had to pass the physical. And God knows I jumped through enough hoops on the field to satisfy them. But inspect me beyond that, no, although I've been probed and plumbed enough by the media and the fans over the years. Sometimes I feel as if my skull has been cracked open and my brains laid bare for everyone to pick over. Why do you ask?"

"No reason, I just wondered."

"It's an odd thing to wonder. Why, what did those geniuses do to you?"

"Nothing, I just, I don't know what made me think of it. But, you know, they checked me out."

Tam hugged him tightly. "Oh, I'll bet they did. Jeez, we live in such a cruel, stupid world."

"Well, they have to protect their investment. "

"God, you are so forgiving of others but never of yourself, I think." Tam turned to face him. "Let me ask you: Why is it that you can't love yourself the way you love others, the way others love you?"

Quinn had no answer but the tears that began rolling down his cheeks. Tam cupped Quinn's face, brushing the tears aside gently with his thumbs. "Let me love you as you deserve to be loved. Hmm?"

Quinn nodded, too overcome to speak.

"Good. Now that that's settled, what say we hit the shower, dress and head for the boardwalk?"

Tam's idea of vacation was not only to stay in a house like the summer place his parents had had but to eat at the restaurants or the kind of restaurants they ate in and go on the rides he had loved as a kid. Quinn was all for it. He had never seen a place like the Jersey shore with its garishly colored amusements, swirling vanilla-and-chocolate soft-serve ice cream cones, fudge shops and crinolined dolls on sticks.

He loved every minute of it, especially Delmar's, the elegant restaurant at the end of the strip with its walnut, red and brass lobby, over which Mr. and Mrs. Delmar themselves presided. He was short, white-haired and vaguely Euro. She was a tall Texas blonde twenty years his junior. And yet, she seemed happy fussing over him as he fussed over everything in the restaurant. As they prepared a table for two—the place was packed— Quinn admired the lobby portrait of a flapper in a moss green swimsuit that clung to her lithe limbs as she rose Aphrodite-like from the gray-green seafoam. Quinn thought her the quintessence of womanhood.

The dinner was scrumptious—lobster dripping in butter and baked potatoes laden with sour cream and chives. Still, something nagged Quinn.

"Hey, you can go back to your healthy diet after our holiday," Tam said. "Eat up."

"No, it's not that."

"Then what?"

"It's just, don't you worry about someone seeing us together?"

Already they had drawn a few double takes.

"So, two NFL QBs having dinner. We ran into each other. You know what? Who cares? I mean it. What business is it of anyone's? Jesus Christ, I'm tired of the whole damn thing—the models as beards, the ready excuses, the looking over the shoulder. Aren't you tired of it, Quinnie?"

"Yes, but what choice do we have? Think about it. If word got out, the press and our families' reactions would be just the beginning. You and I would be marked men on the field, and our teammates would be forced to defend us, regardless of how they felt about it. And don't even get me started on Smalley, that bigot, who has no love for me anyway. Is that what you want for our teammates, our families, and us?"

Tam, who had been eating with relish, suddenly looked dejected. "No, I guess not."

Perhaps Tam was still mulling that as they stared out at a ride that was mounted on the beach. He gazed somewhat moodily, Quinn thought, as girl after girl flew down a labyrinthine slide only to be caught by a guy at the end. The girls' hair stood on end, their voices echoing with shrieks and laughter.

Quinn bumped him, trying to lighten the mood.

"What was your best time at the shore?"

"Oh, that would have been the nights my parents would bring us kids to the boardwalk. We'd stop at the fudge shop to watch the workers make different kinds of fudge in these huge copper bowls. There was always a little blonde girl outside handing out samples. I thought she looked like Alice in Wonderland, with her curls, blue dress and white lace apron. After we bought the fudge, we'd have hot dogs, then cotton candy, then soft-freeze ice cream and then we'd go on all the rides.

"At the merry-go-round, my dad would hand the ride operator a roll of tickets this thick." Tam indicated the thickness with his thumb and forefinger two inches apart. "And say to the operator, 'Let them ride until they're tired of it.' But he and my mother wouldn't go off then. They'd just stand there, watching me, Bev, Kim, Bill and Petey go 'round and 'round, waving at us.

"Afterward, we'd go home and sit on the front porch—looking at our treasures, eating fudge and pistachios and talking until the truck came to spray for mosquitos and it was time to go to bed."

"Wait. Bev, Kim, Bill, and Petey: How did a Tamarind get into the bunch?"

"I was the last of the litter, and it was my mother's maiden name. My middle name's Michael." Tam added, smiling, "Those were great times."

He looked off to the pilings that buttressed a pier jutting out into the water. Quinn had never seen such an expression on Tam's face. It was a look of fear mixed with sadness.

"Hey," Quinn said, "what say we grab a couple of those cones I've heard so much about, head home, and stage our own amusement ride?"

As they made their way to the ice cream stand, Tam's hand brushed his, sending a jolt through Quinn, who looked around quickly—still uncomfortable in the skin Tam so loved to touch.

FIFTEEN

Quinn would savor and nurture the memory of the Jersey shore just as he kept Indonesia like a tiny but steady flame in his heart. He would have to, he figured, with Tam set to leave for the West Coast and training camp. It would be months—not until the two teams played each other in an August preseason game—that they would be together again.

Or so he thought. But two unexpected opportunities would reunite the lovers sooner than later—though they would come at a steep price.

Vienne Le Wood was having a fundraiser at her house in Bedford, New York to support the rainforest, and once again, Quinn, Tam, and Mal were on the short list. Did she intuit something? Quinn wondered. She seemed determined to throw the three together. For an upcoming issue of *Rumours,* she had Elliott Gardener shoot the three on a bed in a provocative motel-room setting.

Tam, clad in an open, pink, floral-print shirt and black leather pants, was posed on the phone while Mal, in an open, blue, abstract-print shirt and midnight-blue jeans, sat next to him, absorbed in an iPad. That left Quinn sprawled across the bottom of the bed—in an open, green-striped shirt and forest-green ultrasuede pants—looking up at the camera. The three barely spoke during the shoot. Quinn thought you'd need a hacksaw to cut the tension. Even the ever-commanding Elliott was on edge. "OK, here we go," he said, sighing.

But it was a measure of how much power Vienne wielded that no one uttered a peep about the scenario she, not Elliott, had conjured for the photo shoot nor the hours the three subjects spent under the hot lights in close proximity, unaware of just how much they had in common, Quinn thought. Now she had again rounded up the usual suspects, as it were—including Elliott, Tiffany, Brenna, and her parents, among others—for a soirée at one of her half-dozen homes.

Like many women who were extolled—and extolled themselves—for their climb to the top, Vienne owed much of her success to a man. Ferdinand Le Wood, nicknamed Freddy, had built his media empire in his native England. When he bought the *Rumours* publications, he installed his French-Vietnamese wife, whom he met in Hanoi, as the editor of the New York edition. Shortly after, Brenna left it to join *The Wreck*. Quinn wasn't surprised by this backstory, nor was he unhappy that Aunt Lena was no longer around to see what Vienne had done with the magazine she had edited. He was quite sure the two would not have gotten along. But he would like to see Great-aunt Josie or his mother take on Vienne. Now there were two matchups for the main card.

Though he had loved Gaucho, the family's Black Lab in Jakarta—and cried when he left him behind and when he learned much later, rather matter-of-factly from Sydney, that he had died—Quinn had always been deeply suspicious of people who preferred animals to their own kind. Vienne was one of those people. In addition to the snapping Papillon Steve McQueen, who was mercifully under house arrest for the evening, there were Miu Miu, Prada, and Gucci—a trio of Persian cats who temporarily scattered whenever the front door opened.

Steve McQueen's fellow rescue Papillons—Alexander McQueen, Butterfly McQueen, and Steven McQueen—stood at attention, wearing huge periwinkle bows that were almost as big as the dogs. They had been bathed, clipped, brushed and otherwise made photo-shoot ready, seated as they were on their matching periwinkle beds. Elliott struggled to get their attention as they looked—longingly, Quinn thought—out the window. He knew the feeling.

"Alexander, Steven, Butterfly, smile for Mommy," Vienne said as she instructed Elliott to snap a photo that would no doubt make it onto the editor's page of *Rumours*. Yet for all of her love of animals, the modern glasshouse was filled with antlers; stuffed birds; animal heads, throws and rugs; hunting prints; and Remington sculptures of horses.

"'I use antlers in all of my decorating,'" Tam sang, coming up behind Quinn.

"Don't make me laugh."

"No, seriously, the minute I walked in that was all I could think of, that line from *Beauty and the Beast*. I mean, Jesus Christ."

Tam turned to the three dogs, quivering in their beds.

"High-five, Huey, Louie and Dewey or whatever your names are. Which one of you is the mini Cujo that terrorizes the photo shoots?"

"He's in solitary in another part of the house," Quinn offered.

"Oh, thank God. I was wondering why Vienne wasn't handing out Hazmat suits at the door."

"Kind of ironic, don't you think?" Quinn asked. "I mean, she loves animals so much. And yet, she has all these animal heads and stuffed specimens everywhere."

"Not a bit," Tam said. "Don't you see? It's all about control. Animals can be neutered, killed, beheaded, stuffed, mounted, and framed. You can't do that with people. Well, you could but there's probably a law against it," Tam added, grabbing a blonde Sangria from one of the circulating waiters.

"Jesus Christ," exploded a familiar voice.

"And speaking of people I'd love to stuff," Tam said.

"Fuck," Mal said, holding up an injured finger that fortunately wasn't the middle one.

"One of those crazy cats was clawing my leg, and I went to brush him off—gently, mind you—and the fucking thing bit me. I hope I don't die of rabies."

"Ooh, baby," Tiffany said, all solicitousness behind him, "I'm sure Vienne has some antiseptic."

"I don't need antiseptic, you idiot," Mal spat. "You don't treat rabies with antiseptic."

"Geez, this isn't the last reel of *Old Yeller*, so stop the melodrama, will you?" Tam countered. "I'm sure, control freak that Vienne is, all her pets are up-to-date with their shots. Besides, most people in this country who contract rabies get it from bats. And I don't see any here."

Just then, one of the housemaids passed by to take the empty glasses.

"I wouldn't venture into the woods around

here at night if I were you," she said, smiling.

"Great," Tam said. "Just great."

"Who the fuck cares?" Mal yelled. "What about my finger? I hope this doesn't affect my throwing motion."

"Let's find Vienne," Tiffany said, trying to placate him. "Vienne, we have a crisis here."

"Oh, my God," Vienne said, coming up to kiss everyone. "What have we here? Did Miu Miu do that? She can be a bit intense. Miu Miu, have you been a bad girl for Mommy? Brenna—"

Brenna had just arrived, grabbing a mini chicken salad cup on the way in.

"Brenna, put down that hors d'oeuvre," Vienne snapped. "With those hips, you don't need it. Help Tiffany and Mal. There are bandages and antiseptic in the powder room on the second floor."

The advantage of Vienne's rainforest tribute was that you couldn't hear Mal complaining about his indisposed digit. Indeed, you couldn't hear much of anything. Between the waterfall and storm sounds, conversation was virtually impossible.

"We're quarterbacks, damn it," said Tam, who was famous for his mellifluous audibles at the line of scrimmage. "We should be able to talk over this din."

"Well, all I know is I'm a real Chatty Cathy," Brenna said. "If I can't talk over this, no one can."

"What did you say?" Quinn asked.

The jungle centerpieces didn't help. Trying to lip-read as guests bobbed and weaved around the towering topiary was hopeless. Finally, Quinn was able to motion to Tam and Brenna, who wandered with him into a conservatory that was one of the few serene spaces in the house.

"At last," Brenna said, settling in, "some peace and quiet."

But not for long. "Brenna Catherine," her mother barked as she poked her head into the solarium. "Stop flirting with men half your age and come listen to this fabulous freelance assignment Vienne has that only you can do."

Brenna looked at Quinn and Tam. "Just kill me now," she said.

When she left, Tam turned to Quinn and said, "Shall we?"

The sliding doors of the conservatory opened onto a garden that was a world away from the Amazon, or Bedford for that matter, with cherry blossom and weeping cherry trees, winding paths and footbridges over a stream crusted with pink blossoms and studded by paper lanterns that guided you deeper into the night.

"I could hold you in a place like this," Tam said. "I could hold you and kiss you in front of all these people and watch our carefully built world fall away and be perfectly content."

"You know holding is illegal in football," Quinn said. "Besides, gardens aren't lucky for lovers, or at least that's what Adam and Eve discovered." He looked down, thrusting his hands deep into the pockets of his skinny black suit as he kicked a pebble down one of the stony paths with the tip of a polished black shoe.

He and Tam remained apart, watching the brightly colored lanterns sail away. In the Far East, they carried the souls of the departed to the spirit world, Quinn thought. He wished they could transport the two of them to some parallel universe where they were husbands and this was their home, this their garden, and it was just the two of them, enjoying an evening alone. Where was that world? And how many strings into infinity would they have to follow to find it?

Tam inched closer, and Quinn was caught between the impulse to turn and bury his face in his shoulder, inhaling his sandalwood scent, and fleeing back into the house where he would be safe from temptation.

"There you are," Vienne announced in a voice that pierced the night and Quinn's reverie. "What are you two doing out here?"

"Admiring your enchanting garden," Tam said.

"Well, stop admiring it and come on in," Vienne said. "It's time for the entertainment."

Vienne had hired Luis José Ortega, a flower reader of Peruvian Indian descent, with long, dark, wavy hair and a heavily lined poker face that looked older than the rocks deposited by the last ice age. He sat by a bouquet of flowers from which each guest picked a blossom and concentrated on it. Then the guest handed it to Luis, who offered insights into the person. He had heretofore been conducting private readings in a small anteroom. Now he was prepared—or rather, Vienne was prepared—for a public demonstration.

"Luis has assured me of the utmost discretion," she said with a smirk. "No secrets will be revealed, despite my best efforts to persuade him to the contrary. Now let's have a volunteer. Quinn, what about you?"

He thought Tam's alarmed look mirrored his own. Mal shifted uncomfortably, while Tiffany patted one of his sculpted thighs, smiling— fascinated and oblivious. Even Brenna, who normally greeted such pronouncements—

especially Vienne's pronouncements—with an amused, quizzical expression, sat down on the arm of a chair occupied by her father.

"Oh, come on, don't be shy," Vienne prodded. She was a scourge when she set her mind to something. "It's all in good fun. And you can trust Luis."

Quinn sat down opposite Luis at a small table that had been set on a platform just for the occasion and picked out a stargazer lily that had been calling him from the moment he first spied the bouquet. He remembered how stargazers dotted the evergreens at the Shangri-La Hotel in Jakarta at Christmastime. How he loved them, loved their magenta and white starfish design, deeper fuchsia stipples, and intoxicating, powdery scent.

He gazed at the flower, then handed it to Luis, who stared at it before closing his eyes for what seemed a long time. Then he opened them. The room hushed.

"You have come a long way," he said to Quinn.

"Yes," Quinn replied, looking at him fearfully.

"And you love two—"

Here Quinn shot him a look that said *don't go there.*

"Places," Luis continued.

"Oh, for God's sake," Mal said. "You could've gotten that out of *Sportin' Life* magazine. Tell us something you couldn't have read."

"All right," Luis said, giving him a hard look. He was a serene man, Quinn thought, but even the calm and centered could be roused to anger by a tormentor like Mal.

"May I have a piece of paper and a pen?" Luis asked.

He scribbled something, folded it and handed it to Quinn.

"Well, I'll be damned," Quinn said. "It's the name of the dog I had when I was five—Rory. Now I know I've never told any reporters that. Let's give him a hand."

And with that, Quinn held up the paper as the guests clapped, tearing it into tiny pieces and thrusting them deep into his pockets before Vienne could snatch any from him.

It was interesting, Quinn thought, that neither Mal nor Tam clapped. Perhaps they intuited something for as they left, Tam said to Quinn, "So what did Luis really write?"

Quinn smiled, suppressing a gurgle of panic. "What do you think?"

He hated misleading Tam. But surely in a perfect world, Quinn thought, Luis would've written, "The one you love above all others is here in the room and wants to be with you forever," wouldn't he? And Quinn would've shared that with the room and sealed the revelation with a kiss as everyone applauded.

But this wasn't a perfect world, and wishes weren't truth. Still, they could be, couldn't they?

Tam seemed satisfied with the response to his question. Not everyone, however, was content.

"You two seem awfully chummy," Mal said, coming up behind them with Tiffany as they waited for the valet to retrieve Mal's Porsche.

"And that concerns you why?" Tam asked, smiling a bit too brightly and tightly, Quinn thought.

"It doesn't," Mal said with a shrug, "except that you two seem like, you know, co-conspirators or something. I mean, it's not like you belong in the same huddle."

"And you and Quinn do?" Tam said.

There was a pronounced silence as Quinn and Tiffany sensed two alpha males about to square off. Quinn was loath to step into the breach. Tiffany, however, was unafraid to go where angels feared to tread.

"Look, Mal, it's late, and I have an early call tomorrow for a shoot," she said.

"In a minute, babe, you go wait in the car."

"Mal—"

"I said in a minute. Go wait in the car."

She left without another word, and Quinn wondered guiltily what her life was like with Mal. It was one thing for him to tussle with Quinn, who was only 10 pounds lighter. But Mal had to have a 120-pound advantage on Tiffany. At the moment, though, Quinn had other concerns.

"What was in the note?" Mal asked, glancing around quickly to make sure the valets were out of earshot.

"What's it to you?" Tam asked, smiling in turn.

"Shall I tell him or will you?" Mal asked Quinn, ignoring a question with a question.

As the three men stood whispering in the shadows, the floodlights occasionally catching their set expressions, it occurred to Quinn that there weren't three of them standing there but three sets of two—him and Mal, him and Tam and Mal and Tam. There was something between them, or at least there had been, something that went beyond athletic rivalry.

"Tell him what was in the damn note," Mal commanded.

"He doesn't have to," Tam said. "Quinn, you don't have to."

"Why?" Mal countered.

"Because I already know what it said," Tam replied.

"And you can stand there with him?" Mal asked.

"Why shouldn't I?" Tam asked in turn.

"You can stand there, knowing I'm secretly fucking him?" Mal spat.

The color drained from Tam's face. Quinn thought he had never looked more beautiful as he did there in the moonlight, like a lovely, lost ghost.

"Quinnie?" was all Tam said. The look of hurt on his face was more than Quinn could bear.

"Quinnie, what's with this Quinnie?" Mal said to Quinn. "Wait, is he fucking you, too?"

Their faces mirrored each other's as they both finally realized what Luis had actually written to Quinn: "Your two lovers are in the room with you."

Mal looked at Quinn triumphantly as he turned to go.

"This isn't over—Quinnie—not by a long shot," he said. "In fact, for you, it's just beginning."

Quinn turned to Tam as he headed to his rental.

"Tam—"

"Leave me alone," Tam said, jumping into the car.

"Tam, I met him before you," Quinn offered as he leaned into it. "Surely, you must've thought I had dated. And I certainly thought there were others before you met me."

"I never in a million years imagined it would be him," he hissed. And with that, he took off. But Quinn wasn't about to let him leave, not like this. He was afraid if he did, what they had would end right there right now forever. So he roared off after him in his roadster and nearly crashed into him as Tam stopped short at the bottom of the long drive.

"Are you crazy? You must be crazy. It figures. I should've known. All my life it's been like this. First him, now you. I must be destined never to be happy in love."

Quinn got into the seat beside him, gazing at him as Tam stared straight ahead.

"For what it's worth," Quinn said softly, "I never loved him the way I love you."

Tam turned to him. "And that great cliché is supposed to make me feel, what? Listen to me, Quinn, I love you. But I could never be with someone who would have the man who raped me."

Now it was Quinn's turn to be struck by lightning.

"Oh, my God, I'm so sorry. I didn't know. How could I? When? I mean, how?"

"How?" Tam said, laughing. "How? I'll tell you how."

He shut off the car and the lights and turned to him. The street lamps radiated weirdly amid the feathery trees. But even in the shadowy, leafy mystery of a spring night, Tam's fury was unmistakable.

"We were high school rivals. We really hated each other. Until we didn't."

Tam's tone softened at the memory. "He was different then. Or maybe he was the way he is now and I just chose not to see it. People don't change, do they? They become more of what they always were. Anyway, he was charming, funny even, and so fucking beautiful. That and his talent went a long way toward excusing a lot.

"It started as a game really—arguing over who was better at football, fighting and then jerking off. We'd drive to the Jersey Shore in his dad's car with a case of Bud and fuck under a pier, the saltwater and seaweed washing over us. It was lovely—as long as I was the number two high school quarterback in Philly and he was number one.

"And then my team beat him and his school for the city championship. Really, it could've gone either way. But I threw one of those once-in-a-lifetime passes down the line for a touchdown, and we won. What do you think is the difference between a winner and a loser, Quinn?"

"I don't, I don't know."

"Is it talent, hard work, desire, all three or is it really just dumb luck? I was so happy. And Mal seemed happy for me, too, more than I would've been had the situation been reversed.

"He suggested we celebrate at the shore, but we were already pretty buzzed by the time we got there. Things started getting rough, and I told him to take it easy, because he was hurting me. But he wouldn't. He pushed me down into the water until I felt my lungs would burst. At the last minute, he brought me up gasping and shoved me against a pile, where he raped me. I begged him to stop. It hurt so much. You know what he said? 'That's how you like it. And now you know who's really number one.'

"I cried all the way home, but I never told a soul. Anyway, who was I going to tell—my conservative Catholic parents? Or maybe my new college roommate, or the coach, or the front office when I arrived at the Miners? Yeah, that would've been great."

"Tam, I—"

"Not your fault. It's just the way things went."

Someone was honking behind them, and Quinn realized that their cars were still blocking the driveway's exit. He got out of Tam's, smiling and waving as he recognized one of Vienne's confidantes and her husband. Whatever else, he mustn't lose his cool now, he thought, even as his world was shattering.

"Tam, come back to my place. We'll talk. We'll work it out."

Tam shook his head.

"Go on. I'll call you. I will."

But the way he took off Quinn feared he'd never see him again.

When he returned to his loft, Quinn's heart skipped a beat. There was Mal, sitting on the sofa.

"You are so going to pay for this."

"Get out. Get out right now. Or I'll call the police. I'll call the press. I'll step out on that balcony and shout it to the rooftops," Quinn yelled. "How could you? How could you do that to him? How could you rape him?"

"Rape? Is that what he told you? Well, I'm not surprised. He was always a bit melodramatic.

"Anyway, one man's rape is another's uncontrollable passion. We were kids then. We were drunk. Things got a little out of hand. No, that wasn't it. I loved him, only he was always such a goody-two-shoes. We mustn't. We mustn't do this, and we mustn't do that. 'We mustn't take your father's car without his permission, Mal. We mustn't drink and drive.' Only he went, didn't he?

"In a way, he was then a lot like you are now— drawn to what he wanted but was afraid to do. I'll prove it to you. You tell me to get out. Fine, I'll go you one better: You go now. You go to the police. See how much they'll care about a supposed crime that happened a dozen years ago. Or better yet, go to your precious Brenna—who called us trog, trog, trog--"

"Troglodytes."

"Yeah, she had the nerve to call us that."

"She said that some members of the NFL act like troglodytes. And anyway, how can you be offended by that when you don't even know what it means?"

"I know when I've been insulted. Anyway, go tell her the whole dirty story, and be sure to include yourself in the telling."

Quinn moved to the door.

"Of course," Mal added, settling in, "it's you who'll be responsible for the hit to your beloved's reputation, because my lawyer and I will have to counter with a portrait of Tam as the miserable little bitch he was, manipulating me until he won the city championship and then blithely announcing he was dumping me as he headed off to U of Penn. I'm sure he left out that part of the story."

"Whatever he did or didn't do, it's no reason to rape—"

"You don't get it, do you? It's not just your little boyfriend, whom I'm sure has already dumped you, and his squeaky-clean family who'll be affected. What about Brenna, your wannabe girlfriend? I've seen the way she looks at you. Think how devastated she'll be to have her worst fears confirmed: That her favorite is nothing but a fag. And how long do you think you'll last in the NFL once word gets out? Oh, I'll survive and probably Tam will, but you, under Pat Smalley? The guy hates you. And what then of all those checks you send to your family down in

Misalliance, Missouri to keep that dump running or to feed the addictions of that whore of an aunt—"

"You watch your mouth—"

"Or support that little pet project of an orphanage back in your little banana republic. And what of my Tiffany?"

"What about her?"

"Well, maybe she'd be interested in playing some of our games. Or maybe not, now that she's pregnant."

"Pregnant?" Quinn broke out in a cold sweat. "You wouldn't do anything to hurt her or the baby."

"What do you care? It's not like you could be anyone's baby daddy. It's not like you even have an example. I mean, who's your daddy?"

Quinn banged his head against the door three times. He would've dashed his brains out, but what good would it do? Instead, he waited for the inevitable, Mal's breath on his neck.

"Don't bother to turn around," he said as he yanked his clothes from him.

SIXTEEN

"I believe in the resurrection of the body and life everlasting. Amen," Quinn said with the congregants at the 5 p.m. Saturday Mass at St. Francis.

But did he? To believe in the Christian afterlife was to believe in that neat tripartite, Heaven, Hell and Purgatory. And what Hell could be worse than the one he was already in? For Quinn, Hell was the loss of freedom, and he was held fast, bound by obligations, expectations, commitments, and, especially, fears. The more feverishly he worked those chains, the more entwined they became.

"Let's play a game," Mal said in his now not-infrequent-enough visits. "Let's play Strip Search."

"I don't like that game," Quinn said.

"OK, let's play Slave Auction. You'll be the slave and I'll be the master and—"

"Are you kidding me?" Quinn snapped. He had been exposed enough to slavery's remnants growing up in a place where people had displayed needlepoints of the Confederate flag until only recently. "After everything the African-Americans have been through, I will not demean their experience, even for your perverted fantasies."

"OK, OK," Mal said. "Spare me the lecture. Strip Search it is. Turn around. Now take off your shirt slowly."

Quinn told himself it was no different than getting a physical. It was no different than being inspected by Smalley. It was no different: This is what he told himself so he wouldn't tear up.

"Don't make me do this," Quinn said. But he did it anyway, because that was all he deserved, he reasoned. He had betrayed the great love of his life. Didn't matter that he didn't know about Tam and Mal. He loved Tam, but he had wanted Mal, too. He wanted to have his cake and eat it, and that never worked. Even now as he reached out to Tam, and tried to explain himself, it was to no avail. Tam didn't return his texts, phone calls or emails. And when their teams met in the August preseason, Tam snubbed him at the end of a game in which the Temps shocked the Miners 45-7—a breach of postgame protocol that did not go unnoticed by the teams, the press, and the fans, thereby deepening Quinn's humiliation.

He tried to tell himself it was all right, that you can't be humiliated if you refuse delivery of said slight, but whom was he kidding? He was more than mortified. He was heartsick, plagued by palpitations, dangerously low blood pressure, nausea, dizziness, loss of appetite, and exhaustion. Before, he hadn't thought it possible to die of a broken heart, to be mad for love. People died from disease, accidents, war, and other acts of violence or something that rocked their core identity and, so, forced their hand. Lovesickness was the stuff of opera and movies. But now that he saw it in reality, he felt like a fool, a stupid, little fool, and the thought that he had brought it all on himself—that he had cost himself the one thing, the one person, he had wanted most—well, that was more than he could bear.

So he turned his anger outward and did the unthinkable: He began to see Mal's point of view.

Tam was a priggish control freak who expected perfection of everyone else. OK, Quinn thought, reviewing the situation yet again, he himself had made a serious mistake. But he couldn't be held accountable for a past that wasn't his. Hadn't he suffered enough?

Would you like to see the scars? he longed to ask Tam. They were the trophies of each encounter with Mal—the night he came over plastered and frustrated, because Tiffany was too sick for sex; the night his team had been crushed in the season-opener, and he, humiliated, had to dominate someone; the night he had been sacked seven times in another losing effort. Quinn counted the brutalities in the bruise near his temple that he covered with his hair, the welts on his back, the marks on his wrists and ankles where Mal bound him. What frightened him even more than the bruises themselves was how much he liked them; how they, along with the meals he skipped and the tiny cross-stitch marks he made on his arms with a penknife, challenged his body; how they represented for him a life pushed to and lived on the edge.

They at least were the signs of passion, preferable to the cold nights when Mal arrived bearing strange gifts, like cigarettes and a football-shaped cigarette lighter with which to burn him.

"What, I thought your people did all that tattoo stuff?" Mal said, flicking the flame.

After that, Quinn determined to get rid of him. He fantasized about killing him, maiming him, phoning Tiffany, sending an anonymous message to Brenna at *The Wreck*, showing up at Tam's doorstep and throwing himself on his mercy— none of which, he knew, were real options and almost all of which would make him no better than Mal.

He searched his Lower Manhattan loft for the card that Dr. Matthew had given him for the domestic abuse hotline. Absent that, he Googled "domestic abuse" and came up with A Place for Us, a shelter not far from where he lived. It took everything in him to walk through the door.

"May I help you?" a young woman said, eyeing him coldly. It was a minute before he understood: He was the enemy, not the victim—a six-foot, four-inch, 230-pound, ripped behemoth in a ski cap, hoodie and dark glasses that he wore not to menace but to shield himself.

"I, I'm, excuse me, I've come to the wrong place," he said, fleeing.

There was no place, he realized, no choice but to endure. He would've buried himself in his work but Lance was back as QB, and he had been demoted to number three behind Nero Jones— this despite protest columns from Brenna and other journalists and boos that rained down as the team began the season 0 and 4.

"You're douches. You're nothing but scum," fans shouted.

Violent emotions but football was a brutal, beautiful and brutally beautiful game, he thought as he went in for Jones in the third quarter of a 34-0 blowout by the Omaha Steers—Lance having left the game with a leg injury that turned out to be another break. Dispensing with the huddle and working quickly, Quinn was nonetheless sacked by two 300-pound linemen. He felt as if his brain would burst through his skull, then his helmet. But what hurt even more was what followed.

"You're no Shepard," one of the goons said,

referring to their star quarterback, Alex Shepard. "You don't even have a daddy from what I hear. You nothing." With that, he flashed Quinn a derisive smile that was almost a leer.

"Come on, bro," the other goon said. "He's a brother, man."

"He may be dark but he's no bro, man."

Why should words devastate more than 600 pounds of blubber ramming you into the ground? Quinn wondered. But they did.

"Shake it off," Derrick said, helping him up, throwing an arm around him and glaring at the opposition. Quinn wanted nothing more then but to shake Derrick off, as well as the hapless trainer who no doubt had his hands full sending crybaby Lance-o-little off to the hospital with his busted leg—to say nothing of consoling Smalley in the wake of his favorite being injured, again—and now came hopping out onto the field to tend to Quinn. He could bear anything but their kindness.

Come on, Novak, Quinn told himself. This is no time to feel sorry for yourself and withdraw like Achilles, sulking in his tent. So he gave Derrick a reassuring pat and waved the trainer away with a laugh, even though his head still ached like a sonofabitch. How he'd love to hogtie those Steers, he thought, mixing his animal husbandry metaphors.

On the next drive, he planted his legs in a perfect triangle, cocked his hips and waited for what seemed like an eternity for Derrick, Greg— someone, anyone—to be open. He felt one of the Steers tug at his jersey, but he yanked himself free and took the ball down the field himself for an 81-yard touchdown. We might lose, Quinn thought as he knelt, crossed himself and rose in one swift, graceful gesture. But he would be god-damned if they would be shut out, if anyone would make fun of him. He may not be Alex Shepard, but he was still himself. And no one—not his mother, Smalley, Mal, or even Tam—would tell him or make him otherwise.

Quinn's touchdown would be the turning point—of the game and the season as the Temps scored five touchdowns to come back 35-34. Quinn gave the stunned Shepard a big grin as he hugged him in the phony postgame ritual.

"Tell Tweedle Dee Dum and Tweedle Dee Dee I said I'm their daddy now," he whispered into Shepard's ear.

He didn't think Shepard got the reference. It was probably too old school for him. But hey, Quinn didn't give a rat's ass. As he sat in front of his locker, he marveled at the strangeness of life and of the game he played, in which "holding" cost you, but it was perfectly legal to dash someone's brains against a bit of bone and plastic before delivering what passed for a verbal coup de grace in the NFL.

That night—or rather, early that morning—Quinn received a phone call that was unsettling though not entirely surprising. His first thought was that something had happened to Aunt Sarah or Aunt Josie and Uncle Artur—that was always his greatest fear. Then he figured it must be Mal demanding phone sex as he often did when he was on the road.

"I'm in no mood for this," Quinn said. Good thing he didn't use Mal's name.

"Well, you better get in the mood, whatever that means," Smalley snapped, "and get your ass down to the 54th precinct, where they're holding

Nero on gun possession charges. This is your fault, mister, and you better make it right."

As Quinn hopped into his convertible, fighting to keep his eyes open, he tried to comprehend how in God's name this was his fault. But then, everything that went right with the team was Smalley's and Lance's doing. (Was Smalley in love with him?) Everything wrong was on Yours Truly, Quinn thought.

At the police station—a depressing place with scarred benches, big, filmy globe lights, dirty windows and, perhaps not surprisingly, unfriendly people—he met Drew Harrington, blond, handsome, and definitely gay, who looked just like Dr. Matthew. Quinn would later discover they were mirror-image twins.

Drew was clearly the commanding yang to Dr. Matt's compassionate yin in his role as legal eagle to the stars. Quinn recognized him from "Nutgate," that tempest-in-a-teapot of a few years back involving the dishy former number one tennis player Alí Iskandar, the equally gorgeous Evan Conor Fallon, the current tennis number one, and an Eagles Airlines altercation that began when a flight attendant refused Evan's request for an extra package of peanuts. Drew, Quinn reasoned, must sleep at the airport, the better to take off to wherever there was a star in need.

In a few minutes, he emerged with a shaken, chastened Nero.

"I didn't do nothing wrong," Nero wailed onto Quinn's shoulder. "I didn't do nothing wrong. A man has a right to protect hisself. That's why I took the gun to the club. How did I know the safety wasn't on? I didn't hurt nobody—nobody except myself, except myself."

Quinn and Drew decided that the best thing would be for Nero to stay at Quinn's loft to throw off the press. With Mal and the Quakers on the road, Quinn thought, there was no chance of awkward encounters.

As Quinn tucked him into bed in an area of the loft that served as the guest room, Nero grabbed his hand and pleaded, "Please, I don't want to go to prison. They'll kill me. I don't want to die."

How young he was, Quinn thought as he soothed him—even though he was only two years younger than Quinn—and how foolish young men were with their little boy-macho posturing. But then, who was he to talk or judge?

The next day, Smalley gave Quinn another of his irrational tongue lashings: "The QB is responsible for everything—everything, do you hear me? Once again, you've let down the team, this time by failing to mentor Nero." Smalley pronounced the word "men-tor" dumbly, with equal emphasis on each syllable.

Afterward, Quinn asked to address the players alone without any coaches present.

"As you no doubt know," he began, "Nero was arrested last night at a club downtown on illegal-handgun possession charges and is facing some serious jail time. He's staying at my place for the foreseeable future. Let's keep that among ourselves.

"Sometimes we make mistakes." Here Quinn flashed on Tam and nearly lost it. "What matters is what we do with those mistakes. There's no question that we as a team have our work cut out for ourselves. But there's also no question that there is a way through this. There is always a way through things, and we'll get there together,

143

because we have no choice and because I not only think we can win but I know that we will."

Quinn listened to his own words. He called plays until he was hoarse. He threw to wide receivers and tight ends until he thought his arm would fall off. He attended Nero's court dates, kept up his visits to Dave, and even dropped in on a fashion show organized by Tiffany under the pretense of wanting to save the whale, or whatever the hell she was saving this month, but really just to see that she was all right. She was as happy and oblivious as always.

"Of course, I'm fine, too big to model right now," she said, proudly showing off her small bump and flashing a huge sapphire and diamond engagement ring. "Just call me fat and sassy."

"Glad to hear it," Quinn said, smiling. "Say hi to Mal. Tell him to keep treating you right, or he'll answer to me, OK?" he added, laughing so as not to alarm her.

He wished he felt as good. He told himself that this then was love: Not that we are loved but that we love and go on loving, even in the void. If he did everything else perfectly—ran the plays, worked out, ate right, kept his overhead low and his loft clean, made sure his family and friends were fine and met his charitable commitments, then it shouldn't matter whether or not he felt loved.

But it did and others were beginning to notice something was amiss.

"You look as bad as I feel," Dave Donaldson rasped. He was confined to a hospital bed now, off the living room of the family's Jersey home. His skin was the color and quality of yellowing parchment, his eyes circled by darkness, his cheeks sunken and his breathing labored. There was more than a whiff of the fetid about him—like the stench of decayed hostas at the end of summer. Quinn thought he smelled like death.

"Well, I was never a beauty," Quinn replied, only half-joking.

"I think you know that's not true," Dave said. "Come on, they say dead men tell no tales, nor do soon-to-be dead men. You can trust me."

Quinn smiled, eyes glistening. "I'm on a runaway train, and I can neither stop it nor jump off."

But he was going to have to try, he decided as he took Mal's call in his car before heading back to Manhattan.

"What the fuck do you mean I can't see you?"

"You can't, Mal," Quinn said. "I'm sorry but Nero's staying here now."

"Are you fucking him?"

"No, no. He's in trouble. You must've read about it. I'm the starting QB again. It's on me to set an example. You know how it is."

"I know I'm not paid to be anyone's babysitter."

"Well, I'm sorry, Mal, but I am," Quinn said, not sorry at all.

"Then we'll use Tiffany's place. She's back at the house in Philly most days now. Or do you want me to make things ugly at your place?"

"I'll text Nero I'll be home in a few hours."

Absence had made the heart grow more inventive if not fonder. He was glad Nero was asleep when he got back to the loft. Quinn turned on the shower as hot as he could stand it. He wrapped his bruised hands. The next day, he asked the team's permission to visit a sick relative in Philadelphia. Instead, he had made a 5 p.m. appointment for himself at Dr. Matthew's office.

Quinn was grateful that the receptionist in the otherwise empty office was more interested in copying his insurance card and filling out forms than in actually looking at him with his knit cap, hoodie, dark glasses, and fingerless gloves.

Once inside Dr. Matthew's office, however, the gloves came off—as did his clothes and any pretenses. Dr. Matthew gently examined his hands, the bruise at his temple, the welts on his back, the burns on the back of his neck.

"Why? Why do you let him do this to you?"

"I don't know. I don't know," Quinn cried. "I tried. I looked for the card you gave me. I did. But I couldn't find it."

His brain, freed from the confines of plastic, was on a tear now, charging down the field of the imagination.

"So I Googled this place in Manhattan, only the woman behind the desk looked at me with such hatred, as if I were the enemy, which I guess as a man I am."

"I'm sorry you had a bad experience there," Dr. Matthew said. "No one thinks of domestic abuse as something that happens to men. But we can end this, you and I, right now. Tell me who did this, and we'll call the police."

"I can't. I can't. There are too many people involved."

"Uh-huh. And what good will you be to them if you're dead?"

"It's a chance I'll have to take."

"Would you listen to yourself? You'd rather risk death than expose this monster."

"He's not a monster. He's just like me—

someone who wants to be loved but is caught up in a very violent world."

"Well, if that's your story, I can't help you."

"I understand," Quinn said, preparing to leave. "I don't know why I came here. I don't know what I was hoping to change when I don't deserve any better."

"Why?" Dr. Matthew said as he reached the door. "What could you possibly have done that would make you think you deserved this?"

"I don't know."

"Yes, you do. What?"

"I betrayed someone I loved. I cheated on him with someone who hurt him, though I didn't know it at the time."

"Then that part doesn't count. But that's not it. So I ask you again, what was it, Quinn? What did you do that was so terrible that you have condemned yourself to a living death?"

PART II

PART II

SEVENTEEN

Twelve years earlier

He remembered his aunt helping him with the oxygen mask, holding his hand and praying with him, even as they were in the tuck position. And then he remembered objects flying—drawn here and there as if by some magnetic field gone haywire—and people crying and screaming as the lights went off, the plane went down and water, lots of water, poured in, cold, so cold.

When he emerged, he was a thing remarkable—a boy like Auden's Icarus, fallen from the sky while others plodded on with their unsuspecting lives. But he had no other memory of the experience till that moment in the Alaskan hospital when he woke, unable to move, screaming for his aunt in Bahasa, knowing somehow she was dead, surrounded by strangers trying to soothe him, trying to understand as he thought to himself, I killed her. I killed my aunt.

"Poor baby. What language is that?"

For days, he drifted in and out of consciousness as sensation gradually reclaimed his limbs. The images his fevered brain received had the staccato rhythm of a slide show—here doctors and nurses touching him, talking; there nurses' aides reassuring him as they bathed and bandaged his racked body; and, finally, a woman who looked like Aunt Lena and his mother, only younger, talking with an older woman, salt-and-pepper haired, who didn't.

"Ooh, I don't know, Aunt Josie." She pronounced the name the French way, "Jho ZEE." "I don't see how we can care for him."

The older woman grabbed the younger by the sleeve of her sweater.

"You listen to me, Sarah Day Novakovic. This is your sister's child. This is blood. And we don't turn our back on blood. We're going to finish what our dear, departed Lena started. This boy washed up on these shores for a reason—to become a real American for the greater glory of God. And we're going to help him do it."

And so Quinn found himself in Misalliance, Missouri, caught somewhere between Jakarta and New York, where he had been and where (he hoped) he was going, what he was and what he wanted to become. At night, he comforted himself with memories of Aunt Lena and their time in Singapore and Hong Kong. It was, she said, their special getting-to-know-you time, and he recalled imagining with excitement that it was what his life in New York would be like with her—lots of shopping, new clothes, dinners with her interesting friends, special treats, visits to museums and historical sites and, mostly, one-on-one time in which they talked about everything.

"Aunt Lena," he called as she took his picture overlooking Singapore Harbor, "if you could be anything else, what would you be?"

She thought for a moment. "A butterfly," she said. "I'd be a butterfly. Remember that. Some day—a long, long time from now—when I'm gone from this earth, I'll come back to you as a butterfly."

Perhaps she had a premonition. The last thing he remembered her saying to him on the flight before they went down was "Don't forget me." Forget her? Would that he could remember only her and forget everything else.

Misalliance was a town of 12,000 with a downtown of one thoroughfare and a few side streets of brick storefronts. There was a hardware store that was a kind of general store, a supermarket, a barbershop, a hair salon, a feed and seed store, a movie theater called the Bijou, and a few other establishments of lesser note. It was a typical American town, Quinn supposed, as he had nothing else to compare it to, save for the moments he was whisked through St. Louis. Even then, he knew St. Louis wasn't as big as Jakarta or as he imagined New York was.

Misalliance stood outside St. Louis, and the house stood outside Misalliance—a large faded pink and green Victorian with scalloped clapboards, gables, gingerbread trim, fluted columns and a wraparound porch. It was partly shuttered, though not for want of money. The Dudevants—for that was the family name of Uncle Artur; Aunt Marie-Josephine, called Josie; and their late sister, Azielle, mother of Aunts Lena and Sarah and his own mother—were actually comfortable enough. But Uncle Artur and Aunt Josie, especially Aunt Josie, children of the Great Depression and World War II, lived in fear of a poverty-stricken old age, and so they deprived themselves of many small luxuries—a freshly painted room, a landscaped garden, dinner in St. Louis—to save money. That they imposed on themselves the very austerity they had striven to avoid was an irony that would've been lost on Aunt

Josie, Quinn thought, a woman serious to the point of literal-mindedness. But the irony was not lost on Quinn, nor was the realization that Aunt Josie's circumspection balanced Aunt Sarah's wantonness.

"That girl is a storm blowing through," Aunt Josie would say, "and I am powerless to stop it."

The more Aunt Sarah spent money and flaunted her "ripe womanliness," as Aunt Josie put it, the more Aunt Josie determined that Quinn, on the cusp of puberty, would not succumb to unbridled ways. That was clear when he arrived in Misalliance after months in an Alaskan hospital and rehab facility and several international phone calls in which Quinn's mother made it plain that she didn't want him back anymore than he wanted to go back to her.

"Do you know your catechism?" Aunt Josie grilled Quinn. "What about your saints?"

"Yes'm," Quinn lied, making a mental note to try to bone up on these at the local library that became one of the few sanctioned pleasures, where Aunt Josie's stern portrait hung in the foyer to honor the librarian emerita.

If Aunt Josie saw herself locked in combat with Islamic Indonesia for Quinn's immortal soul, she also considered herself fighting on two fronts for the integrity of his body.

Uncle Artur, who had lost a leg in the Korean War—yet another subject for library research, Quinn figured—spent most of his time rutting with the various nurses aides, poor, desperate, young immigrant women from Haiti and Nigeria who came and went, as if the urgency of the carnal act would make him whole again and ensure their future in America. The more Aunt Josie tried to hire battle-axes or, God forbid, male aides to care for him as a number of ailments had mostly confined him to a wheelchair, the more he countered with women whose nubile lushness could not be denied no matter how pedestrian the nurse's aide uniform.

"What do you think, Paris?" he said to his latest "paramour," as Aunt Josie disapprovingly called her, appraising Quinn. "Soon this one will be ready for you. Do you have hair on your balls yet, boy?"

When Aunt Sarah repeated the story to Aunt Josie with a giggle that only deepened Quinn's red-cheeked mortification, Aunt Josie issued another of her famous edicts.

"Quinnie Day, under no circumstances are you to venture near the nursing suite," as she called Uncle Artur's rooms.

"Yes'm," Quinn promised, "yes'm" being the operative response to anything Aunt Josie said, he had decided.

Besides, he had once glimpsed Uncle Artur's prosthetic leg hanging on the closet door of his rose-papered bedroom, the memory of which was enough to make Quinn scurry past the suite every time he set foot on the second-floor landing.

But not even that unnerving sight could block out the sounds of Uncle Artur and Paris' lovemaking, nor another sight that Quinn witnessed one night as he made his way to the lilac-papered and scented bathroom, that of an open door and Paris—naked, her dark skin glistening, her full breasts with their dark nipples hanging like ripe eggplants—and Uncle Artur—paunchy, pasty, hairy, sweaty, and naked in his wheelchair—wriggling rhythmically, pleasurably.

She rode him as he clasped her buttocks to move her up and down as if she were a carousel horse, their bloated faces like puffer fish fixated on each other.

In bed, the covers pulled tight around him, Quinn shut his eyes and ears, but the experience was burned into his memory. As was the sight of Aunt Sarah and one of her obnoxious beaus—who looked upon her little, brown-skinned chaperone with contempt—pawing each other in the backseat of her old Mercedes or the balcony of the Bijou.

Still, Aunt Josie needn't have worried. Quinn quickly realized that his nascent passions didn't tend that way, that what excited him about women wasn't their bodies but their position as love objects of men. And he recognized another thing, too—that Aunt Josie's fears enabled him to enjoy his preferences without suspicion. His interest in the ancient Greeks, sporting magazines and art history books were all deemed acceptable pursuits to the woman who saw herself as the doyenne of Misalliance culture.

As she comforted herself with Jane Austen or "Jane Eyre" at night, and Uncle Artur lost himself in Paris, Quinn would hide under the covers with Achilles or some modern athletic equivalent and, stroking himself, imagine a scenario similar to the steamy goings-on he had glimpsed in Uncle Artur's room.

He was both proud of the quality of his come and ashamed of it. He knew it was wrong, or at least he had been taught it was wrong. And he didn't like deceiving Aunt Josie or anyone else. But he knew, too, his was a family of secrets. No one was allowed to bring up Grandma Azielle or "that brutal bounder"—as Aunt Josie described him—that was Grandpa, both long dead.

Quinn rationalized his secret pleasures as his reward for making contributions to the Dudevant household. As soon as he was able to acquire a secondhand laptop—something that practically required creating a PowerPoint presentation for Aunt Josie—he guilted Sydney and Chandler into increasing the amount of room and board they sent her for his care.

"Since you dumped me here, the least you can do is help out Aunt Josie financially," he texted, making things sound worse than they were.

Quinn then persuaded Aunt Josie to use part of the money to improve the house and property by promising to do much of the work himself—a promise he made good on. He had heard the whispers in town—the strange, threadbare Dudevants with their wild Cajun and Black Irish blood and oversexed Croat relations and now the grandnephew of dubious parentage. He'd be damned if they'd laugh at them, at him. To him, it was like laughing at the memory of Aunt Lena. The only way to counter ridicule, he figured, was through self-improvement—at home and at the all-boys St. Gabriel's Academy, where he excelled at academics and athletics with such a degree of humility that he could not help but be popular with the teachers and the other students.

St. Gabe's ended with eighth grade. When it came time for Quinn to enter Misalliance High, Aunt Josie manifested a worldliness that took Quinn by surprise. It appeared when Coach Jim Redfield came calling to express his desire to have Quinn try out for the Wildcats football team.

"Miz Josephine, I know you are a woman of faith," Coach Redfield said over tea served from

Aunt Josie's good blue-and-cream set. "But what you may not know is that football is next to godliness, too. He who plays prays twice."

"Actually, Mr. Redfield," Aunt Josie said as she handed him and Quinn matching plates with thick slices of her delicious pumpkin bread, "it was St. Augustine who said that he who sings prays twice, something I always tell the other members of St. Gabriel's Choir. But I am inclined to believe that life itself, including athletics, is a prayer. And so I will grant permission for Quinnie Day here to try out on several conditions: 1. He must truly want this. 2. Academics must come first. 3. Any unnecessary roughness will signal an end.

"And last but certainly not least, I have read what has gone on between coaches and the students entrusted to their care in the locker rooms and showers of our nation's schools, and I must say I am shocked, shocked. So I will be watching you and your staff at every practice and every game. And if I so much as surmise anything improper, I will rain down on you like a Louisiana hurricane."

Quinn would be playing baseball, too, his real love. But Coach Redfield, a man with his eye on a state championship, had glimpsed something in Quinn beyond the speed of Mercury and a laser for a left arm. He had seen the future.

"Baseball, son, is a great game, but it's part of our pastoral past," he said on the field, putting an arm on Quinn's shoulder and looking over his at Aunt Josie, hawkeyed in the stands. "Whereas football is our glorious present and future."

Quinn would play baseball and basketball at Misalliance High and caddy to make extra money, but Coach Redfield made sure that he knew football was number one. He needn't have bothered. There were plenty of reminders everywhere he looked. Friday nights Misalliance came alive in a way it didn't during the workweek or even on Sundays, its spanking new athletic field beckoning like a glittering oasis to the faithful, who swelled the town's numbers to such an extent that you could hear the shouts, laughter, cheers, and clapping echoing all the way to the Dudevant house. The ball field—with its blue and yellow stands, the school colors—was such that whenever there was a local or national crisis, people gathered there rather than at town hall or the United megachurch, the largest of the seven houses of worship in town. It was only fitting, Quinn thought, for that field was Misalliance's true cathedral and football, its real religion. Coach Redfield always seemed to have scouts from the St. Louis Arches, the New Orleans Gators and the Atlanta Rebels checking out the prospects. These football scouts were personal friends of the coach, who was also visited by baseball and basketball scouting friends. He seemed to spend less time with them, though.

Aunt Josie treated all of them skeptically, as she did anything or anyone who might interfere with Quinn's intellectual or moral development. That included the adorable cheerleaders who were always flitting about him. With Uncle Artur a sexual minefield for any female visitor between eighteen and dead and Aunt Sarah something of a town joke, Aunt Josie had laid down the law to Quinn: She would tolerate nothing less than respectability from him, and that meant guarding his virginity.

It wasn't as hard as Aunt Josie or others

might've imagined, given his developing attraction to the sculpted, fair-haired ancient Greek heroes—including Alexander, Achilles' great descendant—he grew up reading about under the guise of acquiring a traditional, classical, Catholic-approved education. Unwittingly, Aunt Josie and the straitlaced Christianity that threaded Misalliance had given him the perfect cover for his secret life and he felt like a heel—an Achilles' heel?—for using them. Of course, he was far from the only hypocrite in town.

"No one needs to know what we're doing, and we don't have to go all the way doing it to have fun," Abigail purred.

She was the head cheerleader, one who saw the inevitability of the star quarterback that Quinn soon became and the head cheerleader getting it on as a prelude to marriage and having kids.

The petite Abigail was one of the few girls in Misalliance to be Aunt Josied and to have survived the test, afternoon tea at the homestead, followed by a dinner a few weeks later. There, Abigail— elegantly dressed in a maroon sheath and pink pearls, her pale lips and brown hair glistening, her makeup painstakingly applied to suggest no makeup at all and emphasize her cow eyes—was able to hold her own on a variety of subjects. Plus, she was from one of Misalliance's leading families, devout Roman Catholics in a town where Catholics were a minority.

"She's perfect," Aunt Josie said to him as Abigail made a graceful exit after dinner—staying just long enough. Little did Aunt Josie know. Abigail may have been a lady in the Dudevants' salmon, gold and cream parlor, but she was a tigress in the back seat of her car—just as gracefully casting off her pink sweater and bra, unbuttoning Quinn's shirt, bordered by the Greek key pattern, and palming his crotch while guiding his hand to the seam between the legs of her tight jeans, orchestrating their simultaneous orgasms.

As he caressed her well-shaped breasts, he wondered if he was bisexual, incredibly horny, or just a teenager, though he had been imagining Paris—the philandering Trojan shepherd who hung in the Musée des beaux-arts du Canada, not the city or Uncle Artur's put-upon aide—all the while.

Perhaps that's where his deception really began, he would later think. As he held her afterward, he recognized that like Aunt Josie's edict of abstinence, Abigail was part of the perfect cover: She was a girl who had, like him, agreed to wait. But he also realized that whether he was gay, straight or bi, Abigail was not part of his future. What he loved was football—not as he loved baseball, nor as the town and America loved it, as an end in itself—but as a means to an end. Football would be his ticket out of Misalliance to vindication—for himself, his family and, in a sense, for the aunt who had been torn from him with such seeming random violence.

No longer could the town sneer at the crazy Dudevants, nor could Aunt Sarah's thuggish beaus try to intimidate him. Tall, chiseled and, many said, beautiful, with a 4.0 average and scholarship offers from colleges around the country, Quinn was like those Greek heroes whom the gods loved and, in the end he knew, destroyed.

EIGHTEEN

Quinn thought he'd be delighted to leave behind the provincialism of Misalliance. He thought he'd revel in the freedom of university life, particularly as lived on the so-called Left Coast. But what he discovered when he arrived at Stanford was that Aunt Josie, who barely allowed him to kiss her goodbye, had done her job too well. Rather than burst forth from the cocoon she had woven, he found himself knitting it more tightly around himself. Not that there was any time for him to explore and experiment. It was football and studies, studies and football as he was determined to keep up his 4.0 average in an environment in which the learning curve was much steeper—on and off the field.

Head coach Brian Olds was a decent sort, less naked in his ambition than Coach Redfield but ambitious nonetheless that Stanford should win the Rose Bowl. He admired Quinn's running game.

His teammates and classmates seemed less certain. There was a pecking order at Stanford—as Quinn supposed there was everywhere—one that would take longer to climb than it had at Misalliance High. One teammate in particular seemed to have it in for him, Casey Kasmerek. He was a defenseman whose tattooed, fat-dimpled arms looked like marbled hams hanging in a butcher's shop. It was definitely a tribute to just how grotesque they were, along with the belly spilling over his pants, that Quinn didn't first notice his most salient characteristic: He was nuts. Certifiable.

His psychopathic tendencies took the form of a relentless hazing that was characterized as "team-building" by the coaches, who, Quinn thought, were just too lazy or terrified to do anything about it.

Even Coach Olds told Quinn in effect to cowboy up, adding, "Consider it good practice for the day the doc tells you that you have Stage 4 lung cancer."

Needless to say, Quinn was not comforted. He learned to keep nothing of value in his locker, after Casey flushed his cell phone down the toilet and stomped on his laptop. Quinn also repeatedly instructed his absent-minded roommate—science whiz Ivan Ivanovitch, who spent most of his time in the lab—to keep their door locked at all times.

Quinn bore it when Casey shaved his head as teammates held him down or when he found his clothes shredded in the locker. In a way, he thought, it was only the universe righting itself. He had been given so much and deserved so little. Without him, Aunt Lena would probably have still been alive, enjoying her life and career in New York. He deserved to be punished, he thought. But when Aunt Sarah came to visit with some of her friends, and Casey set her in his crosshairs, Quinn drew a permanent line.

"I'm gonna rape her every chance I get," Casey texted him. Quinn, who was genuinely afraid that Casey was as much walk as talk, marched over to his stall in the locker room and in a loud voice announced, "You can say or do whatever you like to me. But if you ever go near my aunt, I'll kill you."

"Why, are you fucking her yourself?" Casey asked, laughing.

The beat down Quinn took after he decked Casey was brutal. His teammates didn't interfere. They thought what was at stake was nothing less than the soul of the team and what was being born of that ferocity was a man, a leader.

While Casey had a 50-pound advantage, Quinn kept fighting back, at times pummeling nothing but air. Casey managed easily to gain the upper hand, pinning Quinn to the locker-room floor.

"Finish him, take him," some of Casey's supporters—more like trembling lackeys—cried. But most of the team was yelling, "Come on, Quinn." No one had ever stood up to Casey. If Quinn could just hold him off, he and they knew, the team would be his to lead. It was at that moment that Coach Olds walked in.

"What the hell is this?" he asked, pulling Casey off Quinn. "Kasmerek, are you fucking nuts? Defensemen are a dime a dozen, but I can't replace a quarterback, not a quarterback of this quality. Understand this, gentlemen—and I use the term sarcastically---this isn't just our starting quarterback. This is a future Hall of Famer, one of the best that will ever be."

When Olds left and Quinn finally rose to confront Casey—who shook and snorted like a wounded bull—he was bloodied but unbowed. Looking around the room, Quinn wiped the metallic taste from his lips with the back of his left hand.

"That's right," he said. "You heard Coach Olds. This is my team now."

If Quinn were truly evil—well, maybe not a

wholly evil person but just an instigator like the goddess Eris, tossing an apple of discord here and there—he realized he would've hacked Casey's email account and sicced him on Trent Birdwell, the president of the student body, who held sway in Professor Marc Dolenz's *The Literature of Rejection* class with a psychological menace that rivaled Casey's physical monstrosity.

Trent was a mediocrity with a huge ego, which meant, Quinn realized right away, that he would one day have a successful career in politics. Like many of those who talked about "serving the people," Trent had precious little interest in them. He was much more focused on sneering at jocks like Quinn, who had been given the rare honor of being admitted to one of the toughest electives on campus as a freshman, and on challenging Professor Dolenz, who, though barely thirty, had already written a number of critically acclaimed best sellers—no small feat given his discipline, the classics.

The Literature of Rejection was an enormously popular class that had students vying for places to plumb literary and historical figures who had displayed a disproportionate rage at being rebuffed—Achilles, Iago, Lucifer, Heathcliff, John Wilkes Booth, Hitler, Lee Harvey Oswald, Timothy McVeigh, Osama bin Laden. It was a controversial thesis, and Professor Dolenz— boyishly handsome with a slight build and wavy, light-brown hair—was already drawing acolytes from both sexes and both sides of the political spectrum. Somehow, this only seemed to deepen Trent's scorn and sense of superiority.

"Jocks sit in the back," he announced to Quinn the first time he walked in the classroom.

"Oh, OK, thanks," Quinn said, already feeling put out and realizing that the caste system of the locker room applied to the classroom as well. It just took a less physical form.

"Don't mind him," the student one seat over said. "Some guys can't help being jerks."

When Quinn studied the face attached to the voice, he realized that this was Achilles or Alexander come to life, if not in temperament at least in sculpted line—the coarse, auburn hair curling over the nape of the graceful neck, the smooth planes of the cheekbones, high and wide; the lips, full and bow-shaped; the nose, long and straight; the laughing gray eyes the color, though not the character, of a stormy sea.

The body attached to that spectacular face was equally splendid—long, broad-chested and well-muscled, though not as big as Quinn's. But then, swimmers didn't have to be as big as football players, for Quinn recognized him as Dylan Roqué, one of the two best swimmers in the world.

If there was any doubt in Quinn's mind about where his sexuality lay, Dylan confirmed it. He was Quinn's first love, first crush, first hero—not that Dylan ever knew it. Quinn was too shy—paralyzed was a better word—to act on or even express his feelings. And he was glad of that, for it quickly became apparent that Dylan was involved with someone else. Quinn could tell from the way he smiled at times when he texted or said, "Hey, you" when he answered the phone. But it wasn't until Quinn saw Dylan at a Stanford swim meet a few days later with Daniel Reiner-Kahn—the top swimmer in the world—that it dawned on him that Dylan's love was a man.

"Hey, Quinn, there's someone I'd like you to

meet," Dylan said afterward, his hair still wet. "Daniel Reiner-Kahn, meet our new star quarterback, Quinton Day Novak. Quinn, Dani."

"Hi, how's it going?" Dani said, giving him a fist bump.

"Fine, thanks, you?"

"Never better."

It occurred to Quinn then that had there been no Dani, he might've been Dylan's type, for Quinn was a slightly taller, heavier version of Dani with the same glossy dark hair and emerald eyes. He might've been Dani's younger brother—his darker, younger brother, Quinn reminded himself.

"Why don't we all go for coffee?" Dylan offered.

Something about Dani's manner told Quinn it would be a bad idea. Maybe it was the way he put his hand on Dylan's shoulder after he beat him in the 200-meter breaststroke. It was a gesture of consolation, protection, and possession, Quinn thought, and it made him realize that he both feared and disliked Daniel Reiner-Kahn.

"Thanks, but I gotta hit the books," Quinn said. "See you in class."

It was there that Dylan belonged to him. "We jocks have to stick together," Dylan said to Quinn with a conspiratorial wink. And Quinn's heart and groin leapt simultaneously as he realized that in class at least he wasn't alone.

"Who here has experienced rage?" Professor Dolenz asked as they prepared to plunge into *The Iliad.*

Dylan's left hand went up as he continued typing on his laptop with the unconscious grace with which he did everything. Quinn—more sheepish, searching to find that kind of courage in himself—looked around before raising his left hand. About three-quarters of the class—most of it male—joined them.

"OK," Professor Dolenz said, spinning a rubber band between his two index fingers. "Now, how many of you have been angry enough to kill? Be honest."

Dylan's left hand shot up again. Quinn's followed.

"It figures," he heard Trent sneer to Rebecca Turing. "I bet the murder rate is higher among jocks."

Rebecca, who was probably the smartest student in the class—in general, the women were way ahead of the men—simply rolled her eyes before disdainfully flipping her long, brown hair and then smiling pointedly, almost provocatively, at Quinn and Dylan. For someone who was in a classics course, Quinn thought, Trent seemed oblivious to having just been dissed by a goddess.

"Right," Professor Dolenz said, exhaling as he glared at Trent, "we are about to encounter a young man possessed of that kind of rage."

"Excuse me, Marc," Trent said to Professor Dolenz, breaching an intimacy that the professor—who always called the students Mr. and Ms.—had never invited. "But wouldn't you agree that the point of war is killing? So doesn't Achilles' rage merely help perfect a killing machine?"

Here Trent flashed one of his "got 'im" grins.

"Well, Mr. Birdwell," Professor Dolenz said, underscoring the form of address, "is killing the point of war? And is all killing in war equal? Is killing a soldier whose gun is pointed at a comrade the same as shooting a child? What about a child carrying a bomb? If killing effectively is the point, wouldn't it be better to kill in cold blood? But that's good. This is the kind of dialogue I want us to have in this class."

It occurred to Quinn then that there were a lot more battles being waged in *The Literature of Rejection* than those on the plains of Troy. There was the tension between the women and the men, forced by Trent's aggressively clumsy wooing of Rebecca, who was, it was well-known—to everyone but Trent, that is—dating a physics major bound for MIT. Not that Trent—with his kinky hair, big nose, oily skin and small, flat fingernails that Quinn particularly skeeved—was her or anyone's type.

There were the class divisions among the pols, the jocks, the artistes and the brainiacs. And then there was the ultimate battle between Trent and Professor Dolenz for supremacy and the soul of the class.

Quinn watched it play out with amusement, knowing that Dylan had his back and he had Dylan's. At night, as he lay in bed stroking himself, he thought of Dylan. He told himself that he needed to be quiet so he wouldn't wake Ivan. But mostly he didn't want to admit to himself what he was doing even as he relished it.

There was something absurd about self-love as there was about all sex—something needy and greedy, naked and raw, terrible and addictive.

"Alexander the Great said sex—what the French would later call *la petite mort,* or 'little death,' referring to orgasm—and sleep were the only things that reminded him of his mortality," Professor Dolenz told the class.

"He mustn't have been doing it right," Trent cracked.

"Yes," Dolenz said, smiling broadly. "I'm sure a man who never failed at anything in his life had trouble in that department."

"Doesn't matter," Trent insisted. "There's a first time for everything. Nobody's perfect."

Here Professor Dolenz would sigh. Quinn knew exactly how he felt. Trent was sometimes, OK often, right, but did he have to be so damn annoying about it? He imagined Trent giving Alexander that kind of lip and the Greco-Macedonian conqueror's response.

"Shall I gather the wild animals to throw in the sack with him?" Quinn, always an aide-de-camp in these reveries of Trent's execution, would ask.

And Alexander, always gleeful, would reply: "Let's use a couple of boars, shall we?"

Quinn found this to be a satisfying fantasy, though not as satisfying as the ones in which he and Dylan were one with the Greeks on the plains of Troy, sharing everything two comrades in arms (each other's) could share, just like Achilles and Patroclus. And just like Achilles and Patroclus on the red-clay kylix that graced the cover of his copy of *The Iliad,* Quinn would carefully bandage a wound on Dylan's forearm as he manfully bore it, looking away.

Or Quinn would imagine himself and Dylan as Alexander and his soul-mate and right-hand man Hephaestion on the plains of Gaugamela, with Alexander applying the aloe vera sap to Hephaestion's wounds as he had been taught to do by his teacher, the philosopher Aristotle, in the mountainous wood that was the Garden of Mieza. "You are so brave, my love," Quinn's Alexander would say, finishing off his ministrations with a discreet kiss to Hephaestion's forehead.

Sometimes in these fantasies, Dylan would shower him with his seed, then water, squeezing a soaked sponge above him, as Quinn, crouching and shaking his wet head, mouth open, laughed, reveling in the sensuous respite from battle. Later he would nestle naked against Dylan's side, trying to make himself small even though he was bigger, and Dylan—older and presumably wiser, definitely more sophisticated—would laugh indulgently and, clasping him by his perfectly molded buttocks, draw the muscular, curling figure to him, he who could never be mean to anyone.

Back in his room—far from the plains of Troy or Gaugamela—Quinn would arc and flood the tissues that enveloped his cock, stilling his staggered breaths as he savored the pleasure that tingled down to his toes.

The reality was, of course, quite different. He would look up to the stands to see Dylan, and his heart would sing. Then he'd notice Daniel was with him, and the same heart would recoil as if stabbed. How could he be so jealous of two people who didn't know he was alive romantically? But he was. And then he'd wonder, should he tell Dylan how he felt? What was the point when Dylan and Daniel were so clearly, in his mind, a twosome? You can't, he decided, build your happiness on the back of someone else's misery. And anyway, who was to say he and Dylan would've been happy? Wasn't there a reason Dylan wound up with Daniel?

As it was, both Dylan and Daniel sent him separate congratulations when he won the Heisman Trophy as a sophomore. Even Trent and Casey had to offer him grudging respect then.

"A tremendous accomplishment," Professor Dolenz emailed him, "made all the greater by your being as fine a citizen and scholar as you are an athlete. You truly embody the Homeric ideal of *arête*."

The honor took him to New York, which disappointed Quinn, not because the city failed to meet his expectations but because his visit was too brief, void of people he wanted to share it with (Aunt Josie and Uncle Artur weren't up to the journey) and filled with those he wished hadn't come.

"Is there someone else?" Abigail asked. "Someone you've met in college?"

"I'm afraid there is," Quinn said, flashing on himself being forced to suck Dylan off while on his knees, a deliciously cruel strap winding its way about his neck down his back and fastened arms to his tied ankles as Daniel prepared to enter him, murmuring encouragement.

"Well, I can't say I'm entirely surprised—or unhappy," Abigail said. "I, too, have found love, at Ole Miss."

Then why had she bothered to come all the way to New York with Aunt Sarah to see him win the Heisman? Part of him—the cynical part—assumed she craved the attention. But maybe she just wanted to let him down easily and felt that the Heisman would soften the blow. What if he hadn't won, for it wasn't a foregone conclusion? Would she have withheld the revelation?

As happy as he was with the Heisman— cradling it, his eyes closed, his head thrown back in sheer bliss—he knew his collegiate career wouldn't be complete nor his NFL ticket punched until he won a bowl game. The Stanford Cardinals had had their chance when he was a junior but had come up short at the Rose Bowl. Quinn was determined that wouldn't happen again.

"I pledge to you and to this school that this time I shall not fail," he said as he did his sun breaths before the makeshift altar on his dresser that included images of Jesus, St. Michael, Alexander the Great, Achilles, and Aunt Lena.

That promise was fulfilled as Stanford blew out USC 42-3 in the Rose Bowl his senior year. Quinn looked up into the stands to see Sydney, Chandler, Aunt Josie, Uncle Artur, Aunt Sarah, her friends, and Dylan, who had long graduated and was now the top-ranked swimmer in the world. By then, Quinn recognized that Dylan had been an infatuation rather than a great love, spurred by a mix of hormones, loneliness, insecurity, and genuine affection. And Quinn marveled at the way you could be so disappointed—no, heartsick—in love only to recognize later that it wasn't love at all, or at least not that kind of love. For by then, Quinn was dreaming of two quarterbacks who were already making their names with the Miners and Quakers.

Still, when the terrible news about Dylan came, Quinn thought, too, about how you could love someone you never really knew and mourn his loss sincerely and profoundly.

"Dylan Roqué came into my life at a time when I was a college freshman in desperate need of friendship and a role model," he posted on Facebook and Instagram. "He offered both, and I will always be grateful for that. I pray that his family and loved ones find comfort in his memory and that God grants him eternal peace."

But that was in the future. For now, Quinn was

delirious to have finally landed in New York as the first-round draft pick of the lowly New York Templars. The team's status didn't matter. Few knew that this was no mere trip across the country. Rather it was a journey of 10,000 miles and twelve years, and he could not help but be moved by it.

As he exited Liberty Newark International Airport, he bent down and kissed the ground.

"You must be crazy," a passerby shouted. "Do you know how many germs there are?"

Quinn didn't care as he sat back on his heels—his hands to his temples as he arched his back, his laughter turning to sobs.

"I'm here, Aunt Lena," he said. "I made it."

PART III

NINETEEN

Quinn's visit to Dr. Matthew changed nothing. He looked a dozen times at the website for the domestic abuse agency Dr. Matt referred him to. A dozen times he started to punch the number into his cell. A dozen times he told himself this time would be different; he would be different. But nothing changed.

He told himself it needn't. After all, he was at the top of his game. The Temps were winning big and winning small—eking out victories against teams they had no business beating, shocking a few rivals and pouncing on weaker opponents.

And since Quinn was driving himself—punishing himself—there was little Smalley could do or say, although he still found ways to criticize. Fortunately—or unfortunately, depending on how compassionate you were and the team ran the gamut from very to not at all—Smalley had a new whipping boy in backup QB Lleyton Starling.

Lleyton was a big, buff blond with an adoring family and an equally beautiful and adoring college sweetheart. Quinn should've been jealous of the guy, who was in many ways Quinn 2.0. But he wasn't. For one thing, Quinn knew that as much as Smalley hated him, the last thing he wanted was yet another QB who could detract and distract from his beloved, injured Lance. For another, Lleyton was such a preternaturally cheery, limoncello-out-of-lemons type of guy that you couldn't help but like him. Unless, of course, you were the teammates determined to break him.

"Hey, easy on him," Quinn told the team, "or I'll be hard on you."

He watched to make sure the hazing rituals weren't Kazmerekian in scope. But Lleyton seemed impervious. When teammates held him down to shear off his stunning blond curls, he just ran his fingers through his stubby hair, smiling, and arrived for the team's workout the next day with a short do that peaked fashionably on top. When Smalley barked at him to step into his office, he was there in a shot, iPad at the ready, as if he were a particularly efficient executive assistant.

He was like the Roadrunner, always triumphing over the Wile E. Coyotes of the world no matter how many traps they set. The most amusing was the Starbucks' gantlet, which involved Lleyton's daily purchase of increasingly elaborate coffee concoctions for the team. The idea was that the order—with its triple-shot this and no foam that—would flummox the rookie. Unfortunately for the team, Lleyton's many gifts included a phenomenal visual and auditory memory.

"That's one decaf venti skinny vanilla latte; one grande skim vanilla latte, no foam; one tall skinny vanilla latte, extra foam and that sprinkle of cinnamon you like, Derrick, cinnamon being very healthy for you; one grande decaf latte with vanilla powder and a pinch of chocolate for you, Jeremiah..."

And that was just the order for the vanilla guys, Quinn marveled. Through mocha frappuccinos and green tea chai lattes, Lleyton—who had worked his way through Harvard at the Harvard

Book Store's Philosophy Café—never missed an order and never wrote one down.

"How does he do it?" Greg asked Derrick. "No, really, I want to know why his toast is always butter side up."

"Beats me," Derrick said. "Maybe if we were nicer to him, his luck would rub off on us."

"He's just good is all," said Jeremiah, who took a fatherly interest in Lleyton, patting his shorn curls and always giving him a five dollar tip. He laughed indulgently at the team's hazing, which only served to make the guys even more caffeine-dependent.

"Damn it," Greg would yell, "where the hell's Starling with the fucking Starbucks?"

As if on cue, Lleyton would appear with the carefully balanced cups. Finally, he drafted a memo to team owner Jimmy Jones Jefferson—which he showed Quinn for his preapproval as he did everything. In it, he requested an espresso/cappuccino machine for the locker room, backing up the request with a cost-efficiency analysis.

At first, the guys balked at being Starbucks-less. Soon, however, they were lining up for Lleyton's signature brews. Such was the machine's hold on the team that it traveled with the players, becoming the subject of one of Brenna's more amusing columns.

Unable to rattle Lleyton with the Starbucks' gantlet, the team set about to humiliate him by forcing him to sing in the locker room. It was a ploy that had weakened the knees of many a rookie linebacker. But no, it turned out that Lleyton, who had also been president of the Harvard Glee Club, had a crystalline tenor that he was delighted to use.

He was particularly fond of Seal's *Amazing:*
Say you don't know how to do it now
So you run.
It's not that you're bleeding but you're through with it now
So you run, so you run.

It became an anthem at Templars Stadium, played after every touchdown Quinn or Lleyton scored. And Lleyton could sometimes be seen leading a chorus in the end zone himself, jumping, an arm overhead, as he twirled around on the words, "Run, so you run."

Quinn, who kept his post-touchdown ritual limited to a quick sign of the cross, punctuated by fingers to lips and thanks to God and Aunt Lena—no point in ridiculing and, thus, riling the opposition—made sure that Lleyton didn't overdo it.

"You know what they say," Quinn reminded him. "You get into the end zone, act like you've been there before—with class."

Still, Quinn couldn't help but indulge him like the baby bro he never had. The fans were equally enchanted with Lleyton, which had the added bonus for Quinn of annoying Smalley, particularly when Lleyton improvised the read option, often with stunning success.

"Starling, when you finish with your waitressing and your warbling, haul your faggotty ass into my office."

Through the door, Quinn and the rest of the team could hear: "How dare you run fucking plays that I don't approve. You do that again, and I'm going to shove a pole so far up you that it's going to push out the white puss that passes for your brain." Afterward, Lleyton slumped down in his locker, put his head in his forearms and wept.

Quinn placed a hand on his shoulder. "Hang in there," he said softly.

Lleyton looked up, brightening through glistening tears. "I'll never find approval there, will I?" he asked.

"None of us will," Quinn said, shaking his head. "And yet, we keep seeking it, don't we?"

Such incidents apart, Lleyton offered the comic bright spot in a season that despite its success was a long, sad slog. Nero had been convicted of illegal handgun possession, yet thanks to Drew Harrington's legal wizardry had been given a sentence of only one year in an upstate New York prison. To Nero, it might as well have been life.

"Don't forget me. Don't abandon me," he said, sobbing and reaching for Quinn's hand in the visitors' lounge.

"Nero, Nero, listen to me: If you show fear here, these people will eat you alive. You have to act brave even if you don't feel brave. My aunt always said, 'Have courage and life will meet you halfway.' Pray, and I will pray for you, too."

When Quinn was out of town, he called or sent care packages. Otherwise, he visited him once a week. Nero had somewhat improbably joined a poetry workshop at the prison led by a birdlike woman, Gloria Halstead. He invited Quinn to Poetry Day. What struck Quinn first, as it always did, were the small windowpanes and the barbed wire, coiled atop the fences like so many crowns of thorns. On a winter day more like spring, guards escorted Quinn and the other guests into the prison yard, where the beefy inmates made Quinn momentarily uneasy.

Not Gloria. "Let's have a poem prayer, shall we?" she said, and Quinn watched, moved, as the hulking inmates bowed their heads under a seamless sky while that slip of a woman read from e.e. cummings' *I thank You God for most this amazing.*

Shuttling between Nero and Dave, Quinn couldn't decide which was worse—prison or a hospital. "I want no funeral," Dave gasped as he lay in a Jersey hospital bed. Quinn could see his soul quitting his body, like a mollusk leaving its crusted home. All that remained was a trace of bitterness. "I want no service, no Mass. Just cremate me and throw me to the wind."

How sad, how awful, Quinn thought, to be in such despair, to feel so alone and abandoned by God that you seek to desert him in kind and wipe any trace of yourself from the face of the earth. Quinn understood—even Jesus felt forsaken on the cross—but he also knew, cruel as it was, that funerals, like life, were for the living.

"Dave, please, I know how you feel," he said as he doled out ice chips to him with a tweezer. "No, no, forgive me, I don't know how you feel. But remember—and I'm sorry to have to say this—but this won't be for you alone. This will be for Kelly and the kids and me and the team. Don't deny us this. That way, some day your children will say, 'My dad was a great man, and I remember how all these people came out for him,' or 'I remember my mother saying how beautifully everyone spoke at his funeral and how lovely it was.' Please, Dave, if for no one else, do this for the wife who loves you so."

What Quinn didn't tell Dave was that he

couldn't bear him taking leave of this world without God's blessing. He knew it was insane. And he knew it was hypocritical. How often had he blamed God for Aunt Lena's death, cursed him for casting him deeper into the land of the unwanted and the unloved?

"Couldn't you show me some tenderness, some kindness, some real love?" The question was not only a prayer to God but a reproach to Mal whenever he pressed Quinn's hot, naked flesh against his bedroom wall or bit his plump lips, drawing blood as he kissed him.

"What kindness do you deserve?" Mal said, grabbing him by his thick hair. Quinn knew he was right; knew, too, that even if this lacked the gentle caress of the butterfly's wings—"Look, Quinnie, he likes you," he always remembered Aunt Lena saying as a white butterfly alighted on his shoulder and she photographed him in Singapore Harbor— at least it was touch, a man's hands on his body, and a man's hands were what his body craved.

"I know this is how you like it, good and rough," Mal rasped in his ear as he pulled hard on his cock, drawing the head back while Quinn leaned against the shower wall and Mal thrust into him wildly.

"Yes, that's just how I like it," Quinn said, panting. "Find me. Take me. Need me. Make me."

Afterward as he lay curled up in a ball, he wondered at himself—embracing brutality and yet speaking with a gentle eloquence so admired at Dave's funeral.

"What is the measure of a man?" he told the packed church—the so-called sea of humanity that included a shell-shocked Kelly, so pale, so lost; the unabashedly sobbing Jeremiah; and even a surprisingly subdued Smalley. "Can you measure him in passing yards or dollars earned? Or do you measure him in the love of his family and friends as you would surely measure David Francis Donaldson?"

But Quinn knew it was all bullshit said to comfort his frightened teammates, suddenly, rudely confronted with their mortality, and a young widow who should have never been left to raise two young children alone.

What was the real measure of a man, Quinn thought as the priest intoned over Dave's remains and he flashed on Mal's rough embrace, but his weight in dust?

TWENTY

In a mid-winter that was already one of the coldest and snowiest on record, the Temps found themselves in the unenviable position of having to win three games on the road to go to the Super Bowl.

"We are road warriors," the ever-optimistic Lleyton said as he set up a makeshift shrine to Dave Donaldson in an empty stall of the Omaha Steers visitors' clubhouse.

It was no small irony, Quinn thought, that Lleyton, who never knew Dave, should take it upon himself to become the keeper of his flame. At Templars Stadium, Dave's former stall was like a Buddhist temple, teeming with tribute. There was Dave's uniform, photographs, fan letters, teddy bears, candles and, always, fresh flowers. This drove Smalley nuts.

"Starling, you ship all this crap to the Widow Donaldson as fast as you can, or I swear I'm going to nail your balls to the wall."

But before Quinn could intervene, Lleyton dug in. "No, Coach, I will not. To dismantle this locker, well, it would be as if Dave never lived at all. A man ought to be remembered, not just by his family but by the people he worked with. We were his brothers, too. And we need to remember him so everyone can see that it mattered he passed this way at all."

Wherever the team went, Lleyton set up a memorial—nothing as elaborate as the one at home but a few items that the players would touch before the game, the way they touched the patch with his number on their jerseys and continued to flash his number with their fingers in the end zone after touchdowns.

Lleyton's gesture—along with Quinn's leadership on and off the field—had a galvanizing, bonding effect on the team when the players needed it most. It was so cold at The Steerage—as The Omaha National Bank Stadium was more colorfully known—that Quinn's face felt like a pin cushion, with icy needles pricking his eyes. He was never more keenly aware of the deep-blue sleeves that were a second skin on his sculpted arms.

"Lance was always bare-armed, even in this weather," Smalley said in the locker room, sneering at Quinn.

"Then he's 'a better man than I am, Gunga Din,'" Quinn said, smiling at a Rudyard Kipling reference that he knew would sail right over Smalley's head.

"I don't know if this Gunga Din ever played football," center Austin Stevens said to Quinn. "But I do know all this mind-over-matter stuff is bullshit in this weather. Cold is cold and hot is hot. Wear the fucking long sleeves."

Tugging at them to make sure they could not be grabbed by the opposition, Quinn watched the players' breaths curl like white arabesques as they strained to be heard over the chanting, cursing crowd and tried not to wince. Each inhalation was like a knife to the core. He wondered if this was what it was like in the Roman Coliseum—so much pain, so much hatred.

The Temps, though, were beyond that. They defied both.

"Who is like you?" Jeremiah screamed, his thick, eye black sporting Dave's old "35."

"No one," they shouted, raising their fists to the night sky.

"Who is like me?" he added, thumping his chest.

"No one," they cried.

"Who is like us?" he added, spreading his arms wide.

"No one," they shouted, beating their chests as their voices rose as one. All that was missing, Quinn thought, were sabers to rattle.

It would take more than bravado to beat the Steers, who had the beefiest D-line in the league. There was a part of Quinn that was afraid—not of being sacked or hurt but of losing.

"Have courage, and life will meet you halfway," he kept repeating to himself.

But how do you have courage? Was it something you could just summon at will, or was it innate? Many people talked the talk but failed to walk the walk. They were all parade, no battle—so great in the regular season, so disappointing in the postseason. The reverse was also true. What was the secret of those who were so clutch?

Quinn had always believed that you were but a strand in the pattern of the universe, and that what you perceived to be good or bad luck—or a good or bad performance—was but the fulfillment of your individual destiny. Yet he realized now more than ever, he couldn't act on that belief. If the Temps were to have a chance, he and the rest of the team would have to believe that destiny was theirs for the making and the taking and simply refuse to be defeated.

And so when they were down 21-7 in the third

quarter at the Steers' 20-yard line, with no one open for Quinn to throw to, he powered himself through a portal in the Steers' defense. It might as well have been a wormhole transporting the team to the far side of the universe, for it enabled him to dive over a sea of Steers into their blue end zone, much as he had seen Dylan Roqué and Daniel Reiner-Kahn do at Stanford swim meets time and again, much as he remembered himself doing as a twelve-year-old in the pool of the Mandarin Oriental, Singapore on the last leg of his fateful voyage to America.

That touchdown, with the score now 21-14, proved to be the game-changer as apple-polishing linebacker-turned-commentator Rufus Washington kept saying over and over on the postgame wrap-up. Quinn threw a brilliant cross-body 70-yard touchdown to Greg to tie it, then led two third-down drives that set up a touchdown to Derrick. With the Temps in control 28-21, Lleyton came in and gave the guys insurance, 35-21.

He twirled in the end zone with joy and more than a bit of defiance, Quinn thought gleefully, as his equally defiant teammates sang *Amazing* at the crowd:

Say you don't know how you do it now
So you run.
It's not that you're bleeding but you're through with it now,
So you run, so you run.

Afterward, Quinn thought of seeking out Tweedle Dee Dum and Tweedle Dee Dee on the field and rubbing their noses in the Temps' victory, but why kick a dog when he's down? He was bigger than that. It was enough that the Temps won.

In the locker room, Lleyton was still riding that high.

"OK, apart from girlfriend time, that was the most fun I have ever had," he said to any teammate who would listen. "I mean, are you guys not jazzed? Are you not overwhelmed by the sheer momentousness of it all?"

"Overwhelmed by the sheer momentousness of it all," Jeremiah repeated, never looking up from his iPhone as he texted one of the many Jere juniors who Quinn imagined were marauding The Steerage.

"If I see even one of those goddamn kids in this locker room, I'm gonna grab him by his little Afro and hurl him into the end zone from here," Smalley had warned before the game.

It was all the team could do to keep Jeremiah from going for Smalley's throat. Though the team hated Smalley, loathing his prejudice, contempt, and toxic commentary—which were equal-opportunity employers—Quinn realized the players feared him, too. They were grown men, multimillionaires for the most part, and yet they were still afraid of their disapproving daddy, Quinn thought, shaking his head.

The visitors' locker room at The Steerage wasn't overrun with Jeres but with reporters, many of whom sought out Lleyton, who was only too happy to oblige.

"And may I add a shout-out, Brent," he said, grabbing the microphone from one network sportscaster, "first to the Lord, then to my parents, Lleyton Starling Sr. and Vivian Morton Starling, and our family and friends, and last but not least to my girl, Dana Farinelli. Dana, I love you. Marry me," he added, holding up what Quinn thought was a spectacular oval ruby, surrounded by diamonds in rose gold that Lleyton said had been his grandmother's engagement ring.

"Well, there you have it," Brent Masters said, fighting for control of the interview. "A proposal on national TV. Dana, wherever you are, marry him, please."

Given Lleyton's exuberance, the media was relieved to turn to Quinn—who was watching the scene, now overrun with Jere juniors, chased by a screaming Smalley.

"Your thoughts on today's comeback," Brent said to Quinn, a smile plastered on his perspiring face as one of the smallest Jeres head-butted his left leg.

"Well, it was obviously a great win for our guys," Quinn said, not missing a beat as he scooped up the child before he could do further damage. "I think we played with a perfect balance of offense and defense and that's what you need."

"What was going through your mind as you scored that stunning diving touchdown?" Brent asked, almost giddy at being back in charge of the questions and answers.

"No one was open and I just didn't want to waste a scoring opportunity," Quinn said with a laugh, "so I thought, 'God, I'm going for it. Help us to score.'"

"Can you say enough about the way Coach Smalley has handled this team?"

It was all Quinn could do to keep from laughing in Brent's face. "I really can't say enough."

"And how inspirational has it been to have Blaine Mahr with you guys this week?"

It occurred to Quinn then that interviews were

structured so that all the interviewee had to do was to repeat the key word in the question. Back in ancient times when the Temps won regularly, Blaine Mahr was the star quarterback. Having ascended to Mount Olympus—in this case, a largely ceremonial job at a Fortune 500 company—Blaine emerged whenever the Temps were in contention, which was virtually never, ostensibly to offer advice but really to remind everyone of the glory days with him that were long gone. The only good thing about it was the way it rattled Smalley.

"As if we don't have enough pressure, I guess I'm gonna have to blow smoke up this guy's ass all week," he griped.

The bad blood went back to their college days, although it wasn't helped by some unkind words Blaine had uttered about Smalley darling Lance. Quinn lapped it up.

"Do you think Blaine would mind posing for some selfies with me for the folks?" Lleyton asked Quinn.

"I'm sure he'd be just delighted."

For his part, Quinn kept his distance. Blaine wasn't afraid to be critical of what he saw as Quinn and the team's need for improvement. But once Blaine arrived to "work" with the players, Quinn acknowledged that he mustn't let his ego—or that of others—get in the way of learning. Blaine had been one of the greatest quarterbacks ever. So he must've done something right, right? After that, they got along fine, but Quinn was still wary of treading into Blaine's space, particularly as he was always accompanied by Tris Meeker, a short, stocky, pasty-faced publicist/gofer/factotum/hanger-on who looked like Truman Capote with a bad comb-over.

His main job was to create demand by running interference and denying access to the demigod. The only thing that made his presence bearable, Quinn thought, was that Blaine—at sixty, a poignantly pale shade of his former radiant self with gnarled hands, a curved spine and one leg that never completely straightened—was utterly clueless that Meeker was in love with him and would brook no one getting too close to his beloved, especially female reporters like Brenna.

"We have to break this up," he said harshly as she approached Blaine. Quinn, who was still talking with Brent, could see that tough as she was, Brenna was put out.

"Excuse me, Brent," Quinn said. "Blaine," he said, smiling brilliantly and putting an arm on his shoulder. "You know Brenna James of *The New York Record*. I'm sure you have a moment for one of the best writers around." With that, Quinn turned to Tris and gave him his best glittering vampire smile. "You guys don't have to leave yet, do you?"

TWENTY-ONE

"Thank you for rescuing me from that garden gnome of a gatekeeper," Brenna said.

She and Quinn were back in New York, having one of their interviews/dinners that he tried to avoid but was just as equally drawn to. He told himself there was no point in getting too close to a journalist and a woman who had feelings for him at that. He imagined that she told herself the same thing. Yet there they were.

"Do you think Blaine knows that Tris is in love with him?" she wondered aloud. "Probably not. He's so self-absorbed, I'm sure he has no gaydar."

Quinn wondered how well Brenna's gaydar worked regarding himself. He broke into a cold sweat. But then she added, "Or maybe Tris is just one of those hangers-on, you know, the nerd who attaches himself to the jock, the chubby girl who trails the beauty queen, the best friend who's happy to be that friend when there's nothing else to be had."

Brenna looked at Quinn and laughed, then looked away. She was wearing a red dress consisting of a layer of lace over a Lycra sheath that hugged her curves in all the right ways. Her long, curly hair was swept back in a casual chignon. Her *Memoirs of a Geisha* facial palette—alabaster skin, smoky eyes, rouged lips and cheeks—was heightened by the coldest winter of the century and the heat of the room that was designed to stave it off, along with the crimson of her dress and the accents of ruby and diamond jewelry.

This was the other side of Brenna, Quinn told himself, the part that had been an arts writer and worked for Vienne at *New York Rumours*, that had loved that world and lost it—or had been forced to relinquish it, same thing. But there was more to it than that. This was also a performance for his benefit, as if to say, "See, this is what you could have, what we could have together."

He thought back to that dreadful night of Vienne's party and the flower reading and something small that he had witnessed and forgotten but that seemed meaningful now. They were preparing to leave—laughing, chatting, if only he could go back and freeze that pre-lapsarian moment—and Vienne put a hand on Mal's shoulder and gazed into his eyes with such longing that Quinn felt something he never had for her. He felt pity.

Brenna was his Vienne, and he didn't want to make her an object of ridicule, to evoke in others the same feelings he had about Vienne that night. Was there anything more ridiculous than a woman in love with a younger man who would never be hers? Oh, Bren, why can't I want you?

As if reading his mind, she said, "You and I, Quinn, are leading parallel lives. We both have glamorous jobs that are not quite what they seem. We both love what we do but hate the people we do it for. And, if I may be so bold as to venture a guess, we're both A+ students in the School of Unrequited Love."

Her eyes glistened as she stared out at a Manhattan skyline that glittered diamond-hard against the indigo night. As Quinn reached for her hand, she moved it away to pick up her notepad and pen. With the other, she turned on her tape recorder. Quinn understood. For the loveless, kindness was often the greatest cruelty.

"Now where were we?" she said.

Where we were was gridlocked, he thought, at the intersection of Fear and Desire. He was no more going to quit his job than she was going to quit hers, and his was a lot more dangerous, he knew. And he could no more forget Tam than she could forget him. He tried. Oh, how he tried. He checked in with Dave's widow and kids—though not too often. He didn't want Kelly to get the idea that he was putting the moves on her. He visited Nero and became a supporter of Gloria Halstead's poetry workshop. He called Aunt Josie, Uncle Artur, and Patience daily. He kept tabs on Aunt Sarah, which wasn't easy, since she didn't always return his texts. And he continued to raise funds for the orphanage he was building in Jakarta.

Quinn prepared for the playoffs until he thought he'd drop, driving himself in the polar cold and snow. But Tam stayed in his head, haunting his thoughts when he least expected it, as Jakarta often did. He had never really understood them, he thought now, and so he had lost them both, and that's what threatened to drive him mad, the realization that circumstances were only partly to blame. Had he made an effort with his mother and stepfather, he might never have been sent away from Jakarta—or rather, would never have wanted to go—and his aunt would never have died. Had he not cheated on Tam with Mal or Mal with Tam—but how could he have known their history?—he and Tam might still be together.

He did, though, and they weren't and that was the hell of it. No amount of avoiding the sports pages would make it otherwise. He would flip on his iPad and catch Tam's image or name and the pain of losing what was in his grasp—of fumbling love—would be as fresh and sharp as the knifing cold. And anyway, there was no end of the talk about Mal and Tam, the Quakers and the Miners, among the Templars. Quinn knew that the way to the Super Bowl—the way home, for it was going to be played at Templars Stadium—was through Mal and Tam. He understood that if he could beat them back-to-back and win the Super Bowl that this would be the first paragraph of his obituary and that would be as good as it would get for him. He would forever be the man who may not have been the best but who beat the best.

First, they had to get through the Orlando Copperheads, this year's Cinderella team, as the press endlessly dubbed them. Gee, couldn't the press do better than that? Quinn wondered. When had writing—thinking—become so lazy? Actually, the Temps had been the Cinderella team du jour for a while, but, no, the Copperheads had been even more forlorn so they got the designated cliché, while the Temps were called "surging" as in the popular meme of the sports networks, the blogosphere and the Twitterati: "Can the surging Temps beat...?" Fill in the blank, Quinn thought. No one, it seemed, save Brenna, some diehard Temps' fans and Quinn himself, thought they could do it. Certainly, no one thought they could get past Mal's Quakers or Tam's Miners, let alone both.

"There are just too many variables with this team and this guy," the International Sports

Network's Ned Harris said of the Temps and Quinn. "He likes to run, which is risky. That's part of what makes it thrilling, too. But you never know what you're going to get. He hasn't proved himself to be an elite pocket passer. Certainly, he's not in the class of Mal Ryan and Tam Tarquin."

"Bullsh--," one poster wrote. "Wonder if Neddy boy would be saying as much if Quinn Novak were white."

There it was, what everyone was thinking but few would voice.

"That's right," one respondent answered, "play the race card."

Quinn told himself he really had to stop reading and watching sports; otherwise, some day he was just going to take the football and shove it down the throats of the haters. He prided himself on being gracious—win, lose or draw. But this was testing him, boring as it did into his Achilles' heel, which was the sense that he would never be good enough.

Mal, of course, was only too happy to hiss as much into his ear, like the serpent in, if not the Garden of Eden then the Garden State of New Jersey. "You better be prepared to go down—in more ways than one."

They were in one of those Jersey no-tell motels off I-95, midway between New York and Philly, that Mal now favored for their trysts. Since becoming a father—Tiffany had given birth to a boy they had named George, Mal's real first name, on Christmas Day—Daddy liked to up the ante, Quinn thought. He had wanted to do it with Quinn in the alley outside some gay bar. But the motel was as far as Quinn was prepared to go and only because it was clear that it was a "See No Evil,

Hear No Evil, Speak No Evil" kind of place. At least it was clean, Quinn thought, clean and dismal with '70s paneling, bargain-basement green print curtains and mustard-colored walls. It represented the new normal, along with Quinn waiting anxiously—which he realized was not the same thing as eagerly—for the new father's arrival, clad in a bathrobe that Mal liked to rip from his shoulders. Quinn had bought a special one for just such occasions—cheap and thin, this not being a Ralph Lauren moment, he figured. Then there would be the endless bitching, a new twist in the torturous—or should that be tortuous? Quinn wondered—relationship.

"She has no time for me," Mal whined. "It's all about that goddamn baby."

"Well, somebody's got to make a new life the center of his or her universe, and it's usually the mother, Mal," Quinn said, enjoying the ability to offer sound advice while twisting in the knife. "Face it, when a woman has a baby, that's her world. Everything else must be secondary. You'll just have to adjust. Why don't you try sharing her life rather than expecting her to cater to yours?"

"Yeah, right," Mal said, slamming Quinn into the wall and entering him so roughly that he cried out in pain. With that, Mal dispelled any illusion Quinn might have had that fatherhood would bring a new vulnerability to him and thus shift the balance of power in their so-called relationship.

"What the hell would you know? Oh, that's right, you're the woman in this relationship, so, of course, you would take her part. But male, female or whatever you are, it's not like you could ever father a child, you loser, you thing of death."

Quinn thought of those words as they stood on

the sidelines of Quaker Stadium, down 14-10 in the final moments of the league championship game. The win against the Copperheads had been a romp, the outcome never in doubt, as good as a bye week, the Cinderella team having apparently run out of glass slippers. Quinn knew the Temps would pay for the ease of that victory in balmy, muscle-warming Orlando when they headed back north. And oh, how they paid—the cold, the snow, the New York-Philly sniping, the snarky press, the battling fans—and that was before the game even started.

Why did they do it? Quinn wondered. Football was war as theater, with the punching and crunching made more pronounced by the stinging cold. There had to be better ways to make a living. But what would he and his teammates—to say nothing of their families and their cities—have if not this? Many of them came from little to nothing. They had given themselves to a game when they were too young to understand what that meant, and, having decided to dance with the Devil, they could not turn back.

And so they endured horrific verbal abuse that began the moment they disembarked from the train that brought them to Philly. Whose romantic idea was it to take a train to the 30th Street Station, where Philly fans would be lying in wait, when they could've taken the usual team bus? Smalley was no help either. "I should've known you guys would never come through," he shouted at the defense on the field as he paced the sidelines in the fourth quarter.

Quinn saw the look of fear, dread and hurt that began to veil the eyes of the players on the sidelines. He called them together.

"Listen to me, look at me," he said. "We are not losers, and this is far from over. Our D-line is going to hold them off, and our O-line is gonna get one more chance on the field. One more, and that will be enough. Believe me: We were born to win."

Don't make a liar out of me, Quinn prayed as he took the field with two minutes to play. Make my words a reality, God, Aunt Lena, he said to himself.

Thirty seconds now. Thirty brief seconds. Thirty long seconds. Time out. Space-time expanding. The ball as big as a flying saucer. Derrick catching it, barely holding it, but hold it he did.

The Miners looking to blitz. Quinn looking to stay upright. Which he did. One more pass now, this time to Greg, who fell backward into the end zone—touchdown. The extra point was the cherry. It was over at last.

"You're gonna fucking pay and pay for this," a stunned Mal said as he clasped Quinn afterward.

The next night. Another no-tell motel. Quinn in a corner bleeding as Mal loomed over him. Quinn wiped the blood from his mouth, triumphant.

"I still won," he said.

TWENTY-TWO

Oh, Tam, I heart you—my lover, my brother, Quinn thought as the Temps and the Miners prepared to face off in the Super Bowl at Templars Stadium. For you are my brother in arms. On this field of battle, we meet as less than friends but more than foes—rivals, former intimates who have left each other and, in leaving, stayed.

The teams emerged from opposite tunnels amid fanfare, all smoke but no mirrors to reflect the ridiculousness of the spectacle, Quinn mused. They stood at attention on opposite sides for "Our National Anthem," as the announcer intoned. It was sung by an opera singer who had been much criticized on the web, as if those "critics" would know anything about opera, or singing the Anthem for that matter, Quinn thought with a laugh. She transcended skepticism anyway. In a deep-blue sheath and yellow-green coat that underscored the team colors and her svelte attractiveness, she sang with lushness and ringing clarity.

"I thought these opera chicks were supposed to be fat," Derrick whispered to Greg. "This one's a real babe."

"Hush up," Jeremiah said. His eyes were closed, his head and body swaying to the music as he communed with something beyond the stadium, beyond himself. Other teammates like Austin were communing, too, their lips moving in prayer. Quinn took it all in as he sang, one of the few players to do so along with Lleyton. He was in his element, singing full throttle in his brilliant tenor, whooping and hollering afterward.

Lleyton had the fearless ignorance of youth, Quinn thought. He'd been playing as if he had nothing to lose. But Quinn had more than enough fear for him and the rest of his teammates, for he had lost much— Jakarta, his aunt and Tam, his everything. He did not wish to lose the little that remained or the possibility of winning. And that, he knew, was no way to play.

The world was a contrary place, and Quinn along with it. He longed for Jakarta. But maybe that was because he was thousands of miles away. If he were back there now, would he want to be here in this snow globe that was Templars Stadium instead? Would he care as long as he was in Tam's arms?

The teams met at midfield for the coin toss. It was macho one-upmanship time. Jeremiah, breathing heavily, was like a bull pawing the ground before charging. Everyone else had his hands on his hips, except Quinn and, he supposed, Tam. Quinn couldn't bear to look at him, that's how afraid he was of seeing hot hatred—or worse, cold indifference—in Tam's eyes. In a world of cold, better fire than ice, Quinn thought, but what did it matter? They both burned.

Blaine Mahr was there for the coin toss, relishing his moment back in the limelight, even if it was only a moment. And for that moment, the officials were all fan-boys with man-crushes. Laughter and back slaps all-around.

"Now, Blaine, none of that," one said, laughing, as Blaine flubbed the coin toss and they started over.

The Miners' captains had called "tails," and tails it was. Luck: So much of life seemed to be luck, didn't it? Quinn thought, particularly beginner's luck. Win the toss and control the game at the outset—at least in theory. The Miners chose to start on offense.

"Good pitching stops good hitting. A good defense stops a good offense." It's all Quinn and his teammates had heard all week—from Smalley, from the media, from the "experts," folks who had never read *The Iliad* or followed Alexander to Persia. Well, we shall see, won't we? Quinn thought.

"I'm going to bury that mutha," Jeremiah was saying, pounding his right hand into his left fist, and Quinn winced, as he did not want to see Tam buried. But he couldn't let him win, even though Tam remained his heart, his love, his own. They were combatants now. If the Temps could hold the Miners in the opening gambit, they would win. It was really as simple and as complicated as that, Quinn thought.

Tam threw a perfect spiral for a first down, but on the next play, the Temps' D brought him down hard. "Yeah," Lleyton said pumping his fist in the air as he noted the play on the chart. (Had there ever been a more enthusiastic note-taker? Quinn wondered.) He scanned the throng, uselessly searching for Aunt Sarah and her crowd, out there somewhere. He looked up into the VIP boxes for no particular reason—except perhaps to avert his eyes from the sight of Tam on the ground—and spied Daniel Reiner-Kahn with Alí Iskandar. Daniel had changed a lot in the years since Dylan died. He'd filled out a bit, becoming more corporate, even on the ultimate casual Sunday.

Alí, whom Quinn had never met in person but talked to once on the phone for a grant from Reiner-Kahn's Ani Foundation for the orphanage, was stunningly ascetic in all black. Quinn could see Dani gesture out to the field, Alí following his gaze, smiling. They looked, Quinn thought with a rueful smile, to be very much in love.

That could be you and me, Tam, could've been, should've been, would've been but for my ability to snatch defeat from the jaws of victory, Quinn brooded. He couldn't think about it anymore. He and the offense were on the field. He crossed himself swiftly, inconspicuously and said a silent prayer to Aunt Lena. "Have courage, and..." He didn't feel courageous, but he couldn't care about that either. Too much was riding on this—the welfare of his teammates, the pride of his adopted city and, at last, his revenge on Smalley, who had been hounding the team all week, unlike Tam's paternalistic coach. No matter. A bad Daddy had his uses, too.

"Krakatoa, Krakatoa," Quinn shouted to the team over the roar of competing Miners and Temps' fans.

"What's this crack stuff?" Greg would say when Quinn first became starting QB. Now they knew "Krakatoa" was the call for a feint play that was always changing. This time the Temps would seem to go right but actually break left—that was if everyone wasn't too nervous to remember, for this was a game like no other and the Temps were a younger, less experienced team than the Miners. Perhaps they had Lleyton's fearless ignorance. Perhaps not. We shall see right now, won't we? Quinn thought.

He took the snap from between Austin's legs—

was there a more homoerotic game than football?—and looked to throw right but actually broke left. He checked to see if Greg was open, but the Miners were on him like a pack of dogs. Quinn felt a tug on his uniform but eluded it and took off running—into the past, into the Jakarta of his dreams, into the arms of the lover he lost, into a time when he was happy and free.

In the end zone, he knelt, rose and crossed himself in the one graceful gesture that had become his signature. He caught Lleyton whirling about as if conducting the now dominating Temps' fans as they sang *Amazing*. Quinn looked up at Dani and Alí, who were standing, clapping, Alí's cane resting against his left leg. The touchdown and their support warmed him and, for the first time in a long time, he felt less alone.

But Tam answered with a beautiful touchdown pass, and the Temps headed into halftime down 10-7—which Quinn thought was brilliant. They were, after all, in their first Super Bowl and were hanging with the defending champs no less. Things looked good for the second half. All in all, the mood was upbeat.

Until the Temps entered the locker room, and Smalley opened his fat mouth.

"That second quarter was an absolute disgrace," he screamed. "What is sport about? Anyone? No, you're too fucking faggot stupid to know, so I'll tell you. The Big Mo—momentum—and you just killed ours, didn't you? Didn't you?"

Quinn could see the players' eyes glazing over with fear and contempt. He had to stop the Big Mo—the one that had swung over to this narcissistic bully—now.

"We've done nothing of the kind," Quinn said.

"We've played the best team in football and perhaps the greatest quarterback of all time almost to a draw, and we're well-positioned for the second half."

"Is that how you see it?"

"Yes, that's how I see it."

"If the game ended right now, we would 've lost."

"And if I were a woman, I could have a baby, but I'm not and I can't. The game isn't over, far from it. We're in striking distance. We can win this. We will win this."

"Well, I'm not surprised to hear you say that since you're the reason we're in this mess. If Lance were here—"

"Oh, please. Lance? He never scored anywhere but in the bedroom. He never took you further than fourth place. What, are you in love with him?"

"You are so gone, mister, after this season."

"Maybe. But for now, I'm the starting quarterback of the New York Templars and the leader of this team. Guys, we can do this. We will do this. Who is like us?"

"No one," they shouted, rising as one.

"Who is like me?" Quinn asked.

"No one," they cried as they ran back out onto the field after the halftime show, which featured a former teen pop star on the redemptive comeback trail.

"There's your answer, Smalley," Quinn said with a grin, emphasizing the "Small" in his name.

He played lights out now. All the Temps did. There was something about cold white anger that was just so bracing, he thought.

It was brutal though. It had started to snow—

the possibility of which had produced much hand-ringing throughout Super Bowl Week. Now that what everyone feared had actually happened, it seemed right, the season's stinging cold and relentless snow, sleet and rain—should that be snain?—providing the perfect backdrop for a game that was more Battle of the Bulge than sport.

The Temps clawed for every yard, the cold making the clash of bone on bone, metal on metal, bite even more. The Miners managed a field goal. It was 13-7 now and late in the evening.

"One touchdown. One touchdown," Quinn shouted. "That's all we need."

Please, he prayed to the D—or the God of D—hold them and give us one more chance. One more chance.

When the Temps got it, Quinn was brought down by one of the Miners' new guys—Casey Kasmerek, his old tormentor from his Stanford days. Did Quinn conveniently forget that the Miners had picked him up? Didn't matter. It was fitting, ironic, ironically fitting and fittingly ironic. Quinn should've expected it. It was payback time for what happened earlier. Still, it was exceptionally cruel, as Kasmerek "accidentally" kicked Quinn—not once but twice. The crowd gasped and Quinn's brain, which had been traveling forward, seemed as if it would burst through his skull and helmet to go on forever. He must've been momentarily stunned, he thought, for it took him a while to react as he was helped off the field. On the sidelines, Dr. Ian Zingracz—the neurologist assigned to the team under the NFL's anti-concussion program—was all solicitousness.

"I'm fine," Quinn said as Dr. Ian peered into his eyes with a light that really hurt.

"Starling," Smalley screamed, "get your ass in there."

But after getting the team a second down, Lleyton was sacked, his collarbone broken.

"I can do it. Let me up," he cried. It was clear, though, that he was in terrible pain, couldn't move his throwing arm, and was having trouble breathing.

"Off with you," Quinn said, refusing to let him say anymore. "When we next see you, you'll be a Super Bowl champ. No, really. Thank you for everything, Lleyton, but it's time for you to get that attended to and for me to finish up.

"Please," Quinn pleaded with Dr. Ian, "I'm OK. I was just a little shaken up. I can do this. There's no else who can." In truth—the truth Quinn surely wouldn't have admitted even to myself—he was feeling a little disoriented, as if he were moving underwater. He tried to shake it off. Focus, he told myself. Just a few more minutes—a few long, short minutes and seven points that were the margin between victory and defeat. He threw a couple of passes that inched the Temps deeper into Miners' territory. I need a miracle here, God, Quinn said to himself. Finally, he saw Derrick open and connected. And Derrick ran and ran, falling on his backside into the end zone, cradling the ball even as one of the Miners' defensemen tried to pry it loose. But that's how some victories are crafted, Quinn thought, ass-backward. Needless to say, the Temps got the extra point.

One point. One point was the margin between victory and defeat, a win and a loss.

Confetti: Quinn remembered the confetti in the team colors, and then red, white and blue, such a waste and a mess, he thought, all that paper, like cut flowers. But flowers are beautiful, aren't they? Quinn couldn't take it all in and, though he should've been happy, he was finding it hard to feel any joy.

There was a swarm of players, reporters, cameramen, family, well-wishers. I must remain poised, Quinn thought, smiling for the curtain calls.

"Is it everything you imagined?" a SNN field reporter asked. Remember the answer-a-question-with-a-word-in-the-question rule.

"Everything," Quinn said, smiling.

Brenna grabbed him. "Congratulations. You so deserve this," she said. "Are you all right?"

"Fine. Fine. Just trying to absorb it all."

Finally, Quinn spied Tam. They couldn't avoid this moment on national TV, though Quinn would've given anything for the earth to swallow him whole right then. He hesitated but Tam—devastation written on his face—wrapped him in a bear hug.

"So close, so close," Tam whispered in Quinn's ear. Was he talking about the game or something else?

"I loved you," Tam said. "I always will." And with that, he was gone. And Quinn was the one left devastated as he wrapped his arms around cold metal instead, the MVP trophy. Jimmy Jones Jefferson tried to pull him into a photo with Jeff Sylvan and Smalley, but Quinn stepped back to let them enjoy the spotlight. He did enough for them. He didn't have to pretend to love them as well.

For the postgame press conference, Quinn dressed carefully, sharply in a black suit with a black turtleneck and black boots. The look matched his mood. Must keep it together, though, he kept willing himself.

Difficult. The questions were interminable, dumber and more unrelenting than on Media Day.

"Is there anyone in particular you'd like to thank?"

"Yes," he said, "I'd like to thank my teammates. And one more person, who is no longer with us— my Aunt Lena. She delivered me into a brilliant life and I'd like to dedicate my MVP trophy to her."

There was, however, always one Wicked Fairy at the party.

"Quinn, do you think this championship and your MVP go a long way to dispelling the rumors that the team may still deal you once Lance returns?"

Nothing was ever enough, was it? It wasn't for his parents. It wasn't for his surrogate football daddies. It wasn't for Mal or even Tam. I will never be able to do enough, be enough for anyone, Quinn thought.

He looked out at the room before answering, realizing that nothing would ever be any different, and he was suddenly tired, no, overwhelmed with exhaustion.

"I can't," Quinn said. "I can't do this anymore."

And that was the last thing he remembered before waking up in a darkened hospital room— with Tam sitting on the bed, touching his cheek as he turned away.

TWENTY-THREE

Darkness, dreaming, darkly dreaming: He was in the water again, Eagles Airline Flight 2095 having gone down over the North Pacific, again. Drowning, sinking deep into the black water, then resurging, fighting for air, being baptized as it were, being born again.

"You're going to be all right, son," the flight officer said, offering a hand, a lifeline. "You're going to make it."

But he could barely hear him, screaming as he was for Aunt Lena, howling in pain.

We die with the dying:
See, they depart, and we go with them.
We are born with the dead:
See, they return, and bring us with them.

He was in a dark room, trying to remember the rest of T.S. Eliot's *The Four Quartets*, which he once knew by heart—Brit Lit, Stanford. *"We die with the dying..."*

Was he dead and born again in the hereafter or in some institution in the here and now? Tam was sitting on his bed, caressing his cheek. And he turned away as if scalded by his touch. *We die with the dying...*

What came after those four key lines? Panic: He couldn't remember and, worse, he couldn't remember anything after telling reporters, "I can't do this anymore."

Why was Tam here and how long had he been here?

"Good morning. And how are we today?" A nurse, maddeningly chipper.

"Oh, wonderful. You?"

She moved to raise the shade.

"No," Quinn cried, tenting his eyes with his left arm. "Shut out the light. I can't. I can't."

"It's all right. It's all right," she said soothingly. A hand patted his right arm. A stronger hand stroked his raised left one—Tam's.

"The doctor will be in in a moment." Footsteps beating a hasty retreat.

"How are you, Quinn?" A male voice, suddenly familiar.

"Dr. Matthew?"

Dr. Matthew smiled. "Yes, Quinn, I'm here. I'm on the case. The minute I saw you collapse on TV, I drove here as fast as I could. You'd be amazed what strings fame can pull. You're the new prince of America, Quinn. Everyone's very worried about you. Do you know where you are?"

In Hell, Quinn thought, but said, "I think in a hospital."

"That's right. And do you remember what happened?"

"I was at a press conference. I remember I was talking."

"Good. Do you remember what you said?"

"I think I said something about how I couldn't do this anymore."

"Bravo. Do you remember anything after that?"

Quinn shook his head.

"OK," Dr. Matthew said. "OK, rest. And you are?" he added, turning his attention to Tam. "What a silly question. Of course, I know who you are. You're the one who got away—from Philly, I mean. I'm from Philly."

Introductions, handshakes, smiles. Then Dr. Matt turned from fandom to doctoring. "Would you mind stepping outside for a moment?"

Tam's face was a kaleidoscope of anxiety, concern, hurt, guilt, misery. Tam pressed Quinn's arm. "I'll be right out there."

When he left, Dr. Matthew's smile faded, and he closed the bed curtains around them like a cocoon. "OK, tell me if this is the one who's been doing these things to you, and I'll have him arrested right now."

"No, no," Quinn cried. "Please. He's the other—the one I loved and lost." *See, doctor, we die with the dying...*

"It doesn't seem to me that you've lost him at all. Quite the opposite: He's here with you now."

Tam was not only there. He had apparently put a rose-gold band with a prominent ruby on the ring finger of Quinn's left hand. He felt something nubby inside—an inscription and another smaller ruby. In the East, Quinn knew, rubies were thought to have healing power. He tried to read the inscription, but his head hurt from the effort.

When had he and Tam become engaged? Had they always been engaged? He wanted to scream. He wanted to run.

"Can I get you anything, my love?" Tam said when he returned, tousling Quinn's hair. He pulled away.

I must stay calm and try to remember, Quinn thought. But in his mind, he was running.

TWENTY-FOUR

Heart like a river; like this river, Quinn thought, frozen with shards of snow-covered ice.

He was staring out at the Hudson through the scrim of a light beige shade, even the buttery winter sun being too strong for his eyes. Or maybe it was too strong for his brain and his mind. Was the mind the same as the brain? Did the mind cease to exist when the brain did, or did it go on in the Great Somewhere? In the weeks after Quinn left the hospital, while others were negotiating contracts, hitting the gym or vowing to come back stronger, faster—whatever sounded good in the press—he and Tam had, unbeknown to anyone, settled into domesticity in Quinn's Lower Manhattan loft.

This is what it must be like to be loved, Quinn thought, as he sat by the window in his sweats, ski cap, hoodie, booties and fingerless gloves and Tam surrounded him with throws and pillows. Someone asking if you want cocoa. Someone kissing your forehead just because. Someone reading with and to you. Someone holding your hand and rubbing your palm as you ate in silence, because there was both too much to say and nothing left to.

They had never been a couple and now they were living together, but Quinn guessed they weren't the first to find themselves in such a situation. It's just that Quinn had always imagined that the circumstances would be different. They would get to know each other first, then one day there would be an engagement with decisions about households and mundane things like china patterns. This seemed so rushed with so many questions left unanswered. Was Tam there partly because he felt responsible for the Miners takedown that led to Quinn's concussion? Then again, weren't Tam and the Miners just doing their jobs? Could Tam really love the man who had defeated him and was now his chief rival?

And what about Mal, the unspoken, sculpted six-foot, five-inch, 245-pound gorilla in the room? He had been at the NFL Awards the night before the Super Bowl to receive the prestigious Walter Payton NFL Man of the Year honor for his work on behalf of the Philadelphia Coalition for the Homeless. It provided one of the few moments of levity for Tam and Quinn, who had not attended and were now catching up with the show—a kind of glorified high school assembly program, albeit one at Lincoln Center—on DVR.

"I just want to thank the people in Philadelphia for needing me so much," Mal said in a speech that raised some eyebrows (notably Brenna's, whom the camera cut to in the press bullpen, taking notes and barely containing her laughter).

"Yeah, I just want to thank the people of Philadelphia for having so many homeless people so I could dump even more work on my wife and stand up there and stroke my ego," Tam said. "Jesus Christ, he really is his own little planet."

Tam had won the MVP Award but had sent his twin sisters, Kimberly and Beverly, to accept it. Quinn was struck by how unalike these fraternal twins were—the petite, pregnant Kimberly, a married nurse, all soft, blonde curves; Beverly, an unmarried teacher, tall, brunette, and angular.

"We just want to say how proud we are of our baby brother," Kimberly said, clearly tickled to be in the New York spotlight. "Go Tam. Go Miners."

Quinn winced at that. He wondered how Tam's sisters would greet the "brother-in-law" who ended their baby bro's quest for a second consecutive Super Bowl. And they were likely to be easier than Tam's older brothers or parents. But wasn't Quinn getting ahead of himself? Was any of this real, or were they just playing house?

Certainly, it was real enough to Tam, who talked at length about his home—someday, their home—in San Francisco.

"I can't wait for you to see it," Tam said, almost desperately, Quinn thought. "It's one of those Victorians—you know, the Painted Ladies—pale pink, in the Haight-Ashbury District. Hey, you'll never guess who lives down the street—Deidre Norquist. She's the artist who—"

"I know who she is," Quinn said. "I went to Stanford with her oldest nephew."

"Oh, right, the swimmer Dylan Roqué. What was he like? I heard, you know, he may have taken his own life."

"He didn't kill himself. He couldn't have," Quinn shot back, willing what he said to be true. "It wasn't his nature. He was compassionate and courageous, though you could hardly blame him or anyone else for wanting to quit this world."

"Don't say that," Tam said softly. "There's never a good reason for ending it all."

"No?" Quinn countered. "There aren't any circumstances under which you'd kill yourself? Because I know there are situations in which I would."

"Sounds as if you were in love with him," Tam said, changing the subject while getting to the heart of the matter.

Quinn shrugged. "I was a freshman with a schoolboy crush on a senior, and he was the love of someone else's life." Quinn flashed on Daniel with Alí in one of the boxes at Templars Stadium—laughing and clapping, Daniel whispering in his ear, their heads close, almost touching.

Quinn felt a heart-pang at the memory. Daniel had loved Dylan, that much Quinn was sure of. But now he had made a new life with Alí. Does the heart forget, or does it merely go on, tethered nonetheless to the past? *We are born with the dead, Tam. See, they return, and bring us with them.*

Quinn didn't want to be mean to Tam, really he didn't. But he wasn't going to let him tell him anything about the people he knew, his past, himself. He wasn't going to let him back in, let him get too close again. He still hadn't forgiven him. He still hadn't forgiven himself.

At night, they shared Quinn's bed, spooning. The first night, Quinn made to undress, pulling down the sweats that doubled as pajama bottoms. Tam grabbed Quinn's hand and held it with the bunched-up sweats in front of his crotch, and Quinn felt himself stirring. It had been so long since the last time between them. He couldn't imagine anything he feared and wanted more. So he was both relieved and crushed when Tam said, "No, no, it's too soon. We'll wait till you heal."

Yes, Quinn thought, wait till I'm no longer the damaged goods you made me. He let Tam bury his face reassuringly in his neck, but he lay awake most of the night. He wished Tam weren't there, wished he had the courage to throw him out. Why didn't he? Maybe because what he feared most was that Tam, having found him, would abandon him again. The next day Quinn thought that fear had been realized. He woke to see Tam's duffel packed.

"I have to head to my golf tournament," he said. "Come on, don't look at me that way. If you were well, you know you'd be out there playing at the tournament with me and preparing for the next season."

But Quinn wasn't so sure. He didn't know if he'd ever go back to football—not that he expected anyone to miss him, even though his teammates sent texts and gifts. In the wake of the Super Bowl, his collapse and absence from public view had met with a mixed reaction.

"I just don't know if he's tough enough," one commentator intoned. "I've always thought he was something of a head case anyway."

"Head case? He could've been killed," another answered. "The Temps will be lucky to see the return of the man who led them to their first Super Bowl in thirty-five years."

Quinn tuned them out. He wanted to be alone. Then why did Tam's departure fill him with such panic and grief?

"Come on, don't be that way," Tam said. He took him in his arms before Quinn could protest and kissed him, the rhythm deepening as the kisses became slower, more sustained. But just as Quinn was melting, Tam pulled away.

"I'll be back in a week," he said with a devilish smile. "In the meantime, I'm sending you a surprise to keep you company while I'm away."

The surprise arrived a day later in the form of

Beverly and Kimberly—or Kim and Bev as they introduced themselves. They hugged and kissed Quinn enthusiastically, Kim more so, but then she was the more demonstrative of the two. Quinn looked around to see if the rest of Tam's family was with them. Tam had a helluva nerve sending the sisters to his place—probably to watchdog his investment, Quinn thought bitterly. But he found himself smiling and saying, "Please, come in."

"We're just in town for a few days," Kim said, moving right into the loft and eyeing everything as she took off a bright red coat to reveal her tight butterball stomach. "A shopping spree. Well, really to see you. Tam thought you could use the help and the company."

"And I said, 'Tam, we don't want to invade his space,'" Bev said, almost reading Quinn's mind. "'We might be more of a hindrance than a help.'"

"And I said, 'Nonsense,'" Kim said. "When our brother told us he was getting married, well, you can imagine. We were shocked."

Quinn smiled. "Oh, I can imagine that the only thing that shocked you more was whom he was marrying."

Kim began to demur, but Bev would have none of it.

"We were stunned," she said. "I mean, Tam always had the odd girlfriend, emphasis on the word 'odd.' I suppose that should've told us something. But just because we were surprised doesn't mean we're not delighted."

"And are your parents and brothers equally delighted?" Quinn saw the answer written on their faces. "Thought so. They don't know, do they?"

Kim squeezed his arm. "One step at a time."

The twins were staying at a nearby boutique

hotel. The plan apparently was to draw Quinn out, back into the world. *We are born with the dead: See, they return, and bring us with them.* Not so easy. For one thing, he didn't feel like doing anything, let alone appearing in public. For another, appearing in public reminded him precisely why he didn't want to—all those people with their cameras and their questions, however well-intended, all those reporters parsing his every move as if there were meaning in a forkful of spinach salad. But Bev and Kim proved irresistible company, arguing passionately, finishing each other's sentences and desserts. They reminded him of being with Aunt Lena or Brenna, sharing their kaleidoscopic interests, which teemed with color and life.

It wasn't long before the New York tabloids were wondering if the Temps' QB was dating the enemy—in the form of Tam's sister Bev, with Kim serving as chaperone.

"Congratulations," Brenna said during one of their quasi-professional interviews/heart-to heart phone calls.

"Brenna, it isn't what you think."

"No?" She sounded hurt.

"No, we're just friends." God, was a lamer thought ever uttered? He longed to tell Brenna the truth, to take her into his confidence. But he couldn't. Not yet.

And he and Tam's sisters were friends, maybe more than that.

"It's nice," he said one day at lunch in his loft. "I never had siblings."

He started to cry, no, sob in great, uncontrollable gasps. He felt so useless, hopeless, embarrassed and alone. Bev put a hand on his arm as Kim drew him to her. He could feel her baby stirring. "It's OK," she said. "It's OK. My brother loves you. It's going to be all right. You're going to get better and marry him in a big wedding that I can't wait to help plan and have babies and be very happy. Remember how small Tam was when he was born, Bev? He was like one of those newborn pandas, no bigger than a stick of butter, he was so premature. Remember when he got strong enough, how Mom let me dress him in my doll's clothes and put him in my doll carriage? I think I thought he was more my baby than hers. And if people think I'm going to let them get in the way of his happiness or yours, well, they've got another guess coming, buster."

Quinn didn't quite believe her, but he sent them off with lovely parting gifts—handbags with golden map patterns.

"Quinn, you shouldn't have," Kim said, proceeding to dump the contents of her handbag into the new one immediately.

"Thank you," Bev said, hugging him. "We'll be in touch. Remember, you have sisters now."

Quinn was sure that was the last he'd hear from them. But no sooner had they left than he found an exquisite, camel-colored Italian leather appointment book from the twins in which Kim had marked what to do—and when to do it—to prepare for the wedding, with a detailed list of stores and services to consult. And while en route back to Philly, Bev texted him a number of articles on recovering from a concussion. The twins were true to their word: This was the beginning, not the end, of a relationship—or relationships, plural.

The next day, Tam returned as promised with a different kind of gift—a plan for getting Quinn back into shape.

Quinn looked at him, fingering the ring on his left hand.

"OK," he said. "Let's do this."

TWENTY-FIVE

As winter eased its icy grip, Quinn felt an unexpected lightening of his spirit, which responded to Tam's promptings. The pair rose while it was still dark and went for their run in Battery Park, then headed to the Juniper Tree Café for oatmeal, Greek yogurt parfaits and latte. After breakfast it was time for their gym workout, which they did back at Quinn's place, using equipment Tam had ordered and set up. Quinn figured if Tam ever lost his quarterback job—yeah, fat chance, he was "F***ing Tam Tarquin," after all—he could be a trainer. Or drill sergeant.

"Come on, one more set," he'd say.

"No, no more."

"OK, then, just half a set."

Part of what made Tam great was that he knew when to push and when to back off. But he did push.

"Do you want to lose your starting job to Lleyton?" Tam asked, looming above Quinn as they panted. Why couldn't this be from hot sex rather than exercise? was all Quinn thought. "Well?" Tam insisted.

"I don't know. I honestly don't. It's probably inevitable. I mean, let's face it: One day Lleyton Starling will be hailed as the greatest quarterback who ever lived after you. But for now, I have no guarantee either Lleyton or I will be the starter this coming season. We'll probably both be playing behind Lance, assuming I'm there at all."

"Oh please, that glorified playboy. He's no match for either of you. And Lleyton's not ready to be number one. He needs a few more seasons behind you, by which time you can punch your ticket to a team that will really appreciate you."

"Again, if I play that long, or at all."

"What is it with you? Don't you want to come back?"

"And risk another concussion or sub-concussion or whatever it is I had and possible brain damage? Don't you think about it?"

"No, I don't. It's what we do, just like any other job, like being a miner—lower case 'm'—only much better paid."

"By people who make even more and don't care what happens to us once we're used up."

"By which time we'll be doing something else—or nothing at all. Maybe we'll just be raising our kids and sitting on our porch, watching the sun rise and set over San Francisco Bay."

"Do you really think that's ever going to happen, Tam? Do you really think we're going to have a moment's peace in or out of the league, not to mention our poor children, who'll be TMZ-ed to death? Don't you see, Tam? This is going to be the first paragraph of our obituaries."

"Well, good. I always wanted to be famous. I always figured, though, that it would be for something like most passes thrown. Still, it might as well be for this."

"And you have no fear?"

"No, I never fear what I know is meant to be."

"Well," Quinn said, "you might as well not, because I'm afraid enough for both of us."

"Then I think you're a pretty courageous guy, because fear is the first step to courage. Without fear, there's nothing for courage to overcome. Fear can paralyze you, or it can set you free. So which would you rather be, paralyzed or free, Quinnie?"

Free, he thought as he slowly made his way back into the world. Whenever Tam was busy with commitments to his sponsors—"You know I'm coming back, don't you?" Tam reassured him—Quinn ventured out on his own to see Nero or Kelly. It was good to remember that there were other people much worse off than him. Or he called teammates or met Brenna for lunch.

"It's good to see you on the mend," she said, patting his arm as they lunched at Saigon's. "Are you looking forward to returning?"

"Is that the reporter asking or the friend?"

She smiled. "The friend."

"We'll see when training camp starts this summer."

"What did you mean when you said, I can't do this anymore?"

"I honestly don't know." But he did. He just felt he couldn't tell her—at least not yet.

"Mmm. Might this imply a career change? Well, you wouldn't be the first. Indeed, I have some news on that front."

"Do tell." Quinn was eager to deflect the conversation from himself.

"Well, no doubt you heard about Vienne." Vienne? Had he been buried alive so deep that he was oblivious to some earth-shattering revelation—or at least some juicy morsel—among their circle? Quinn shook his head as he leaned in and took another dollop from their shared caramel fudge sundae.

"Boy, you really have been out of commission." Brenna leaned in, too, barely able to contain her schadenfreude. "Well, then you might not know that she and Freddy Bear had been having their problems. Things apparently came to a head when Mal Ryan paid her a visit at Shady Nook Farm, you know, the Bedford estate we visited. It was all pretty innocent, at least at first while Tiffany was there. But then she went back to Philly, because the baby was sick. Anyway, I don't know if the household staff caught Vienne and Mal *in flagrante delicto* or what, but before you knew it, the staff—whom I heard she always treated badly—was reporting her to Freddy. And I guess that was the indiscretion that broke the billionaire's back. I heard he had her locked out of the *Rumours'* office and fired her inner minions. She's history."

"Just like that?"

"Just like that. I mean, Freddy can do that. He owns the *Rumours'* empire. The best part was that he flew in for the housecleaning and could be heard shrieking at the COO, 'And I never want to see another fucking animal in this place.'"

"Gee, I wonder if he were referring to Mal or the Papillons?" Mal, Quinn thought with a pang, yet another thing he'd have to confront.

Brenna giggled. "Good one." She paused for a spoon of sundae. "I'm sure, knowing control-freak Vienne as I unfortunately do, that she has an iron-clad prenup that will be keeping the McQueen pooches in kibble in perpetuity. But here's where things get bizarre: Guess whom Freddy has asked to be the new editor?"

Quinn paused. It was so delicious to hear someone who always used proper grammar. Wait, what was she saying? Was it her? Should that be she?

"Oh my God. Congratulations. This calls for some Champagne. "

Quinn asked for the wine list. "Waiter, we'll have a bottle of Bollinger Special Cuvée."

"A very good choice, sir."

"Ooh, Bollinger. Aren't we the little sommelier," Brenna teased.

"I have my sophisticated moments and my go-to treats—Champagne, Coca-Cola, ice cream sundaes. So, when do you start?"

"Well, I haven't said 'yes'—yet. Don't forget: I have the same ambivalence to reporting and editing that you have to football. I never wanted to be anything but a writer. Columnist suits me fine. Plus, I have no illusions about working for Freddy Bear. The job will be unending. And it will mean going back to my old world just when I got used to the new one. It will mean giving up covering the NFL."

And seeing you regularly. She didn't have to add that. He knew that's what she was thinking.

"We'll always be friends," he said, reaching for her hand. "That will never change."

What was left unspoken between them was what could never be, and the conversation veered from gleeful gossip to sober sorrow.

"I've never told you this but you remind me a lot of my Aunt Lena, in your glamorous command of all life's situations. And I have a funny feeling she's up there willing this to happen, guiding you to her old job. Your dad must be tickled."

"He is," Brenna said, taking a sip of the Champagne. "Mother is another matter. You know she and Vienne were—are—very friendly. I can't help but feel I've stabbed them in the back."

"No. No," Quinn said, taking both of her hands

in his and looking her in the eye. "You get rid of that goddamn useless guilt. You did nothing wrong. Vienne overplayed her hand by apparently shitting where she ate, surrounded by people she mistreated who had no reason to cover her ass. And let me tell you something else: You don't take this job, someone else will. Come on, it will mean more money, exposure, opportunity. You don't have to do it forever, just till you get what you want out of it."

"Temporary situations, though, have a way of turning into forever. But what about you? Will you follow your own advice?"

"Football is a lot more dangerous than the magazine world."

"Wanna bet? OK, then. Will you be my first cover? Freddy's decided to rip up the April cover and start fresh—deadlines be damned. So how 'bout it?"

Quinn laughed as he nodded yes. "You're not even editor and already you're acting like one, driving a hard bargain." He raised a glass. "To editors past and present."

She clinked his glass with hers. "To editors and their nephews."

TWENTY-SIX

"Mal huh?"

Quinn was bringing Tam up to speed, the story having not reached the evening news plateau necessary for Tam, who did not generally indulge in gossip. "Not surprised. I mean, we could people Wikipedia with the wrecks Mal has left in his wake."

"To be fair," Quinn countered, "it often takes two to twerk. Had Vienne not been interested or had she treated her household staff better, she might not have fallen from grace. But then, who am I to talk?"

Silence of a Grand Canyon-size chasm.

"Tell me," Tam said softly, "what sexual experience did you have before you took up with Mal?"

"None," Quinn said. "But I wanted him."

Tam took Quinn's face in his hands. "You were a virgin and innocent, just as he took advantage of my drunkenness that night under the pier."

There was no point in arguing how defenseless—or not—he himself had been, Quinn thought. He understood that Tam was constructing a narrative and was eager to help him do it, just as he offered up his face hungrily to be kissed and guided Tam's hands to his swelling pecs, not to mention his burgeoning cock.

"Not yet," Tam murmured as frustrated as Quinn.

"Why ever not?" Quinn said. "Look, if you're

here out of guilt rather than love, then please, go. I don't need the baggage."

"It's because I love you that I want to wait till you're stronger, healed. I don't want to take advantage."

Quinn could see in Tam's face that he loved him, that what he said was true. Why Tam should feel that way was another matter. Quinn had to content himself with their forays into the public as a couple, although the public wasn't aware of their coupling. As far as the public was concerned, they were just two of the sports celebs who'd been invited to World Tennis Day at Madison Square Garden. Why the reigning NFL MVP and the rival reigning Super Bowl MVP should happen to be taking in the match together from the JPMorgan Chase box seemed to intrigue the spectators not at all. They were content to worship two sports luminaries—captured on the Jumbotron—paying homage to other sports luminaries. The ovation for Quinn was particularly loud and long, about as long as it was for Tam.

"See, they love you and want you back," Tam said, smiling and clapping. Quinn, who was embarrassed and somewhat startled by the outpouring, wasn't so sure. He was more interested in the match between Australia's Evan Conor Fallon, the number one-ranked player in the world, and the number two-ranked, America's Ryan Kovacs.

In a way, Quinn thought, tennis was as brutal a game as football. It just went about its brutality in a more elegant manner. Evan and Ryan were like prizefighters playing chess. The power with which they hit the ball during long rallies; the intense concentration, as if they were the only two people in the house, was, well, thrilling, Quinn thought. He, like the rest of the Garden, held his breath.

Evan and Ryan had grown up a lot, Quinn thought. Gone were the eye-rolling, sighing, crying, looking-up-to-Heaven (or, at least, to-the-coach's-box) days for both—although they were still capable of racket abuse, albeit with a smile, particularly in this, an exhibition match. At one point, Evan even went over to Ryan's side of the net as if to coach him and Ryan moved over as if to play doubles. Only there was no one on the other side of the net. They both shrugged, and Evan walked back to his side of the net, hitting a moon ball of a lob to the rafters that Ryan returned with a sharp slice. Evan went to return it only to whiff at it as it veered off course for a winner. The crowd went wild.

"The Magnus effect," Tam shouted to Quinn amid the applause. "Like in football. You think the ball's spiraling one way but it heads in another direction."

Quinn nodded. How many moments in life were Magnus effects? For him, the most moving one of the evening came right before the match when the International Tennis Hall of Fame introduced the inductees who'd be honored later that summer in Newport, Rhode Island. Among them—and the only one present, the rest appearing via video—was Alí Iskandar. Tam and Quinn watched, as touched as the audience, as Alí took the hand of the tiny towel boy and carefully made his way out onto the court for the remarks, looking natty but almost painfully thin in black skinny jeans, turtleneck and moto jacket. Even his cane—more of a walking stick—was black, threaded with silver and topped with what Quinn thought on the big screen looked like a silvery skull. He leaned on it lightly as he took the cordless mike in his left hand—a man bridging the land of the living and the land of the dead. *We die with the dying. See, they depart, and we go with them...*

"Thank you, thank you for your kind words and welcome," he said to the crowd, speaking English with an inflection that had long since ceased to betray an Iraqi accent. "It is a great honor to be chosen for the Hall. I've had the great pleasure of watching Étienne Alençon and Alexandros Vyranos being inducted, and I know what joy it has brought them. In fact, Alex said to me, 'You're next,' and he was the first person to call to congratulate me, making the honor doubly special."

Here Alí paused as if gathering his emotions or maybe just his strength. "I'd like to thank my family for their love and support always. They're flung to the far corners of the earth for their work these days, but they are never far from my thoughts nor am I from theirs. I'd like to thank the late Private Michael Smeaton, who made my journey to America and my career possible. He is gone from this world, and yet remains through his widow, Kathy, who has done so much for me and for veterans and their families. She is here tonight with their daughter, Michaela."

With that, Alí gathered the mike to his chest and applauded as he gestured to an attractive blonde and a younger, willowy one whom Quinn thought looked like a model. Seated with them was another blonde who was a real one, Kahrin Klaus—she of the sculpted cheekbones and even more sculpted figure—rumored to be Alí's longtime girlfriend, though Quinn thought that more of a relationship similar to the one he had with Brenna. He searched the crowd, scanning at last the other private boxes. Where was Daniel Reiner-Kahn?

"There are others I wish to thank privately," Alí said, at which the crowd giggled as the kiss cam found Kahrin pointing to it and chuckling. "Why is everyone laughing?" he asked, blushing and laughing himself. "There is, however, someone else I would like to acknowledge publicly and that is the late Dylan Roqué. It is my pleasure to announce tonight the winners of the Dylan Roqué Scholarships for academic and athletic excellence, which are awarded through the Ani Foundation of Ari Kahn LLP."

With that, ten high school seniors scampered out onto the court to pose with Alí.

"Last but never least, my thanks to God and to you for listening and for your love. You have been one of the great joys of my life. And now I've played with and against Evan Conor Fallon and Ryan Kovacs. I know we're in for a great match."

With that, the crowd rose as one for an ovation that only grew. Alí tried to quiet the crowd and even went to take his seat courtside, only to have Kathy, Michaela and Kahrin gently push him back out onto the court. Alí had had such an up-and-down relationship with his adopted country, Quinn thought. Now leukemia—and time—had made him beloved. As Quinn and Tam stood with the others clapping, Quinn finally caught sight of Daniel in a corner of a private box, wearing a pinstripe suit and wiping his eyes.

Finally, the throng was sated but the Tennis

Hall of Fame official was not. "We can't let you go without asking you, do you miss playing as much as we miss you on the court?"

"Oh, why don't they leave him alone," Tam muttered to Quinn.

Alí brought the mike close and said, "Ah, in a word, 'No,'" which made the crowd roar. But they both knew what he really meant. Not only did he no longer want to play; he couldn't.

"Still," the official persisted, "would you oblige us with a hit?"

"This guy's getting on my nerves," Tam whispered.

Quinn could see Alí's reluctance but the crowd was into it, so he said, "OK," motioning to the towel boy who had come out with him. The child took his place on the other side of the net—a slip of a thing whose racket covered about a third of him—and Alí lobbed a ball that his "opponent" returned sharply. Alí, who never moved, shrugged, applauded and, turning to the crowd, said, "Let's have a round of applause for a future Hall of Famer."

Nicely played, Quinn thought later in the quiet of his loft as he and Tam did their yoga stretches. But he couldn't help but think of how cruel life was, particularly to athletes, how it drained them of their talent, just as death could slowly rob someone as lovely in every sense of the word as Alí of the life force. *We die with the dying: See, they depart, and we go with them...*

"Penny for your thoughts," Tam said. "No, wait, the economy still sucks. I'll give you a whole quarter."

Quinn laughed. "No, I was just thinking..."

"Yes."

"My back needs an extra stretch. I've got an idea. Get down on all fours and stretch like a cat—your arms out in front of you, your face and upper body on the floor, your heels resting on your butt."

"Hey, I don't like the sound of this."

"Just trust me, will ya? Now I'm going to sit on your tailbone and—"

"Wait a minute. You're gonna what?"

"I'm going to sit on your tailbone and then do a backbend over your back, resting my head next to yours and stretching out my arms to reach yours in reverse. And then we'll change places. It's a fantastic stretch for the back, you'll see."

"It better be."

"Comfortable?" Quinn asked as he placed his tailbone on that of his lover. It had been so long since they had touched intimately that this was like sex—hot, wet, dripping sex. Quinn thought he'd explode.

"OK," he said, trying to keep his mind on his breathing and the pose. "On the count of three, I'm going to do a backbend over your back, rest my head in the curve of your neck, and extend my hands to meet yours. One, two, three."

And with that, Quinn dove backward as if he were Dylan or Daniel diving into the water for the backstroke in the old Stanford days. Immediately, he felt buoyed by Tam's breathing, spine and back. Indeed, Tam's whole body lifted him on a warm wave as if he were Cabanel's Venus. Quinn nestled his face against Tam's head, taking in his intoxicating, spicy sandalwood scent and wondering at the luxuriant strands that were not quite blond, not quite brown as he nuzzled them.

For his part, Tam seemed content, too, his breaths lengthening and deepening as they slowly ebbed and flowed, making a hollow, hissing sound. After a while, Quinn wondered if he had fallen asleep. "You OK down there?"

"Marvelous," Tam said.

"Is that sarcasm?"

"No, no, really marvelous," Tam said luxuriously.

"Time to switch places."

"Do we have to?"

Quinn laughed but there was nothing funny about the hard-on he was getting as Tam settled on his tailbone. Tam bent back over him, and Quinn felt enveloped and protected in a cocoon of warm, woodsy flesh. I could die here and be reborn, he thought, a chrysalis becoming a butterfly of love.

"Are you sure you're all right?" Tam kept asking.

"Yes, shh," Quinn murmured. He didn't want to break the spell. He just wanted to rest there in an extended child's pose with Tam's head close to his, their fingers entwined. It wasn't sex but it was, he thought, the biblical bone of my bone and flesh of my flesh, so much so that he loathed Tam releasing his hands and rising slowly.

"Wow," he said, exhaling. "I'll have to remember this when my back aches from other exertions," he added, teasing as he kissed Quinn deeply, his tongue alighting on Quinn's.

"We could be enjoying those exertions now," Quinn said. "I feel nice and stretchy."

Tam shook his head. "No, my love, not until I am really yours and you are truly, finally mine."

When would that be? Quinn wondered. Wasn't that Triple Crown winner out of that barn? A plot formed in Quinn's mind to make that occur sooner rather than later. He turned it over as he sat after hours in the anteroom outside Brenna's new office at *New York Rumours* one early evening in late winter—his left leg resting at a 45-degree angle over his right as he circled his left foot nervously.

To distract himself, Quinn took the full measure of the office. Gone were the animal and rainforest accouterments that had been set against a harsh gray modern backdrop. It was as if Ferdinand Le Wood had erased every trace of his former wife. In their place were rich moldings, saturated pastel and jeweled colors, Renaissance and Neoclassical paintings, books of all kinds and male Greco-Roman sculptures, busts and heads. Clearly, this was Brenna's influence and it looked as if Freddy Bear were giving her carte blanche— for now.

Soon an officious young woman with a tablet and a headset came clicking along on four-inch heels.

"I'm Alessandra Moroni, Ms. James' executive assistant, and you must be her 6:30."

Normally, Quinn didn't care if people recognized him or not. So it amused him to no end that the ever-efficient Alessandra thought of him as no more than Ms. James' 6:30.

"Brenna, your 6:30 is here," she said into the headset. Brenna in turn must've set her straight, for Alessandra said, "Yes, of course" and then, smiling at Quinn, said, "she's just finishing up a conference call, Mr. Novak. May I get you some still or sparkling water, or perhaps some tea?"

"No, thanks, I'm fine," Quinn said, even more amused at the change of tone. He didn't have much time to speculate on what Brenna might've said as he was ushered into her office, which was an extension of the anteroom, and, Quinn imagined, Brenna's home with its comfortable, elaborately carved furnishings.

"I'll be out at my desk now if you need me," Alessandra said, setting down a silver tray with two glasses, a crystal bucket of ice and bottles of still and sparkling water.

"No, no," Brenna said, laughing, "you, out, home, go, do something fun.

"She is so funny," Brenna told Quinn after Alessandra left. "You know what she told me the other day? She said she wants to be just like me— a great writer and editor, never get married and never have children. Can you imagine? You know what I told her? 'Keep an open mind and an open heart. Don't close either to the possibility of love,' which is what I did.'"

As she talked, Quinn saw her as if for the first time. She stood behind a high-backed chair, one hand resting on it, the other on her hip, emphasizing her curvy figure, as did her structured, royal blue bandage dress. Her hair was drawn back in a loose, curly chignon, her skin highly polished; her fine nose underscored in profile as she gazed out the window of the One World Trade Center office at the dense resurrection that was Lower Manhattan, momentarily lost in thought. The transformation—of city and woman—was extraordinary, complete and yet, it seemed an utterly natural extension of the place and the person he knew. But there was a rueful quality to both now as well.

"You can do this," Quinn said. "I know you can. You're strong, and you were born for this."

"Really? I'm not so sure. Anyway, let's talk

about you. Are you up for this? Poor choice of words. Are you ready for the photo shoot?"

"Yeah, I guess. I can't believe I'm doing this. I can't believe Freddy's letting you do this."

"Are you kidding? He wants to shake up the magazine, and I think he believes this is one way to do it. I also think he assumes that if the issue fails or if there's a huge backlash, he has the ready fall guy in me."

"You're not going to fall. I won't let that happen."

She let out a long sigh. "All right then. Elliott's waiting for you in the studio."

She led him downstairs to another floor past several locked doors that required keycards and codes.

"Freddy's just as control-freaky as Vienne was," she said. Outside the door, she kissed him goodbye, adding, "Have a great shoot."

"Wait, aren't you going to stay?" Suddenly, Quinn felt uneasy.

"I trust you. I trust Elliott. Besides, if I stay, I might embarrass myself."

"Now I'm really nervous."

"Don't be. Hey, what you said to me: You can do this."

But Quinn had never done anything like this before. His previous shoots for Elliott would seem tame in comparison. Maybe he was just a male slut punishing himself—for what? For not measuring up to others' and his own expectations? Maybe he was a supreme narcissist for thinking anyone would want to see arty nudes of him. (He remembered the ribbings he'd gotten from his teammates over his previous photo shoots.) Or maybe he was just a guy in love trying to prove something to the guy he loved. All he knew was that he was a long way from Misalliance.

He sensed that the others thought so, too—or something similar—for there was a reticence on their part, a hesitance from all except Elliott's assistant, Christian, who had been undressing him with his eyes from the moment he walked into the studio.

"Right," Elliott said, "let's get you ready. No, not you, Christian. I need you on the set."

Brenna had thought of everything right down to the iced hibiscus Champagne he loved and the playlist, which included the apt *Ready to Go, Won't Back Down and, of course, Amazing.*

"You must be sick of it," Tonya, another assistant, said of the Temps' anthem.

"No, actually, it never gets old," he said, hoping to keep the focus on the music to stave off his nervousness.

He soon realized there was no need of it. Elliott's team managed to undress him and apply body makeup without ever exposing one body part or touching him intimately. They left him alone as he donned a navy hoodie, a pair of jeans and blue-and-white spectator sneakers, sans socks. He was feeling relaxed and sort of sexy already.

"OK, here we go," Elliott said. He unzipped Quinn's jacket slightly and brought up the hood, smiling. "Now just look at me. That's right. Let me do all the work."

His was a compassionate eye, a soothing voice, a gentle presence. Greatness needn't announce itself, Quinn thought. It only had to be. Plus, Elliott made him feel like a collaborator in the process—ensuring he was comfortable, telling jokes, asking him for his ideas. And, shyly at first but then more confidently, Quinn offered them.

The studio—with windows along the top that let in the light while keeping out prying eyes—had been divided into various environments.

"Wow, would you look at this," Quinn said, entering a space that was a tropical set with rocks, plants and a waterfall. For a moment, he was back in Indonesia and then back in the black water. *We die with the dying...* Don't think, Quinnie, he told himself, just give yourself over to the experience.

Elliott didn't tell him what to do here. He just let him explore the rocks in nothing but ripped jeans that exposed a tuft of man-fur. Quinn stretched out on the rocks—on all fours at first, then on his back—or clung to them under the waterfall as he turned to look at the camera, damp tendrils caressing his powerful neck.

"Yes, you see, you've got it," Elliott said. "You're a natural."

Quinn climbed some of the rocks and rested his cheek against the stone wall. He ran his fingers through his hair, arching his back, his tawny chest muscles melding with the stones. He could feel the syncopated beat of his heart. What was he really doing here? Playing to an audience of one that wasn't Elliott but, he hoped, the one he loved and who loved him.

In a pale green room with a huge white bed and soft lighting, he tented his face with one arm and stretched out, a rumpled sheet covering his sex but otherwise leaving his body bare. It was a languid Venus pose, one that had belonged to women throughout art history save for that period in the early-nineteenth century when it was co-opted by Endymion, Cephalus, Rinaldo, and other fortunate—or, depending on your viewpoint, unfortunate—young men who found themselves captives of a witch or a goddess.

"I want you to think of, well, nothing," Elliott said, "absolutely nothing. Can you do that?"

How could he do that? Even thinking of not thinking was a thought. But Quinn tried to still his mind as he did sometimes in the meditative part of yoga—"tried" being the operative word. If he were thinking right now, he said to himself slyly, he would think that the camera lens was the moon to his Endymion, making love to him as he lay there. He was completely vulnerable, he thought, except that he was conscious, not oblivious like Endymion and nude not naked, the nudity being a kind of armor, a kind of performance. He was acting nude, acting vulnerable and unconscious of the camera's admiration and love's moony embrace.

The last room was black and blue, tough and tender with raunchy rock playing and dragon projections in the background. Quinn sported a robe in the Temps colors. "OK, let's just do this," he said, opening it with one sweep and dropping it on a black leather couch.

"Oh, my God," Christian said.

"Christian, are you going to be professional about this, or am I going to have to send you to the time-out corner?" Elliott admonished.

"I'm professional, I'm professional, but oh my God. I feel as if I should get down on my knees and worship, or maybe something else."

Quinn had to laugh. It was just a cock. No big deal. Well, actually it was a pretty big deal but no big deal, if you knew what he meant. And, anyway, he wouldn't be sharing it with the world, just a certain someone and him alone from hereon in.

He lay face down on the couch, the leather against his own hide—skin to skin—sending an erotic charge throughout his body. He could feel the foreskin retracting and his cock swelling, and he arched his back, reveling in the sensation. No one spoke. He stretched out, resting on his forearms, and, turning, peered out of the corners of his eyes, the mossy shadow of his underarm peeking at the camera, too.

Finally, Elliott spoke. "I want you to raise yourself up on your forearms, tilt your head down and look at me. Yes, that's it exactly, like an undulating snake, shedding its skin, being reborn."

When the shoot was over, Quinn, wrapped again in his robe, took Elliott aside. Elliott dismissed the others and led him back to the last set.

"OK, do whatever you want," Elliott said. "I'll follow you."

Quinn lay face down on the couch, eyes closed, stroking himself. He pulled back the foreskin gently—was there any better sensation in all the world than the rubbery, tingling, nervy feel of drawing back the hood with no lubricant, just skin on skin?—then traced the throbbing vein beneath the shaft. His face flushed. It was bad enough that he would be splashed all over the April body issue of *New York Rumours*—and that Christian was probably tweeting descriptions of his member right now. But if these photos ever got out, well, that would be the end of his career. Maybe that's what he wanted after all.

He turned over at last and arched his back and cock upward, looking directly, boldly at the camera, his face lush with lust, the moans escaping from his body, which jerked involuntarily. It was one thing to pose artfully nude, quite another to perform sex. This was, he almost hated to admit, a tremendous turn-on, and he gave himself over to it as he would his lover, had he been there.

"Yes, beautiful," Elliott said thickly as Quinn's rhythm quickened and he exploded over himself. "You're beautiful. And very brave I think."

He took Quinn's face in his hands and kissed him on the forehead and then on the lips.

"These, I take it, are for a certain someone, yes?"

"Yes," Quinn said, turning over with a smile on his face.

Elliott couldn't resist taking one more close-up of his face.

"I'm going to submit this last shot to Brenna," he said. "It's the cover, I think. The rest of these I'll make into a photo album for you after I take a month's worth of cold showers."

Quinn felt like a spy when they met a week later and Elliott delivered the finished "product."

"You have my word that no one has or will eversee these," Elliott said.

"Not even the famous Christian?" Quinn teased.

"Especially not the famous Christian."

Quinn shrugged. "I trust you, Elliott. And I tell you what? I'll keep these images safe with the understanding that twenty-five years after your death and mine, they can be exhibited."

"You sure?"

"Hey, we'll both be dead. Who will care then, right?"

But Quinn did care very much when he shyly

presented the leather-bound navy photo album—wrapped in a bright lime grosgrain ribbon—to Tam.

"Oh, you devil," Tam said. "I'm going to have to drink this in later and often."

He in turn presented Quinn with an envelope. "I have a surprise, too. Mine isn't as sexy—nothing could be—but I think it might also have a certain shock value."

Quinn opened the envelope to find two sets of first-class tickets with a complex itinerary that ended in two words—Jakarta and Bali.

Tam watched as Quinn fingered the tickets silently.

"It's time," Tam said, "for you to go home."

PART IV

TWENTY-SEVEN

Quinn and Tam boarded an Eagles Airlines Boeing 777 for Tokyo at Newark Liberty International Airport on a rainy and windswept April day. Quinn didn't know what they were doing—or, more specifically, what he was doing. He hadn't been on an international flight since the one carrying him and 261 passengers—including the late, loved, deeply lamented Aunt Lena—went down in the North Pacific when he was twelve. The way he got through the many domestic flights he and the Temps took was to remind himself that at least they wouldn't be flying over any oceans. Still, when he was invited to the Pro Bowl in Honolulu his rookie year, he had a hard time convincing himself that, technically at least, New York to Honolulu was a domestic flight. He was glad that the Super Bowl broadcasting gig, to which he had already committed himself, preempted his participation.

Now he was staring at a screen that said, "New York to Tokyo—6,573 miles, 14 hours." He would be crossing the international dateline where it was already tomorrow. Already tomorrow, he thought, except that he was really flying back into yesterday.

Tam had bonded with the flight attendants in first class, who had recognized them—as had many they came into eye contact with—but were playing it cool. His people had put out a carefully worded press release explaining that as Quinn had been such a big supporter of his golf tournament, Tam was returning the favor by going on a "fact-finding" mission with him to Indonesia to see how the orphanage was progressing. "Fact-finding": Wasn't that what Congress called all those golf junkets to Puerto Rico? Quinn wondered whom they were kidding. But Tam was "F***ing Tam Tarquin," and if he said he was going on a fact-finding mission, then damn, he was going on a fact-finding mission. And if he, oops, let slip that it was just his luck that his sister Bev was smitten with his Super Bowl rival, well, who was anyone to question him?

Just what kind of game Tam was playing was anybody's guess, Quinn thought. All he knew for sure was that it was a dangerous one and that Tam was much better at it than he, whose mind was still back in New York, where reaction to his most recent photo shoot was crashing on the Jersey shore.

"These soft-porn photos—along with his post-Super Bowl press conference 'performance'—call into question what kind of team leader we have, what kind of mind he has," an indignant Smalley told *The Wreck,* INN and just about anyone who would listen to him. "And you have to think that his questionable judgment—his very stability—will be on the agenda come contract time."

Quinn wondered why someone like Vienne could get canned for adultery yet a bigoted sadist like Smalley held on to his job---probably because Smalley's transgressions, for the most part hidden from the press, were against his troops not his bosses.

Fortunately for Quinn, those bosses—Jimmy Jones Jefferson and Jeff Sylvan—couldn't have cared less about his provocative *New York Rumours* photo shoot. What they cared about was winning and anything else that put fannies in the seats. The *Rumours* issue was a hit. Brenna was a hit. And Quinn was a hit with everyone except the old school segment of the male population that doubted his manliness in offering himself as a sex object—which they viewed as a feminine occupation. What if they knew about the other photos, which Tam had hidden in plain sight on one of Quinn's bookshelves?

Quinn broke out into a cold sweat considering them now. What had he been thinking? Oh, that's right: He hadn't been thinking, for had he been, he would never have instigated the mother of all selfies. Fat good it did, too, because for all Tam's quiet licking of his lips as he incessantly perused them—often alone in the bathroom—he still hadn't touched him sexually. And yet he acted like a husband for all intents and purposes.

"You should try to eat something, my love," he whispered when the elaborately prepared Chilean sea bass arrived.

Quinn shook his head and pulled the airline blanket up near his face. He was living on Coca-Cola, crackers, vanilla ice cream and Dramamine until—twenty-two hours later, God willing—they landed in Jakarta. He marveled at how Tam could eat everything first class had to offer and delight in all the freebies. "Mom and the girls will get a kick out of these makeup samples," he said, looking at all the little bottles in the ultra-suede pouches. To Tam, it was all a lark. Quinn wished he could be as easygoing.

Or as beautiful as Tam was when he slept, his head like a sculpted marble bust, the sandy curls winding about an oval face that framed long lashes sheltering eyes the color of the sea, perfectly arched brows, a straight nose and a bow-shaped mouth. Quinn longed to kiss that mouth as Tam's sleeping form unconsciously—or maybe not so unconsciously—nestled near him. But they might as well have been the distance of the dark ocean they were crossing.

While Tam slept, Quinn read *Travels With Epicurus*; watched game film on his tablet until he was bleary-eyed; listened to the airline's classical and rock playlist—twice; saw a twelve-part BBC documentary on The Bible; walked the length of the plane—three times, pausing to greet well-wishers or sign autographs; freshened up; did his stretches and calisthenics; caught up on his emails; paid some bills; wrote in his journal; and, when all else failed, charted the plane's arc across the Pacific on the screen in front of him. The tiny plane sat on the top of the screen like a logo on letterhead stationery, hovering for what seemed an eternity off the Bering Strait between North America and Asia. Honestly, it was like watching paint dry, Quinn thought, or grass grow—or anyone play golf.

At one point, he forced himself to peek out the window at clouds over Alaska that looked like glaciers. Inside, the plane registered the outside temperature—minus 55 degrees. They were cruising at an altitude of some 35,000 feet in a glamorous sardine can, outside which they couldn't survive. How had he ever let Tam talk him into this?

"You should try to rest," a steward offered, as much for his own sake, Quinn thought, as for his.

"Is your friend all right?" he thought he heard

another flight attendant say to Tam as sleep fought to claim him.

"Oh, yeah, he's just a nervous flyer," Tam said.

What was left unsaid was what the flight attendant might've known and Tam surely did: Quinn's fears were not irrational, particularly to those in the press who liked to psychoanalyze their subjects under the guise of faux sympathy. He had been Icarus, the boy who fell out of the sky. It was a tempting narrative that played out before, during, and after Super Bowl Week. Not only was he interviewed about it then but also on every significant anniversary of the event and every time a plane crashed, as if having been a victim made him an expert.

One thing he was an expert on was his own experience. Few had survived the crash, particularly as time went on, and each person's perspective was unique, though his was limited initially by Aunt Josie's insistence that he be kept from the details he himself did not remember.

"What you need to do is think of our dear, departed Lena as she was, not as she is in that watery metal grave," Aunt Josie told him, "and to live your life as she would've conducted hers."

"Yes'm," Quinn still found himself saying in his daily phone chats with her.

He had prepared her, along with Aunt Sarah, Uncle Artur and Patience, for his nude pictorial in the April issue of *New York Rumours* and was surprised by her equanimity.

"Well, as long as it's artistic," she said. "We wouldn't turn our noses up at a Michelangelo, now would we, Quinnie Day?"

But would we turn our noses up at our gay fiancé? That was the real question, Quinn thought.

All Aunt Sarah cared about was the laundry list of products she wanted from the Far East. Brenna, too, had an agenda:

"I want a field report from you on the orphanage for the July issue," she said. "And a gamelan, to be paid for by me right down to the last cent of postage and I won't take 'no' for an answer."

"Gee, what should we send Mal?" Tam asked maliciously over noodles at a Tokyo International Airport bar during their brief stopover. "How about a big stuffed Hello Kitty?"

Mal, Quinn thought miserably. Tam had to bring him up. Mal was still trying to fly under the radar outside the eye of Hurricane Vienne. Quinn could not take Tam or Brenna's pleasure in the affair's scandalous aftermath. What about Tiffany, their son, the Quakers, and their fans? Private acts, public consequences.

He would have to come to grips with Mal sooner or later, as well as the Temps and Sydney and Chandler, whom Tam had taken to texting.

"I heard from Syd. She'll be meeting us in Jakarta with Sumarti," Tam said, as if he and El Syd were old friends. It half-annoyed Quinn that his mother and Tam were already texting buddies.

"Well, I can't rely on you, can I?" Tam said as they went through yet another security screening as they boarded yet another Eagles Airlines flight, this one bound for Singapore (3,301 miles, six hours).

No, he could not, Quinn thought as they settled into another first-class cabin and adjusted their watches yet again. Quinn's entire correspondence with his mother had consisted of a text reading, "Arriving in Jakarta Holy Week. Staying at the

Shang. Looking forward to seeing you and Chan before we head to the orphanage and then push off for a brief holiday in Bali."

Tam, on the other hand, had connected with her email, Twitter, Facebook, Instagram, and LinkedIn accounts in what Quinn thought was a misguided attempt to ingratiate himself with a woman who would find fault with God. Still, Tam persevered in a relationship that he already thought of as son- and mother-in-law.

"Such a sweet text from Syd," Tam said, smiling as he settled into his seat for the flight to Singapore. "She says she won't hear of us staying at the Shang, though she and Chan will be taking us there for Easter Sunday brunch. Instead, we'll be staying with them at their place. Gee, I can't wait to see the house you grew up in."

And I can't wait for you to get a full picture of that scene, Quinn thought. He wondered if Syd and Chan would be so accommodating if they knew the real nature of his relationship with "Mr. America," as *Sportin' Life's* Ken Ransom had described Tam in a recent "kiss-ass profile"— Tam's words.

"Syd says there's going to be a party in our honor. Wow, we really rate," Tam added, turning to Quinn with a smile before drifting off—again.

No, you do, Quinn thought, drawing a blanket up—again. But no matter how many blankets he drew up to his chin, he remained vigilantly awake.

"This is your captain speaking," he heard over the public address system.

Oh, captain, my captain, Quinn thought—one with Walt Whitman—as he looked around at Tam and the other slackers snoring, tongues lolling. I await your instructions, Quinn added mentally.

"The South Pacific is notoriously turbulent so I'm going to keep the seat belt sign on for just a bit longer."

I've never taken mine off, Quinn told him silently.

"Well, someone is prepared," the flight attendant said as she tugged at Quinn's secure belt. She smiled at him and he looked at her with the same wide-eyed gaze that greeted the flight officer who had reached out to him in the icy waters: "You're going to make it, son. You're going to be all right."

"I'll take care of his belt," Quinn told her, looking for any excuse to touch Tam. He stirred for a moment and Quinn brushed his hand. Such a touch was electric when there were no others to be had. Hours earlier, when they had passed the spot where he thought the plane went down—for unbeknown to Aunt Josie, he later read everything he could about it—he prayed:

Eternal rest grant unto them, O Lord, and may perpetual light shine upon them. May they rest in peace. Amen. May the souls and all the souls of the faithful departed through the mercy of God rest in peace. Amen.

Now he added:

We die with the dying:
See, they depart, and we go with them.
We are born with the dead:
See, they return, and bring us with them.

In Singapore, Quinn felt like a chrysalis shedding its cocoon before spreading its wings. He and Tam stripped down to polo shirts, jeans and navy-and-white boat shoes in the men's room of the Crowne Plaza. The entire hotel was a black-and-tan fantasy.

"This sure beats the Crowne Plazas back home," Tam said, as they shaved in the men's room. "I mean look at this bathroom. You can just imagine what the ladies room is like."

"I remember Aunt Lena saying it had a very pretty lounge," Quinn said, laughing at the memory. "But then Aunt Lena said she'd never been in a powder room that didn't have a lounge where you could immediately begin an intimate conversation. Women are amazing like that."

And men were not. If they were two women, they could walk arm and arm and no one would be the wiser. As men, they could not. Freedom was the price men paid for power.

Quinn considered himself and Tam in the mirror. "Asia has lots of five-star hotels and lots of over-the-top malls—if you have the money, that is. There's tremendous wealth—and tremendous poverty. I just don't want you to expect too much. Many of these countries are still developing."

"Would you stop," Tam said, waving his razor. "I'm going to love it," he added, mouthing, "as I love you."

In truth, Quinn was divided between wanting to ensure that Tam wasn't disappointed and wanting to shield his native land from any rejection by his lover. So he employed the same tactic he did on any given Sunday: He lowered expectations. But he didn't have to with Tam, for whom it was all new and wonderful. And it helped that Singapore—the Monaco of Asia—eased Tam's introduction to the Far East, with its gleaming white art museum and adjacent Protestant churches; its Broadway-style shopping district on Orchard Road; its orchid-lined highway, along which the army engaged in early morning maneuvers; and, best of all, its spectacular harbor, anchored by the Mandarin Oriental and a mall that made Madison Avenue and Rodeo Drive look like a collection of discount stores. For Tam—who believed fervently with Louis Pasteur that "Chance favors the prepared mind"—Singapore was like a long-lost twin.

"I am so glad we're going to have some time here on our return trip," Tam said, smiling at the flight attendants on Singapore Airlines—pretty, young women in expert makeup and upsweeps as tightly wound as the culture and colorful costumes.

Now they were headed to the land where tight upsweeps need not apply. The Jakarta of Quinn's childhood had been like New York without the Rudolph Giulianis and Michael Bloombergs. It remained to be seen how time had changed it—or not—and how the one he loved best would react to the place he loved most. Quinn could hardly breathe as the plane seemed to skim the tile roofs, palms trees and rice fields—a patchwork of red and green.

Outside, it hit him like the wall of humid air: Here was the place that had first formed him, that had set him on his course, where he most felt the spirit of his beloved Aunt Lena. It was all too much, and he was glad he was wearing shades, for the place of his birth moved him more than the elegant blonde in the white sheath who stood just beyond Customs and offered him a cheek.

"And this must be Tam," Sydney said, breaking into a grin that was like the sun emerging from the clouds and embracing him so heartily that an unsuspecting observer would've thought he were her son and Quinn the stranger.

They walked to a teeming curb, where Syd cautioned Tam to mind his wallet and passport as they dodged men hawking designer colognes.

There Sumarti—older, grayer, and slightly stooped—waited and Quinn embraced him, overcome with emotion. Sumarti, too, had tears in his eyes.

"Sumarti, this is Tam," Quinn said, quickly recovering. He longed to say, "This is Tam, my fiancé" but contented himself to watch his lover shake hands warmly with the man who had influenced his young life more than Sydney and Chandler combined.

"Sumarti, take the boys' bags," Sydney said, more concerned with logistics. "I'll sit in the front with you so the boys will have more room in the back. You'll want to shower and change, but we haven't much time. Chan's meeting us for drinks first at B.A.T.S.—that's the Bar at the Shang, Tam. And then we're joining the Parkers upstairs there for brunch. Everyone's dying to meet you, Tam."

Sumarti shot Quinn a look in the rearview mirror, but Quinn's face remained impassive. He was used to his mother's games. Once they'd had the power to hurt him. Now he put them on a shelf in his mind, like so many dust-collecting tchotchkes—or so he hoped.

"I would think everyone would be eager to see the native, favorite son and reigning Super Bowl MVP," Tam countered.

"Oh, we don't pay much attention to that here," Sydney said. "No one in Indonesia follows the NFL. It's all soccer, cricket, baseball—and tennis, especially from Australia. Which reminds me: You know who was just here, Tam? Evan Conor Fallon and Ryan Kovacs—the number one- and number two-ranked tennis players in the world. They came to play an exhibition and promote Indonesian tourism, an event I helped organize. Honestly, you should've seen how adorable they were in their Indonesian jackets and how respectful they were meeting the president and visiting a mosque— although I don't think their rivalry is as great as that of Alex Vyranos and Alí Iskandar. They were my favorites."

"And how much did all that adorability and respect cost your corporation and the Indonesian government?" Quinn couldn't help needling his mother.

"Oh, Evan and Ryan made a little more than four million dollars each," Sydney said. "But it was money well-spent as it goes to their charities, and their appearance here will generate millions more for my company and tourism. When you appeal to millions you make millions."

"And tennis players appeal to far more millions worldwide than American football players do," Tam added, "one of the many reasons I've always enjoyed traveling abroad in the off-season. No one notices me. Which still begs the question: Why would anyone here care about meeting me?"

"You transcend football, Tam. Everyone here knows who Tam Tarquin is."

"Well, I'm sure they'll be glad to see Quinnie, too."

Now Quinn caught Sumarti's eye. Yes, this was going to be an enlightening visit, he thought as the eclectic architecture, comforting in its familiarity, whizzed by and the baseball players in their unchanging yellow, green and white uniforms sent balls arcing in the morning mists on the fields of memory.

TWENTY-EIGHT

At home, nothing had changed, Quinn realized. Oh, his mother had long since converted his bedroom into a purple and gold guest room. (She probably did that the moment he left, he thought bitterly.) And Gaucho, his beloved dog, had long since given way to Gaucho 2.0, one of his pups. But nothing else had changed. His mother still knew how to push all the right buttons.

"Don't lollygag, Quinn," she called to him in the shower. "We don't want to keep your father waiting. Honestly, Tam, I don't know what he's doing in there. He's not prompt like you."

There were three or four insults in those remarks, Quinn thought as he scrubbed away twenty-two hours of stale airline air. First was that masturbatory inference, Sydney. And then a dig about his supposed tardiness. But most of all, stepfather, Sydney: Chan was his stepfather. Let's not pretend we're one big, happy family, even for the guest.

Indeed, his mother was so eager to go to brunch that he barely had time to present Nimen with the floral shawl he had brought her. If being in Jakarta and encountering Sumarti had brought him to the brink, seeing Nimen again had been the breaking point, and he wept openly as she sobbed in his arms. Nimen had changed. She was still pretty but also pretty worn. Adhi, her youngest, was now a medical student whose studies Quinn was funding. In return, he would one day be the doctor on staff at the orphanage. Now she was trailed by her oldest grandson, Ari, who loved the ball and glove Quinn gave him and immediately commandeered Tam for a game of catch.

"Tam, I'll show you all the places where you can get your mother and sisters designer shawls dirt cheap," Sydney said.

Was that another dig? Quinn wondered. She didn't seem to object to the expensive gift Tam gave her—an Alexis Bittar necklace with big celadon stones and a matching cuff bracelet. Quinn had to admit that it looked stunning on her white sheath. Now he sat in the front, chatting with Sumarti, as his mother monopolized her new best friend in the backseat.

"Excuse me," Quinn said, bracing himself as Sumarti careened around one traffic circle after another, "but, Tam, this is the statue I told you about, the Figure of Youth. Doesn't he look like Prometheus bringing fire to earth?"

Quinn could just imagine what Tam was really thinking about the rippling stud as he snapped a picture of him holding a disc aloft.

"I hope Quinnie hasn't been boring you, Tam, with his passion for the classics," Sydney said, smiling.

"Quinnie" was trying not to fume as they turned off the highway and swept onto a thoroughfare of McMansions, pausing before a large, white building with a circular drive. Sumarti popped the trunk and several officers inspected its nonexistent contents before waving them toward the entrance. He jumped out to open the door for Sydney, who set off the metal detector with her Alexis Bittar set. Quinn and Tam removed their cell phones, watches and matching engagement rings—which so far had gone unnoticed—and put them in a basket on a conveyor belt before passing through the metal detector.

"Tam, I think you're trying to get me in trouble," Sydney said as she was wanded by a female guard in a long dress and flowing head scarf. Was Syd flirting with him? Quinn thought, thunderstruck.

The Shangri-La in Jakarta was one of the most Western hotels in Asia, an ornate marble and gilded affair whose spacious, multi-tiered lobby had wrought-iron balconies and cream-colored furnishings. There was an art gallery in the back that sold the kind of middle-of-the-road Western art Brenna always said no one could object to even if it wasn't very good. A little bungalow labeled *Peter Rabbit's Hut* was designed to make the majority of Christian tourists feel right at home, as were the trees festooned with pastel-colored Easter eggs, the chocolate bunnies, and the endless playing of *Easter Parade.*

"I thought this was the most populous Muslim country on earth," Tam whispered to Quinn as they made their way through the lobby.

"Darling, money knows no religion," Quinn whispered back, smiling.

Or border: The kitchen at the Shang might as well have been a wormhole to New York. The brunch was filled with delicacies from Little Italy and a pizza to rival the former Famous Ray's. The chocolate pizza was still the best dessert Quinn ever had.

Jakarta, he recalled, saw itself as New York's sister city. Both had been colonized by the Dutch and the British. Both had an affection for deep dish apple pie and Delftware. Both were great going-out towns with big building projects and plenty of money changing hands under the table. But Jakarta still lacked the infrastructure and water supply that made New York attractive even on its most challenging days, not to mention the quality of life laws that the Big Apple had long since made its peace with, especially post-9/11.

If Tam was disappointed in Jakarta's shortcomings, he didn't let on as Sydney, chatting away, led them to the light-wood paneled bar where Chandler waited—still blond, still fit. Quinn glanced at the booth where he and Aunt Lena had dinner that night so many years ago. There, too, it had all begun for him. And there the ghosts quickly faded, giving way to a room filled with people who seemed to be on hand expressly to meet him and Tam—or at least Tam. Indeed, it quickly became clear why Sydney was so eager to get to the Shang. This was no ordinary brunch with the Parkers. This was like a full-out promotional event, complete with raised iPhone cameras and well-wishing expats clutching footballs, waiting for their moment with America's Son. Quinn was furious with his mother. But Tam took it all in stride—slapping the men on the back, complimenting the ladies on their outfits, kneeling to pose with the kids for selfies, signing every football.

One little boy shyly asked Quinn for his autograph. Quinn smiled and, crouching, signed the child's junior-size football, then produced one of the silver dollars he kept in his pockets for youngsters.

The boy ran off with a look of bliss and rapture on his face as if he'd just been given a million dollars. It made Quinn feel good. It was the only thing that did.

"Boy, if you had told me years ago that Syd and Chan's scrawny, little brown boy would grow up to become a big NFL star, I would've said you're crazy," Dennis Parker said, toasting Quinn over a drawn-out brunch.

Out of the corner of his eye, Quinn saw Tam wince. He put a restraining hand on his lover's knee under the table and with the other took a sip of Malbec. Nothing like drinking Argentine wine in Indonesia, but then, we're all internationalists, Quinn thought bitterly.

As the brunch group, which had swelled to include far more than the Parkers, posed for more pictures at an assortment of chocolate Easter bunnies afterward—no wonder movie stars despised the paparazzi, Quinn thought—he begged off, saying he needed a breath of air. He hurried down the stairs past a Chinese birthday party, the guests all dressed in red, and out the door down the winding paths that bordered the brimming kidney-shaped pools, pausing before the white, domed mosque. He listened to the melismatic call to prayer and answered it with a prayer of his own as there was for him only one God, who protected the weak and the strong alike and held them both accountable.

When he was a child, his mother would scold him when he ran off to visit the mosques. "Don't you know how dangerous this country is?" she'd say, shaking him. Now he thought wickedly of parading his lover inside one.

Speak of the devil. "There you are," Tam said, coming down another path. "This mosque is absolutely stunning. I'd love to visit it."

"We can arrange that," Quinn said, smiling.

Indeed, Quinn blessed the mosques, the cathedral and the National Museum for the precious time they gave him with his lover. At the National Museum, the two wandered among the voluptuous goddesses and rippling gods that dotted the sunken, grassy courtyard like figures on a chessboard—remnants of Indonesia's Hindu past, which had been exiled to Bali. The museum was a musty affair—mainly tribal artifacts—that seemed to be perpetually under construction. Despite this, or maybe because of it, Quinn was both sad for the place and terribly protective of it. His people were trying so hard. His people: Were they really his people? He had been away now slightly longer than he had lived there, long enough to imagine that the museum must've seemed threadbare to someone as sophisticated as Tam. A poor thing but mine own, Quinn thought, misquoting Shakespeare.

"Of course, it's not the Philadelphia Museum of Art," Quinn said.

"Would you stop," Tam said, grabbing him by the wrist in the courtyard. Quinn didn't know if anyone was watching, and he didn't care. He wanted Tam to kiss him, to take him right there, to love him and tell him everything would be all right. But Tam, having made his point, let go quickly. And Quinn turned away just as quickly. Why had they come halfway 'round the world when they could have been just as alone together at home?

Oh yes, the orphanage, his baby, for which he endured so much back home. All those Vienne Le Wood photo shoots and soirées; all the introductions to Brenna's influential Van Doozie relations, who'd embrace you one moment and cut you off the next—you never knew if you had those people by the head or the ass; all those probing questions from the press that left you drained and psychically naked; all the sponsors who thought they owned your soul; all that groveling in the hopes of a check, a contact. It was all worth it to nurture his child, and so were all the anxiety, anger, and anguish that welled up inside him now that he and Tam were with his family.

He couldn't wait to show Tam the actual site—five acres near the present orphanage. Blueprint in hand, Quinn walked him through the footprint of a state-of-the-art school and residence—more home than orphanage—a complex in bisque stucco with burnt-orange roofs surrounded by date palms, flower gardens and a pond with lizards and exotic birds for the children to observe and draw. There'd be a hydroponic garden and aquaponic farm where the students would learn the basics of agriculture as well as classrooms, a laboratory, and a library, all staffed by the best teachers he could find.

Quinn knew he was on dangerous ground. For every Indonesian official who applauded this extraordinary gesture by a native son who had made it big playing a sport called "football" that was somehow not soccer, there were many who worried the school would lack traditional Islamic values. Only Quinn's promise to include Islamic studies and personal reputation for religious tolerance—along with Syd and Chan's corporate connections, he thought, wincing—had gotten him this far. What if officials knew the real nature of his relationship with Tam? Quinn's skin flushed then turned clammy. He hadn't really thought that through, had he?

Tam was at Quinn's elbow, interrupting his disquietude with his teasing. "What, no sports?"

Quinn smiled sheepishly as he showed him where the ball field, tennis court, and swimming pool would be. Beyond them would be the dormitories. He wasn't merely showing off to Tam. Among the pre-wedding gifts Quinn had received from Tam was a pledge for most of the money to cover the building and startup costs. Quinn didn't feel right about accepting it. He had always made his way alone, though when he stopped to think about it, there had always been so many helping hands along the way, from dear Aunt Lena to Brenna and his teammates. Even Vienne and Mal had taught him valuable lessons. *I am a product of all that I have met*, Quinn thought with Tennyson's Ulysses.

He still felt funny taking the money. Was it because he had a hard time believing Tam when he said, "This is going to be our baby, as much as the ones we're going to have"?

Hope replaced fear when they visited the present orphanage, next to the building site. Quinn wanted Tam to see it for himself, to understand what he was really investing in, but perhaps more so to understand just what was at stake in their relationship. Tam had always been good with kids. Here they clung to his legs and climbed into his arms like creatures seeking shelter amid the branches of a spreading oak. All but two. They were brothers with brush cuts and large, dark eyes who, until recently, had worked the streets selling chewing gum—all at the ages of seven and six. They were hesitant, though, to receive the backpacks filled with goodies that Quinn and Tam had for each child and that were nearly as big as they. Only after Nir, the elder boy, gestured that it was all right did Lan come forward.

As they ran off to explore their newfound bounty on their own, Quinn watched Nir throw a protective arm over his brother's shoulder. They were all they had in the world, and yet, they were happy, giggling and chirping between themselves. Quinn almost lost it then. Fortunately, Adhi arrived at that moment to give them a guided tour. Strolling and chatting with him and Tam, Quinn found it hard to imagine that the poised young man before them was the same carefree child with the bad mushroom haircut who had once trailed his mother with her laundry basket.

Outside the orphanage—which was clean and bright but nothing like the place Quinn was planning—Adhi took his leave of them, and Tam grew quiet as he and Quinn waited for Sumarti to pick them up. He could see tears brightening Tam's eyes through one side of his sunglasses.

"I want to take them all home with us but especially Nir and Lan," he said.

"I know, I know," Quinn said. "But you realize that we could never adopt any of these children."

"Because we're gay," Tam said with bitter finality.

"That isn't even on the radar," Quinn said, "or, at least, on the public radar. There is no gayness here beyond don't ask-don't tell. There's no prohibition against it, although in northern Indonesia, open affection between men might earn them a caning. So it's not discussed or displayed.

"What I mean is that the Muslims have something called kafala, by which you can become a guardian or foster parent, as it were, but not the actual parent of an orphan. They don't believe in the mixing of blood. And then you'd have to be a Muslim to become the guardian of a Muslim child. Besides that, in Indonesia, we'd have to be a heterosexual couple of a certain age who'd been married for a number of years and living here for at least a couple as well. We wouldn't qualify for a whole host of reasons."

"I thought you said, 'money knows no religion.'"

"And it doesn't when it comes to catering to tourists. But this is a whole other thing."

They fell into a silence that left the next logical question unanswered: How the hell were they going to square their roles as orphanage benefactors in Indonesia with the reality of being fiancés?

It was all so sad, Quinn thought—the prejudice against others, many of whom had so much love to give as potential parents, as well as the orphanage itself, filled as it was with people who had been an afterthought in other people's lives—or no thought at all. Or who may have been greatly loved and relinquished only with unending regret.

He supposed he should've been grateful to El Syd. She had kept him, clothed him, fed him, educated him, and continued to support his efforts, at least in front of her friends. But she hadn't loved him—that was the hell of it. She couldn't bring herself to love him, and he couldn't forgive her for it—an attitude that calcified with each moment he and Tam spent with her and Chan. How is it that you can feel more for a complete stranger than you can for your own child? But Syd and Chan did. They couldn't seem to get enough of Tam, even planning a huge party that was ostensibly a fundraiser for the orphanage but that Quinn believed would never have materialized without Tam's presence.

Though she talked a good game, Syd thought the orphanage a fool's errand. Her idea of construction was the Regatta, a group of waterfront high rises in north Jakarta shaped like the sails of the tall ships, each oriented to the city for which it was named. Chan took "the boys," as Syd kept referring to them, to the New York Tower.

"This is just amazing," Tam said to Chan as they stared out from a penthouse balcony at the Java Sea. "How much would something like this set you back?"

"Oh, it's prohibitive," Chan said with a rare laugh, "for all but those with Tam Tarquin-size salaries."

"So what are we talking, a couple of million?" Tam asked before adding to Quinn sotto voce, "We could live here and have a weekend house in Bali—or vice versa."

"Are you crazy?" Quinn whispered back. He didn't know what to think with the mixed signals he was getting. On those rare nights when Syd and Chan weren't waltzing them all over the city—Turkasz for great Turkish food in a setting that looked like an Orientalist painting, all peacock blue and teal scalloped arches, cutouts and shimmering tiles; Aloïs for German food in a lodge that boasted wood, brass and waitresses in peasant blouses, matching white caps and floral skirts; and The Four Seasons hotel for the most elaborate international buffet brunch Tam had ever seen—they dined at home with Tam fitting right in, seated opposite Quinn and between Syd at one end of the table and Chan at the other. Sometimes Quinn would wander through the kitchen, where Nimen now held court with Ari, smiling at her as he did in the old days before heading out and acknowledging Sumarti, who still polished the SUV with the company plates—albeit a new, white one—endlessly.

In the backyard, the fallen frangipani blossoms still withered on the hard, almost plastic grass. As he walked amid their stout, sinewy trees, he could see Tam, Syd and Chan in animated conversation at the table, their bobbing heads reflecting various shades of amber and gold.

They went together, Quinn thought. Tam could be their son in a way he himself never would. And that aroused in Quinn a quality he always denied in himself, because it was so hateful to him— jealousy.

"It's worse than cancer," Aunt Josie had always cautioned him. She almost didn't have to. Whenever jealousy threatened to well up inside, he quickly countered it with gratitude for all he had and another Aunt Josie-ism by way of Jane Austen: "Till I have your disposition, your goodness, I never can have your happiness." Translation: To have what someone else has, you'd have to be that person with all the attendant qualities you might not otherwise have and all the challenges you might not otherwise want.

It was a lesson lost, he knew, on others. From a young age, he had seen the way jealousy ate at teammates, who compared everything from the size of their cocks to that of their contracts. In the Temps' clubhouse, everything was a competition, from who could remember the most Beyoncé lyrics to who had the prettiest wife and/or girlfriend. Though Quinn thought the latter a tie among Kelly, Dave's widow; Dana, Lleyton's intended; and Shawna, the baby mama of several of Jeremiah's brood, he believed no woman could hold a candle to Tam in the looks department. It wasn't just that Tam was an Apollo Belvedere come to life. It was that men in general burned as the hotter sex. Oh sure, they had long since ceded the beauty contest to women in their quest for power, but the best-looking guy was still better-looking than the best-looking woman, with a face that you could read across a room, a lushness, a musculature, a musky scent, a thrilling power that women lacked.

Multiply that to infinity and you had Tam. There was just something about him that went beyond bone and sinew. When he walked into a room, he was the one around whom others revolved, as they did at Eastern Promise, the bar near the "10,000 Block," the area of the city that contained all those houses that resembled the mansions on Sunset Boulevard. It was "Pressure Hour" at the Promise, with the anticipation of free Bintang, the mild, pale-yellow native brew, as long as no one quit the room—not even for the restrooms—for at least an hour.

Quinn and Tam sat at the bar, nursing the same glass—neither were huge drinkers, especially of beer—as the clocked ticked down the moment to free Bintang. They had not been long in the smoke-filled, wood-paneled bar—was there any smoke-free place in Jakarta?—when American and Canadian expats started drifting their way. And all to see Tam, Quinn thought. They were less interested in him, even though his team had won the Super Bowl. But he got it. He was a star. Tam was a legend.

And something more. The waiters and patrons who didn't know who Tam was gravitated to him. Even his polite refusal of a smoke was met with sympathetic smiles.

"That's all my sinuses need," he said. "No, seriously. It's one of the many reasons I never did drugs."

No one thought it odd that the great Tam Tarquin had Achilles sinuses. He had that ability to be believed no matter what he said, because he was so thoroughly himself—so calm, so comfortable in that oh-so-golden skin—whether he was at the Promise or a presidential press conference on fitness.

Quinn envied that ease. But more than that, he knew why he didn't possess it. And he traced it all back to her. If adulthood was a reaction to childhood, then Syd and Chan were the perfect training camp for Coach Smalley and company. It was, he realized, no mere coincidence that he seemed to wind up with hypercritical people to whom he was always proving his self-worth. It's what he had been bred on. And maybe it was just who he was, so that the person who did the most reproving was actually himself.

Quinn recognized that during the fundraiser at Syd and Chan's home a few days after Easter and before he and Tam set out for their Bali holiday. The cocktail party was like a microcosm of the universe—the guests, the planets in various orbits around the sun, Tam, impeccable in white pants, a white shirt open at the throat, and a navy blazer, with Syd clinging to his arm. She, in diaphanous sky-blue, never looked more radiant, guests said.

Chan, unable to compete, leaned in nearby. Quinn seethed on the fringes. Why? By every measure, the party was a success. They had raised $500,000 thanks in large part to auctioning off a clinic with Tam. But then, he was always good at selling himself, Quinn thought.

"Everyone," Syd said, raising a glass of Champagne—not her first, Quinn recognized---"I want to propose a toast to the man who has made all this possible—Tam Tarquin."

Quinn was stunned. Even Tam was embarrassed. Several guests glanced sideways at one another. Had she publicly repudiated him, her rejection could not have been more complete, Quinn thought.

"Well, actually, the person who has made all of this possible—the new orphanage and thus, this party—is Quinn Novak," Tam said in response. "Quinn, come up here and take a bow."

But Quinn demurred, a smile frozen on his face. It was awkward as hell—or at least he hoped it was. How dare they, Quinn thought. Who the fuck did she think she was? And what in hell was Tam doing?

Quinn held it in for the remainder of the party. The fate of the new orphanage depended on his composure. But he barely said a word through a joyless dinner at B.A.T.S., and turned in early the minute they returned to the house. It was not long before there was a knock on the door.

"May I come in," Tam said.

"If you must."

"What's wrong?"

"As if you didn't know."

"No, I honestly don't. I mean, apart from you acting like an asshole."

"I'm acting like an asshole?"

"Yes. You were uptight all night with the guests whose good will, not to mention cash, we're going to need if we're going to make that new complex a reality, and you were rude as hell to Syd and Chan at dinner. Now out with it: What gives?"

"Oh, forgive me, but if you recall, the new orphanage was my idea, my project. As for Syd and Chan—as you so chummily call them—there, too, I've been at it a lot longer than you. So you'll have to excuse me if I'm a bit possessive of this place and their insults."

"Excuse you? A bit possessive?" Tam's voice got softer but more urgent. "Listen, honey, I came halfway 'round the world with the intent to charm, kill everyone with kindness and present the face of the un-Ugly American and why? Not for me. Whatever you think, I do not need an audience 24/7 and, so far, this has not exactly been my idea of a vacation. But I did this with one purpose, or rather one person, in mind—you. Cultivating my future mother-in-law and father-in-law, getting to know the people and the culture in which you were raised, making your cause my own—all for you."

"Wow, that's so big of you."

"Well, actually it is. But I'm not looking for any thanks. I'm merely looking to share a life. Yet you keep pushing me away."

"Me? You're the one who hasn't touched me in months, at least not as a man should be touched."

"Because you were sick. You weren't ready."

"Bullshit."

"Because I was scared, OK? Because we hurt you, not intentionally but sort of intentionally on the field, because I knew how Mal had hurt you, had hurt me."

"I never held that against you. It comes with the territory. It's part of the job. We sacked you, too.

"But no one on your team kicked me the way Kasmerek kicked you. We knew what kind of guy he was, an enforcer. And when I saw you collapse at that press conference..."

Tam stood there with his hands in his back pockets, tears streaming down his face. Quinn looked at him but said nothing.

"Look," Tam said finally, "maybe this trip was a mistake. Tomorrow morning, I think I'm going to head home. I'll make some excuse about being called back for training. You should head back, too. I don't think it's any good for you here anymore, Quinnie. I don't think you'll ever find the answers you're seeking, because I don't think you really want them."

Don't, Quinn thought. Don't let him go. But he did. And that night, he cried himself to sleep, feeling powerless to move.

You are such a coward—a jealous, stupid, foolish coward—to throw the chance of it all away, he thought in the harsh light of the next morning. When he emerged from his room, however, he didn't find Tam packed to leave. Rather he, Syd, and Chan were sitting in silence at the dining room table—one of Nimen's fabulous breakfasts, a mix of American and Indonesian foods, spread before them. Only the scene was anything but a congenial meal. Instead of gazing at Tam with her usual rapt adoration, Syd had that look—halfway between anger and sorrow—of a parent whose golden child has just been expelled from college with criminal charges pending. Chan, too, seemed stunned.

"What time is Sumarti taking you to the airport?" Quinn inquired, defeated. "I'll come see you off."

"I'm not going anywhere, except to Bali with you," Tam said. "Sit down. Please."

"Yes, I think you'd better," Syd said.

Now it was Quinn's turn to be exultant and Syd's to seethe. Quinn had to admit to a certain first-time schadenfreude. It was, however, short-lived as he realized Syd's discomfort was somehow about to become his own.

"Tamarind has just informed us that you and he are lovers. Is this true?"

Tamarind—ooh, the use of a formal name, always the kiss of death, Quinn thought.

"Look, Syd—"

"Is it true?" she asked again in her iciest manner as if she were a "just answer the question" trial lawyer.

He realized this was the moment in which he could free himself of her at last. "Yes," was all he said.

"You could not have hurt me more deeply than if you said you were a murderer. Although you have always been a mean person. I remember how mean you were as a child. No matter how I tried, you were always mean, especially to me."

"Wow," Quinn said. "A murderer, huh?" They were about to trade blows. "And mean? Pot, meet kettle. Or should that be cappuccino machine meet Keurig?"

"Snark doesn't become you," Chan chimed in. "Have you considered how this would reflect on your careers?"

"Thank you," Syd said.

"To say nothing of how it would affect your

mother and me," Chan added. "You two will waltz out of here the way you waltzed in. But we live here amid these people. I wonder, too, if you've given any thought to what this will mean for the orphanage you are both so intent on building. Guess not."

"Honestly, Chan, I don't think anyone gives a damn about this stuff anymore," Tam offered.

"Really?" Chan countered. "The very fact that you two haven't 'come out,' as you people would say, shows that others do care very much about this 'stuff'—or at least that you must think so, otherwise you wouldn't have felt the need to hide your relationship. And have you been having sex here? Is that why you're going off to anything-goes Bali?"

"Please, Chandler," Syd said. "Not at breakfast."

"No, not at breakfast, Chandler," Quinn said sarcastically. "God forbid that we should have a conversation about me fucking my fiancé."

"If you're going to be vulgar, Quinton Day Novakovic, you can just go to your room," Syd said.

He and Tam looked at each other and burst out laughing.

"With all due respect, Sydney, your son is not a child anymore," Tam said.

"With all due respect?" Syd said, incredulous. "With all due respect, sir, this is still my house, and you have proved to be a major disappointment, not what you appeared to be at all. We'll leave off for now how and when you corrupted my son."

"Trust me, the corrupting was mutual," Quinn said, and he and Tam started giggling like conspiratorial truants. He hated to admit it, but he was beginning to have fun with Syd and Chan's discomfort.

"Look, we can head over to the Shang right now," Tam said sharply. "We were going to stay there anyway."

"Why not? You'd fit right in with the Saturday-night hookers," Chan said. "I think they're the wrong sex for you two, though. But I hear there are young men as well."

"Chandler, please," Syd said, exasperated.

"Before we clear out, though, I think we need to set a few things straight," Tam said. "I—we—came here to inform you of our engagement and make our peace and build a relationship. We both very much want that."

"I doubt very much that Quinton wants that," Syd said.

"Typical," Quinn said.

"You've always wanted to hurt me from the time you were very young."

"And whom did I learn that from, mother, huh? When were you ever a mother to me?"

"Oh, God, this is not to be borne. Always on the same binge. 'Mommy and Daddy didn't love me.' Take a number, Quinnie, and get on the end of a very long line. My own father beat my mother mercilessly. They both died too young and too late, and we were raised by a disapproving aunt and a randy uncle, which is why we all escaped—me overseas, your Aunt Lena into her writing and your Aunt Sarah into whatever she's into—as soon as we could. God, Sarah—and Selena. You killed her, Quinn. She wouldn't have come back here and been on that flight if she hadn't come to get you."

"That's below the belt, Syd," Tam said as Quinn

sat there, crushed. "He didn't kill her anymore than I hurt him when we sacked him in the Super Bowl and Kasmerek kicked him. Yes, we make choices. But the plane might not have gone down. Quinn might not have gotten a concussion. Things happen. Anyway, you forgot one thing about your relationship with your son. You were the one who got pregnant."

Now who was hitting below the belt, Quinn thought.

"Yes, I got pregnant," Syd said, stunned. "I made a mistake."

Here her voice quivered for one of the few times in Quinn's experience, but Syd quickly recovered as she looked at Chan. "And then I met a wonderful man who understood, who was willing to make a life with a woman who was pregnant with another man's child. That's no small thing."

"Sydney, they can't understand," Chan said, exhaling. "It's not like they could produce a child together."

"Maybe not," Tam said quickly, "but we can certainly father children and we can adopt. And we intend to once we're married. But I don't think we can before you set Quinn free, Sydney. Whether or not you two can forgive each other, he needs to know who and where his real father is. A man has a right to his identity, his whole identity. And I think at last this will set you free as well."

That night, as Quinn was prepared to drift off again alone, there was another knock on the door. It was Tam in nothing but a robe and a finger to the smile on his lips. He tossed off the robe, revealing himself fully alive to his passion, and slipped into bed.

"Obviously, I can't save this for Bali," he said. "Now you are mine at last."

"I think," Quinn said, falling into his arms, "that I was always yours as you were always mine."

They dozed and woke throughout the night, making sweet, tight, quiet love in their waking moments.

"Sex is always hard," Quinn said, panting as they faced each other, straining, their legs entwined, their bodies beaded with sweat yet quivering slightly, exposed to the air conditioning.

"Hard is a good thing," Tam said, laughing, shifting slightly inside Quinn.

"No, I mean, it's difficult, isn't it, not an easy thing to give yourself and receive in return."

"Uh, is there a football metaphor in this, Quinnie? Hey, lover, I'll go deep," and he planted a long, slow kiss on his mouth then turned Quinn on his back and thrust inside him.

In the morning, Quinn woke content in his lover's arms. Was there anything more delicious, he thought, snuggling next to Tam, than lying in bed with your lover, knowing you didn't have to get up for work? He reached for the sheet quickly, though, as the door opened. Tam had forgotten to lock it. Damn. Nemin. But she merely laughed while putting a finger to her lips as she gathered the scattered clothing into her laundry basket and just as gracefully and silently exited.

Tam will just have to shower with me and wear some of my clothes, Quinn thought, shifting in his arms with a smile on his face.

When they boarded the Garuda Airlines flight a few hours later, Tam handed Quinn a piece of paper from Sydney with a name, a lead that might hold the key to Quinn's past and their future.

Quinn shook as he put it in his left pocket and patted it.

"Are you traveling to Bali for business or pleasure?" the pretty stewardess in traditional dress said as she handed them hot hand towels in preparation for the breakfast after takeoff.

"Bit of both I think," Tam said, smiling.

He looked around, muttered, "Oh, hell," and as the plane took off, threaded his fingers through Quinn's.

TWENTY-NINE

If Jakarta were New York in July, Bali was New Orleans—or, better yet, Florida—in August. Quinn and Tam arrived mid-morning at the revamped Ngurah Rai International Airport in the capital city of Denpasar, where they were met by Pierre, the driver from the Grand Hyatt Bali in Nusa Dua.

Pierre was an amiable, talkative type— emphasis on talkative—who spoke perfect English. He peppered Quinn with questions about life in New York, which Pierre seemed to think was a cross between *Home Alone 2* and *The French Connection*, and especially the nature of their visit.

"Business and pleasure," Tam said, smiling. Quinn thought he looked a little peaked after the plane ride. But he revived with a complimentary fruit cocktail on the balcony of one of the Grand Hyatt's fiery, red tile-roofed stucco villas, connected by a series of footpaths and footbridges that cascaded down to the Indian Ocean.

"Would you look at that," Tam said, watching the teal-colored water break foamy on the shore.

"So was it all worth it?" Quinn asked, standing on the balcony beside him, drink in hand.

"And then some," Tam said.

Their suite consisted of a large common area— kitchenette, living room, dining space—between two bedrooms with king-size beds and baths with showers and Jacuzzis.

"It's a shame that we're going to have to

unmake two beds when we're only going to be using one," Tam said playfully, "you know, so no one's the wiser to what we're up to."

"But we could take turns," Quinn said, licking his lips, "my room for love in the afternoon..."

"And mine for steamy sex under the stars," Tam said, chasing Quinn into his bedroom. Tam fumbled with his iPhone, dialing up Martin Solveig's *Ready 2 Go*.

"Subtle, Tam," Quinn said, laughing. "Real subtle."

But he pumped up the volume and wriggled beneath him in anticipation as Tam tugged at the flies of their jeans. Was there anything Tam didn't do gracefully? Quinn thought, marveling at the way he could slip Quinn's jeans and Calvins down, caressing the curve of his butt as he trailed his fingers across his mossy groin and cupped his balls before stroking his cock upward and unrolling a condom downward. Taking Quinn's hand, Tam instructed him to do the same to him before he rested at the gateway to Quinn's pleasure.

It was at such moments that Quinn was his sexiest and happiest, relishing the tickling tease before the thrust and parry, when he could feel the skin at the tip of his shaft retracting and the vein behind it throbbing, and he didn't think he could take the pleasure and pressure anymore. It was always over too soon—no matter how skillful and athletic they were going about it, lightly tugging on each other's balls to hold back the floodtide of orgasm. The only consolation was that there was always the promise of next time.

"Was that what you would describe as a quickie?" Quinn said, resting on his lover's wildly beating heart.

"Think of it more as an appetizer with a fruit cocktail chaser," Tam said, reaching for his drink. "Let's hit the showers together and then the beach I've been hearing so much about."

But they didn't make it down to the beach until late afternoon thanks to a shower that echoed the rapture of an hour before.

"OK, that has to be an NFL record," Tam murmured as they shivered in each other's arms. "Swimming in the Indian Ocean is going to seem like nothing after this."

Ocean swimming—particularly Indian Ocean swimming—was, however, even more of a challenge than two titanic orgasms in one afternoon, Quinn thought. The Indian Ocean may not be as big as the Atlantic or as vast as the Pacific, but it was deep—"tideless deep," to borrow a phrase from Henry James. I may be smaller than my sisters, she seemed to say in a whisper that grew to a roar, but I am mighty and mysterious. Quinn thought of the tsunami and all those souls on Malaysia Arilines' Flight 370, who rested beneath the ocean's deceptive waves. He watched fearfully as Tam swam against them, only to be turned back. He swam out after him and together they found themselves borne back to the shore on white foam, like a pair of Aphrodites rising from the sea.

Certainly, the other beachgoers looked at them appreciatively—Tam in his long black lace-up swim shorts, Quinn his negative image in white ones. At first, Quinn wondered if the other guests were staring at them, because they secretly intuited that they were a couple. Or maybe they somehow recognized who they were. But how stupid was that, Quinn thought, when those around them—Russians, Japanese, and Indians—were unlikely to have a real awareness of the NFL. No, people were glancing at them, Quinn finally realized, blushing, because theirs were easily the two best-looking bodies on the beach.

That didn't stop Russian grandpas with potbellies from wearing Speedos, however. Even the ladies—who could be counted on, Quinn assumed, as the more discerning, fashionable sex—favored itsy-bitsy, teeny-weeny bikinis, forget the yellow polka dots, regardless of figure types.

"Maybe it's the place itself," Tam said as they strolled up a stone path to their villa. "There's a sensuality here I've never experienced before, a languor. You don't want anything to stand between the sun, sand, and sea and your bare skin."

They paused before a Hindu temple at the edge of the hotel property that was a study in filigree with soaring, dark brown wood spires and niches filled with gods and goddesses, limbs entwined in various gymnastic, *Kama Sutra*-style poses, the female figures' globular breasts and buttocks sculpted to bursting.

"And yet, here's a sign that says, 'No menstruating women may enter,'" Tam said. "Wonder how they'd feel about two gay men?"

"There's actually a pretty active gay scene here," Quinn said, "and plenty of gay 'weddings,' by which I mean you would have to get married somewhere else. As you've surmised, Bali's a mass of contradictions. There's no gay marriage and yet, plenty of ceremonies. Basically, they don't think in terms of gay and straight so much as married and unmarried. The big strike against us is that we're not hitched."

"Yet." Tam looked at Quinn with a smile. "I think we're going to need another shower."

"Three for three," Tam announced triumphantly at dinner, twirling his spaghetti carbonara. "And we haven't even been here a full day." He considered a forkful of pasta. "I thought carbonara was made with prosciutto."

"It's some kind of beef substitute. There's no pork in a Muslim country," Quinn offered.

"Got it. No, it's delicious. You couldn't find better spaghetti carbonara in Philly or San Fran. I think the buffet is the second best thing about the trip so far."

Tam took two spoons and scooped a generous helping on a side dish for Quinn as they sat in a colonnaded pavilion by a pond filled with lizards, birds and fish.

"Eat up," Tam said. "We're going to need our strength if we're going to begin our search tomorrow. Where did you say we were off to?"

Kuta: about a half-hour drive from Nusa Dua and a world away from the wealthy tourism of the Grand Hyatt, with its yoga spa and village-like network of sleek shops selling $500 sarongs. To get to Kuta, you careened around jug handles and traffic circles enveloped in the dust of construction. Occasionally they yielded a marble like the ripped Ghatotkacha driving his equally well-muscled steeds into battle. As Pierre sped over the road and chatted away, country music blared from the radio—Pierre having decided that since Quinn and Tam were Americans, they must be country music fans—and Tam captured the hunky Ghatotkacha with his cell.

There were more such bodies to behold in the flesh at their destination. Kuta was where the kids from Perth on a shoestring budget hung out, their skin gleaming like the tin shops that collided with improbable portico-ed marble buildings on the main drag.

Kuta, Quinn knew, was also where anything went and you lived to make the rupiah today, for who knew what tomorrow would bring? So you pressed the flesh to close the sale, and you could not walk down the street but for the pressing merchants. Quinn worried how Tam would react, being stopped and touched every few feet, but he needn't have. Back home, no one was more used to people coming up to him, touching him, imploring him, even occasionally snipping a lock of his hair, as if he were a gridiron Ghatotkacha. On that demigod's home field, Tam just smiled or laughed as he and Quinn moved on, saying, "Thanks, but shopping later." He would allow nothing to dissuade them from their mission.

"I mean," he was saying, "how hard could it be to find someone named Tjok? That's an unusual name."

They were eating a vegetable, rice and meat dish at one of the local eateries. "It's chicken," Quinn had advised. "It's always chicken."

Tam considered a piece of meat he had speared, tasted it and inclined his head as if to say, "Good."

"And to answer your question, it's as if someone had written down the name John on a piece of paper in America. Tjok is a very common name here, and it's only the name of a guy who might lead us to my real father. Face it: this is a needle in a haystack."

"Maybe so but you don't give up before you've even started. When you're down 33-5, you don't throw in the towel. You dig in and start chipping away and that's what we have to do. Now we have a place, here, and a name. This place is not that big. Someone is bound to know or remember something."

They waited until the sun went down and hit the beach. That's where the "Kuta cowboys" plied their trade, lining the shore to service the rich, mostly European ladies—and, more discreetly, gentlemen—in search of a little adventure and sexual release. Most of the cowboys were married with wives who approved of their husbands' adventures in the sex trade as a way to earn extra Euros or even American dollars. There was no shame in "cowboying up" in a culture of such fluidity. But that didn't make it any easier.

"We're looking for a guy who's my fiancé's father." The concept was met with confused stares, giggles, head-shaking and, once, even an offer of a child sex slave.

"Look," Tam said, the color rising in his face, "the last thing we would ever do is harm an innocent and if we see or hear of anything like that we're reporting it to the authorities."

Not long after that encounter, he and Quinn were approached by two English women who were friends and looked like bookends, if bookends were short, lumpish creatures with rounded calves, chicken-wing arms, steel-wool bobs, and whose most distinguishing characteristic was a nondescript doughy quality.

"How much?" one said as they both smiled, then laughed.

"How much for what?" Tam said.

"Ooh, coy. I like that. You know. How much for a bit of fun with what's in there?"

She reached over and tugged at the waistband of Tam's shorts, revealing smooth, golden skin and a hint of man-fur that sent a current through Quinn's cock.

But he looked at Tam with a horror that he could only imagine matched Tam's own.

"No, ladies, I'm afraid you have the wrong idea. We're tourists like you."

"Ooh, tourists looking to earn a little pocket change perhaps?"

"We have jobs," Quinn said softly. "We're football players."

"Did you hear that, Audra? Footballers. Which team are you with, luv? I don't think we've seen you play Manchester U."

Actually, Quinn thought, Tam had appeared at Wembley Stadium in London when the Miners and the Steers had faced off in an early-season game. Somehow, he didn't think the two women had caught that one.

"No, we're American football players," Quinn corrected.

"No doubt that's how you got those big muscles," Audra's friend offered, sidling up to him. Audra clearly preferred Tam, who smiled and said, "Look, ladies, Quinn and I are lovers. In fact, we're going to be married."

"Congratulations," Audra said. "When's the big day?"

"We haven't set one yet," Tam said. "But we're committed to each other."

"That's wonderful. But while we're all here, may we watch? We'd be happy to pay. Think of the fun of it, Gretchen. It would be like live gay porn."

THIRTY

"Well, I think we've hit a new low," Quinn said.

They were at The Mulia, one of Bali's newer hotels, later that night, sipping Cosmos and eating shrimp tempura in a blue room the size of half a football field, with huge, cream-colored egg-beater chandeliers, floor-to-ceiling niches filled with cinnabar jars and at least nine stations serving different kinds of cuisine. The dessert station alone had a separate room.

"Really? I think we're making progress," Tam said.

"Progress? We were mistaken for child molesters and hustlers."

"Exactly, in that order. Being seen as a prostitute is a lot better than being thought of as a child molester. We're getting closer to our goal of finding your father. We keep putting ourselves out there, we're going to meet someone who knows something."

"We keep putting ourselves out there and we're not going to need the NFL, because we'll be in a whole other league, if you get my drift."

Just then, something caught Quinn's eye—or rather someone.

"Oh my God, it's the ladies from the beach."

He and Tam tried to shrink in their booth but the women spotted them, trailed by two men—clearly their husbands—who had put two and two together, come up with five and were none too happy about it.

"What are you boys doing here?"

"Audra, how do you know these men?" her husband said.

"Oh, we met your wives while we were all shopping in Kuta," Tam said, smiling at Quinn as they rose to kiss the ladies on the cheek and shake hands with their husbands.

"Ladies, did you find those Rolex watches you were looking for? Oops, I hope I haven't spoiled the surprise for your hubbies?"

By the time Tam finished weaving the fiction of the shopping excursion and encounter, making it clear that he and Quinn were a couple, the men were slapping them on the back and inviting them to visit whenever they were in the UK.

"Nice folks after all," Tam said. "We should invite them to the wedding."

"You're irrepressible," Quinn said as the couples moved to their table and he and Tam resumed their seats.

But Quinn wondered if even Tam's irrepressibility would be enough. Afterward, they strolled through The Mulia's own version of the Hanging Gardens of Babylon, watched over by lotus-bearing caryatids that crowned a series of palm-studded marble terraces. As Quinn and Tam threaded their way down the marble staircases, an electrical storm arose, the lightning piercing the waves to a soundtrack of thunder as the light rain gave the steps a slippery, silvery sheen that was reflected in Quinn's tears.

"What's the matter, my love?" Tam said. "Oh, Quinnie, don't you see? Even if we never find him, I will be your father, mother, brother, everything, and you will be mine." He took him in his arms.

"Don't, Tam, someone might see."

"Oh, who's going to see or know? And anyway, who cares? It's the twenty-first century, for God's sake."

But even in the twenty-first century, there were still people who cared, especially in this part of the world, Quinn thought as he kissed Tam lightly at first, then deeply, feverishly, hands roaming wildly, his whole body lit by lightning, still playing with fire like the young Prometheus who had been his touchstone. From the restaurant, he could hear Adele wailing *Fire to the Rain*—or was it merely the soundtrack that throbbed in his head?

They rode back to the Grand Hyatt wordlessly. Wordlessly, their mouths found each other the moment they shut the door of the suite behind them. Wordlessly, their bodies crashed on each other's shores, no barriers now just skin on skin in the cool air.

It wasn't until they were about to drift off—cradling each other—that Tam spoke. "I love you, fatherless child."

THIRTY-ONE

"We're looking for a man named Tiok," Tam said. "We think he can help us find Quinn's father."

They were back on the beach, explaining the situation, flashing rupiah or U.S. dollars when they thought it would help, getting nowhere. And time was running out.

"Let's just enjoy the rest of our vacation and forget this," Quinn said as they took a break from the beach with burgers and fries at the Hard Rock Café. "It was always a long shot anyway."

"No," Tam said, putting his burger down and wiping his mouth. "It's going to happen. I can feel it. We just have to have faith and keep up hope."

"What about love, or are we only interested in two of the three theological virtues?"

"We'll always have that," Tam said, smiling and patting Quinn's arm.

Back on the beach, the sun was setting, along with Quinn's patience. Tam was as indefatigable as a pollster, stopping people, mostly men of a certain age, left and right. Quinn became aware that they were being watched by a young man.

"Do you know a guy named Tjok?" Tam asked.

"Maybe," the young man said. He was slight, brown, smiling and cagey, with a thatch of dark hair and a side part so deep that it looked like a comb-over, not that he needed one.

"You," he motioned to Quinn, "look like someone I know. Come and see."

Tam shrugged. "What have we got to lose?"

Quinn thought it a wild goose chase at best. Maybe the guy was just stringing them along for cash. Worse, maybe it was a trap. But they got in a cab with him, Tjok—whether or not that was his real name was anybody's guess—excitedly directing the driver of the Blue Bird taxi in Balinese. Tam and Quinn observed from the back seat, holding on as they hurtled from one roundabout to another.

"Do you have any idea what he's saying?" Tam asked Quinn.

"I think he's directing him to a house not far from here."

It was about halfway between Kuta and Nusa Dua in a quiet area filled with orange canna lilies and red bromeliads. The modest house, which stood by the water at the end of a long dirt road, would not have been out of place in a coastal suburb in the American South. Tam paid the driver but instructed him to stay. He was taking no chances.

"Wait, please," Tjok said. He ran into the house and, soon, those outside heard raised voices. Not long after that, a woman emerged with Tjok— pretty, slender, and of that indeterminate age that many women in midlife, particularly dark-skinned women, are. Quinn figured she was, however, old enough to be his and Tam's mother and was indeed Tjok's mother. She smiled at Tam as any polite hostess might but gasped and burst into tears, a hand covering her trembling lips, when she looked at Quinn. She embraced him then and after a while, he, arms open, embraced her as well, not knowing what else to do and not wanting to be ungracious and cause her any more distress.

"You," she said at last, "are my husband's son. You come in now, please."

Inside, the house was small, clean, and white—more beach house or cottage than a formal home, with comfortable wicker furnishings, lived-in cushions, and books, pictures, and mementoes strewn haphazardly if no less lovingly. Quinn thought about his own mother's palatial home with everything arranged at right angles for dynamism and the strangeness of a life in which a man could possibly make love—if you could call it that—to two such disparate women.

Of course, Quinn's father—if indeed the man who had yet to appear was his father—had not loved his mother. He had merely serviced a young woman who had too much to drink one night and took a dare from the friends who had always been more important to her than family, earning a souvenir she neither wanted nor thought she could get rid of.

Tjok's mother, Pina, disappeared into the kitchen, returning with oolong tea in a red, yellow and blue teapot with a dragon pattern and a bamboo handle and matching cups, along with a plateful of ginger cookies.

"My husband in back," she said. "He not well."

Her eyes pooled. "He dying. Please. You wait. I tell him, then you come."

Up until then, Quinn had been enjoying the house, the tea, the cookies, and the young, curious faces that peered at him and Tam and that belonged, he assumed, to Pina's younger children.

"I think we should go," he said to Tam. "We've obviously come at a bad time. I mean, what are we doing here? Even if this man is my father, and that's a big if, we've come too late."

"No, I don't think so," Tam said. "I think we've arrived just in time."

Pina returned to the living room then. "You come."

In a back bedroom, Quinn saw a thin man with a concave chest propped up in a white bed, gasping for air as he drowned in the sea of himself. Here is the other half of my soul, Quinn thought, as he looked at a face that was an older, ravaged version of his own.

He sat by the bed and took one of the man's— Artha's—offered hands.

"Hello," Quinn said softly. "I've come a long way—across a lifetime—to find you."

The man smiled faintly and turned slightly to gaze at Tam, who took his other hand as he sat on the opposite side of the bed.

"This is my friend," Quinn said. "No, this is my lover, my fiancé and soon my husband."

"Thank you for that," Tam said. "Sir, we're glad we found you and are happy to help you and your family in any way we can. We ask only one thing— your blessing on our marriage. You see, I love Quinn, but I don't think he can love me, love anyone really completely, until he's whole, until you give him your blessing as his father and let him go. Can you do that, sir?"

Tam turned to Pina. "Does he understand?" She was weeping now but composed herself to say something in Balinese.

Artha looked from Quinn to Tam, then upward at something they could not glimpse. He nodded and then closed his eyes, drifting off, but only for a short while.

They sat there a long time holding his hands, the three—father, son, and lover—connected by circumstances and their deepest desires. After a while, Artha drifted off again and Tam rose first, kissing him on the forehead and placing his hand on his groaning chest. Quinn followed suit.

"We'll be back tomorrow," Tam said to Pina, pressing some cash into her hands as he engulfed them with his own. He patted Tjok on the shoulder and tousled the younger children's hair—his future brothers- and sisters-in-law.

"You realize that this could all be a scam," Quinn said back at their suite.

"You don't really believe that, do you?" Tam said.

No, he didn't. That night, Quinn dreamed that he and Tam were at a theater in New York. Artha, healthy and brimming with bonhomie, came in and sat down, smiling as he opened the program for the performance. But when Quinn rose to speak with him, he morphed into a mummy who slowly undid his wrappings to reveal—nothing but air.

Quinn woke with a start, went to the bathroom and settled back in bed, nestling in Tam's contented arms. The man could sleep through a nuclear attack, Quinn thought. Eventually, he, too, fell asleep and dreamt that he was back at Templars Stadium, only it wasn't a stadium at all but an office building afloat on the Jersey marshes, and Quinn had to work with others at a long bench in a hallway.

"But I can't concentrate," he told Smalley, a suit behind a big desk.

"If you can't concentrate, that's your affair," Smalley said before he, too, vanished.

Quinn woke with a start at five, fell back to sleep and didn't wake again until Tam, dressed and leaning over him, shook him gently, kissing him.

"Hey," Tam said softly, "Tjok called. Artha passed at two thirty. He waited for you, Quinnie. He waited for you."

Artha's body was cremated and his ashes cast into the sea after Pina and Tjok were rowed several yards from shore. Quinn watched with Tam and his half-siblings from the beach, having witnessed the burst of cremation fire from the temple as competing gamelans played and various relatives chatted, moved about and danced even, as if at a rock concert. Then they saw Pina, with Tjok at her side, holding the red urn, one hand on top, the other on the bottom as the two stepped carefully into the boat. Quinn thought back to Dave's funeral and how someone could be alive, however sickly one moment, and then reduced to a box no bigger than a tea caddy. He trembled slightly, Tam's arm steadying him as Pina released Artha's remains and his essence returned to the elements.

"Now we no see him," she later told Quinn. "But he watch us."

As the senior men in the family paddled Pina and Tjok back to shore, Quinn, Tam and the others there set lit paper lanterns adrift on the water, symbolizing the souls of the ancestors. Quinn and Tam crossed themselves, bowed their heads, and prayed.

At the house, they shared a meal with the family in the backyard, while dancers in red, green, and gold costumes performed. Quinn wandered alone along an overgrown stone path toward a wooded area.

"Tam," he called, "come look at this."

In the dusky wetlands, fireflies twinkled, like so many fallen stars.

THIRTY-TWO

Tjok called early the next morning. "My mother would like to see the two of you," he said.

At the house, she spoke in Balinese to Tjok, punctuating her words with gestures to make sure he understood.

"My mother has a request," he said, half-embarrassed.

"Tjok, whatever you need, we're happy to help," Tam said.

"No, no, it's nothing like that," Tjok said, laughing, "only that she wishes to dance at your wedding."

"Well, how 'bout it?" Tam said to Quinn.

"How 'bout what?"

"Getting married."

"Here? Are you kidding? I can just imagine it now: The selfie seen 'round the world. Are you crazy?"

"Look, Quinn, I know gay marriage isn't legal here. But a ceremony of some sort would please Pina, and it would be a sign of our commitment to each other—a preview of the real thing. Besides, we owe it to our future children."

"Will there be future children? Will there be a future, is what I suppose I'm really asking."

"What's the matter, Quinnie?"

"I can't, Tam. I can't marry you."

"I know all this is sudden, but—"

"No, you don't understand. I can't marry you anytime, anywhere. I can't ever marry you."

Quinn walked out of the house then and wandered down the path to where he had seen the fireflies. He didn't have to turn around when he heard footsteps. He recognized Tam's footfall.

"That's it? We've come all this way—I don't mean in miles but in time—for it to end like this? Because I've got to tell you, I won't let it. I'm going to fight for us even if you won't."

"Don't you see? We can't do what we were meant to do—and I don't think I fully understood that until this moment—and be openly gay and married. I don't know. Perhaps I'm more Indonesian than I thought."

Tam was quiet for what seemed like a long while, taking it all in.

"So what you're saying is that the only way I can hold on to you is to let you go. I'm sorry, but that's not good enough."

"I get it, really I do. Let's shake hands then and part right now as friends."

"No, I mean I'm not willing to let you go. If a life, a commitment in secret is what it takes, then that's a price I'm willing to pay. Because wherever I am, it will be all right as long as I know that you're in the world, and I belong to you and you to me."

Tam's eyes appeared large and glassy, Quinn thought. Perhaps they merely reflected his own.

"All right," Quinn said, exhaling. "You do understand the conventions of having a commitment ceremony in the style of a Balinese wedding?"

"I'm sure I can get with the playbook," Tam said.

"OK, then, prepare to be kidnapped."

"Kidnapped?"

"Yes, the bride is kidnapped by the groom's relations and taken to his village."

"Wait a minute, how come I'm the bride? I thought we were both the grooms."

"Perhaps then neither of us will be kidnapped."

Since Quinn was half-Indonesian and thus playing for "the home team," as Tam put it, the family decided that Tam would be kidnapped. The evening before the wedding, Quinn kissed Tam goodnight and went to stay with Pina and her family. The next day, Quinn's newfound senior male relations arrived at the hotel and "kidnapped" Tam, escorting him to the family home. Quinn grew solemn though when he saw his beloved, a mirror of himself in a light-gray suit with a gold sash and woven crown. Now it was Tam's turn to tremble and Quinn's to take his hand reassuringly as they exchanged scaly silver dragon rings with gold heads and flashing ruby eyes by John Hardy, whose verdant, terraced complex they had visited an hour away in Ubud.

The only thing missing was any photographic record of the event, everyone present understanding the importance of keeping it private. It saddened Quinn. In a selfie world it was as if the moment didn't exist without a camera to take note of it. But then that made it all the more necessary to live the moment and cherish it, didn't it?

"This will just have to remain in our minds and memory," he said after he and Tam exchanged their individually written vows.

At Pina's backyard party, she wept as she led some of the ladies in a graceful dance. A gamelan group offered traditional music, then accompanied Tam's iTunes selections most harmoniously, including the song the couple had chosen for their first dance, George Michael's *Father Figure*. The guests clapped rhythmically as Quinn and Tam took turns leading, whirling each other around.

As the song reached its plagal conclusion, with its Eastern flavor, Quinn and Tam kissed. It was, Quinn decided, however secret, the perfect marriage of East and West.

THIRTY-THREE

"It's all for the best," Syd said—in a manner that was somewhat self-congratulatory, Quinn thought—when they returned to Jakarta and informed her and Chan that not only was the wedding off but the past—hers, Quinn's and whatever happened in Bali—would remain there.

"Well, I have to say that took real courage," Chan said, raising a glass to both of them at a farewell luncheon. "I salute you both."

Oh, yes, everyone will be perfectly happy—except perhaps us, Quinn thought. But no one likes a martyr. And no one has everything.

"So what will you two do now?" Chan asked.

That was the question, wasn't it? There were NFL careers to consider, Quinn thought, a relationship to navigate privately and to balance with those careers, people he would have to confront or, at the very least, contend with, like Mal and Smalley; people who needed him, like Kelly, Nero, his teammates, and the kids at the orphanage.

The kids: Quinn and Tam had vowed on the night of their commitment ceremony—after Quinn had presented Tam with an Indonesian canoe paddle, symbol of a warrior, and Tam had given Quinn a potted evergreen studded with stargazer lilies, like the Christmas trees of his childhood—that the orphanage would be their life's work, whatever it took. And in this, Quinn now understood, Syd and Chan would help them.

So what did it matter that he would probably never love her just as she had never loved him? Tam would love her. Tam would be the bridge, Quinn's gift to her. And she in turn would use her influence to complete the new orphanage. Quinn could see it all now, could see that it was meant to be and that it would be enough.

At the orphanage, he and Tam waited in a garden to take their leave of Adhi before flying home. It was a place that offered balm to Quinn's fears, where everything was as it was before. Soon Adhi appeared with Nir and Lan, backpacks in tow.

"They've been waiting every day for your return," Adhi said, laughing. "They have some things they've made for you."

Nir nodded then and Lan came forward with a card made out of heavy, cream-colored construction paper, with the word "Thank You" scrawled in red and green crayons and decorated with stickers. Nir had a card, too. It showed four stick figures—two adults and two children with arrows pointing to Nir and Lan's names. He presented it gravely to Quinn, who knew who the two adults were meant to be.

"Thank you for our presents and for all you do for the children," Nir read aloud.

Tam crouched down. "Come here, Nir. I want to ask you something, man-to-man, because you're the head of your family and very grownup. Would you and Lan give me and Quinn the honor of watching over you especially?"

Nir stood there solemnly, mulling things as he always did, but Lan broke into a grin and, reaching out, threw his arms around Tam's neck. The thinness of his small body contrasted with Tam's muscular physique, and Quinn was struck by the tenderness and power of the moment, by life's fragility and love's endurance.

And by the realization that at last he was where he was always meant to be, with the people to whom he belonged and who belonged to him, his family. He had come full circle. He was truly home.

Quinn stood there weeping quietly as Nir nodded and leaned in to embrace Tam, who closed his arms about the boys and sobbed.

After a while, though, he laughed and said, "Well, what do you think? Shall we let the big kid in? Altogether now, group hug."

Quinn crouched down then, and the four linked arms, heads touching.

"OK," Tam said. "This is a kind of huddle. I'll tell you what." He rose and rummaged through a bag of gifts for the kids to find a junior-size football.

"Oh, please, Tam," Quinn said, wiping his eyes and smiling.

"No, no, just a version of flag football, nice and gentle." Tam tossed the ball lightly to Lan, who ran with it in circles as Nir chased him.

"OK, good offense, I think," Tam said. He made the T sign for "time-out."

"Flag on the play, boys. Stop for a minute and let us show you how it's done. Nir, you go left and Lan, you go right. That's it, spread out."

For a moment, a tiny white butterfly alighted on the ball, then flew past Quinn before vanishing.

Hello, Aunt Lena, he thought, and goodbye.

As he prepared to throw, Tam twirled the ball, laughing. "Hey, Quinnie," he said, "go deep."

Fin

About the Author

Georgette Gouveia is the editor-in-chief of WAG, a luxury lifestyles magazine, and a former Associated Press Award-winning cultural writer with Gannett Inc. "The Penalty for Holding" is the second novel in her series "The Games Men Play," which is the name of her sports/culture/sex blog. The first novel, "Water Music" (Greenleaf Book Group), was published in 2014. Gouveia is also the author of "The Essential Mary Cassatt" (Harry N. Abrams/Wonderland Press). For more, visit thegamesmenplay.com.

CPSIA information can be obtained
at www.ICGtesting.com
Printed in the USA
LVOW03s0111120318
569503LV00001B/122/P